Need You

Robyn Reed

The Sweetwater Series

Robyn Reed

AUTHORS NOTE

Need you, book 2 of 3 in the Sweetwater Series, the first series written by myself. I've loved writing these and hope you enjoy them as much as I do.

These books are interlinked standalones, so you can enjoy them as a series or by themselves.

My books all have a lot of spice and a happy ending, as I myself can't read a book without one.

So, if you enjoy a slightly possessive alpha male and a good love story with a little drama sprinkled in, you've come to the right place.

Please note, this book is strictly 18+

Enjoy reading. X

This book is a work of fiction. Names, characters, venues, and incidents are the products of the author's imagination or used fictitiously. Any resemblance to the actual events locales or persons, living or dead is entirely coincidental.

To all the girls who want a guy with
golden retriever energy
and a dirty mouth…

CONTENTS

CHAPTER 1: Rose
CHAPTER 2: Rose
CHAPTER 3: Luca
CHAPTER 4: Rose
CHAPTER 5: Luca
CHAPTER 6: Rose
CHAPTER 7: Luca
CHAPTER 8: Rose
CHAPTER 9: Luca
CHAPTER 10: Rose
CHAPTER 11: Luca
CHAPTER 12: Rose
CHAPTER 13: Luca
CHAPTER 14: Rose
CHAPTER 15: Luca
CHAPTER 16: Rose
CHAPTER 17: Luca
CHAPTER 18: Luca
CHAPTER 19: Luca
CHAPTER 20: Rose
CHAPTER 21: Luca
CHAPTER 22: Rose
CHAPTER 23: Rose
CHAPTER 24: Luca
CHAPTER 25: Rose
CHAPTER 26: Luca
CHAPTER 27: Rose
CHAPTER 28: Rose
CHAPTER 29: Luca
CHAPTER 30: Luca
CHAPTER 31: Rose
CHAPTER 32: Luca
CHAPTER 33: Rose

1

Rose

"Are you fucking serious right now?"

The kitchen I'm currently working in looks like a bomb has gone off, all because the new staff member has decided to somehow throw an industrial-sized pack of flour all over the place. I puff out a breath, blowing white powder into the air. My hands find my hips as I glare at the new intern.

He shrinks in on himself a little, but I'm so done caring right now. I've been on this job far too long, and my patience is wearing thinner by the minute. I try like hell not to berate him for his stupidity, but when I glance down at myself, I look like the abominable snowman.

"You seriously need to start watching what you are doing. You literally knocked a load of food onto the floor not a day ago, and now you're causing more chaos". My words come out a little harsher than I meant them, and the poor guy looks at me like he's about to burst into tears. I probably shouldn't have been so mean to him, but this is going to take forever to wash out of my hair. "Look, just clean up this mess. I'm going to change and clock off for the night".

It's the last shift at the restaurant where I've been sent to work for the past eight weeks before I head home tomorrow to start my new journey.

It's a typical Thursday evening. The chefs are preparing the food for the weekend, and I am finishing up the new dessert menu, ready for them to roll out for the new year. Or I was until the intern somehow managed to blast flour all over the place.

I take great pride in my desserts, but I love baking more. The tiramisu is my prized dessert here, but honestly, give me a cookie or a blueberry muffin any day. As much as I love travelling around the country and being able to work in different restaurants, it's not the same feeling I get when I think about setting up my own little bakery. I know for a fact it will be a hell of a lot harder work than what I'm doing now, but I feel like I'm ready for the challenge.

The dream has been one of mine for as long as I can remember, using my easy-bake oven to make muffins for my dad when I was younger or to try and impress my mother with my skills. She was only interested in what I could do that would make her look good, and much to her disappointment, I didn't become a socialite or some sort of influencer like she wanted, and I'll never live it down because in her eyes, if it's not something she would have wanted for me, then it was a failure.

My dad pushed me to follow my dreams, though, and that's how I ended up attending college to get my culinary degree and become a baker.

That dream is about to become a reality because tomorrow, I finally get the keys to my new place. It's fitted out and ready for me to begin work, with just a touch of paint needed here and there. It also has the added bonus of a little one-bedroom apartment above it. I can live there while I wait for my place to be ready.

The house my two best friends and I shared was set on fire about two months ago by Grace's psychotic ex-boyfriend. They managed to find places to live, and I was on the road, so it didn't matter until now. The house is taking forever to be done, so this way, I still have a roof over my head. It's not the greatest of places to live, but it will do for now, and I've poured my life savings into making this work. And at twenty-seven, this is all I have, so I need to find a way to make it work.

My mind comes back to the present as I stare down at the intern. Seeing the angry look on my face, he quickly shuffles to the side, allowing me space to get past him as I make my exit for the staff room. It's only a tiny space that around twenty people have to share, but there are men's and women's bathrooms just through the back of it. I make quick work of opening my locker, grabbing some spare clothes, and darting into the bathrooms.

It takes me longer than I thought to clean up the flour mess that's all over me, and I don't have the patience to wash my hair here, so I grab my things ready to leave, opening the door to the staff room where my co-worker Freddie is waiting just outside. He's leaning against the opposite wall, a little further down from the staffroom door, one leg propped up against the wall, and his shaggy blonde hair falls over his face as he types something out on his phone.

His head snaps up as the door shuts behind me, and a smile takes over his face as he straightens himself up, putting his phone in his back pocket. He walks over to me, crowding me as I crane my neck to face him. He's a nice guy, but sometimes, he needs to take the hint and give me some personal space. Trying not to be rude though, I clear my throat and turn to give him my attention, "Can I help you with something Freddie?"

He gives me a cheesy grin, looking down at me. "I know you are going back to Tennessee tomorrow and wanted to know if you would, um... Like... Maybe you want to go grab a drink before you go?"

Oh, sweet baby Jesus, how the hell do I let this guy down nicely? "Oh, um, that's really nice of you to offer, but I'm just swamped and need to pack before I go back home, so I really should just do that as soon as I get to my hotel. I'm really sorry; I wish I could".

It doesn't deter him. "Oh, I could help you? We could order in or grab some food". He's giving me his sweetest smile, but all I can think of is how I'm going to get out of this situation. He's a good-looking guy, tall and athletic and with the bluest eyes, but he has the personality of a wet mop, and for someone as bossy and outspoken as I am, I'd end up embarrassing the guy on our first date.

The groan that tries to escape me is pushed back down with every ounce of willpower I have as I give him a tight smile in return and try to figure out how to get out of this situation. Thankfully, my phone chooses that moment to ring in my bag. My eyes dart down to it, and I fiddle with the zip on my bag to get it out quickly and see my best friend's name on my screen.

Lifesaver! "Uh, sorry, I'll have to take a rain check; I've gotta take this," I say as I press to answer and put the phone to my ear, giving him an awkward wave as I shuffle past him, out of the door and into the cold December evening.

"Hey, oh my god, Grace, you have the best timing right now. You just saved me from having to embarrass myself by turning down a guy from work." She giggles into the phone as I turn and walk down the street to the hotel work has put me up in.

"Oh good, I'm glad I can be your scapegoat for the evening. Anyway, that's not actually why I'm calling up. It's Jaxx's birthday this weekend, and I know you will be back in town, so I'm calling to invite you to ours. He didn't want to do anything big, so I suggested we have our friends round for drinks and some food. I know it's super last minute, but you know what we're like. Pleaseeeee tell me you'll be there".

Her peppy voice filters through the phone as she talks to me, reminding me why I can never say no to the little ray of sunshine that is Grace. Jaxx's birthday is two days before Christmas, and Grace loves to be at the last minute if nothing else.

I let out a small laugh on the phone. I miss my friends so much when I'm away, and I'm really not cut out for the travelling life. I'm really a homebird and cannot wait to get back into town. "Of course I'll be there, I wouldn't miss it, I'm assuming Hallie will be there too". She hums down the phone, "Oh yeah she's coming as are my brother and Luca, you remember him, don't you?" I stifle a groan as I press my hand to my head, stopping in the street. "Is that supposed to be funny? I assumed they would be there; it is Jaxx's birthday after all". How can I ever forget the guy who offered his place to me after meeting me twice?

"Mmm hmm, I saw the way you were watching him the last time you were together at ours. Don't think I'm not on to you, missy". My mouth twists as I think of the cocky man that is somehow bossier than I am. "I am not attracted to Luca. He called me Red for a start and then offered his place up to me like we're best buds. You'll find me buried in a bottle of wine for the night, thank you". The laughter that echoes through the phone lifts my mood slightly as I continue my journey to the hotel. "All right, that's fine by me. Oh wait, does that mean you have somewhere to live now?"

"Ah, um, well yeah. I didn't want to tell you until I'm with everyone, but yes, I have somewhere to live. I'll give you all the details when I see you". She lets out an excited squeal down the phone, causing me to pull it away from my ear slightly, "Oh my gosh, this is the best news! Does this call for the good stuff?" I huff out a laugh at Grace, "It always calls for the good stuff. I'm just getting to my hotel now, and I need to pack, so I'll see you on Saturday, yeah?"

"Yeah, see you then". We hang up, and I make the rest of the walk back to the hotel; the Christmas lights twinkle against the night sky all the way down the street as I wander down the road, my mind going through everything I need to do when I get back to town. I'm hoping to have the bakery up and running by the beginning of the new year, so I've got a week to get things sorted, and since I don't celebrate with my parents, it makes for another quiet Christmas.

Once back in my room, I jump in the shower, trying to scrub off the rest of the flour that's stuck in my hair and the stench from my body because I smell awful from the longest day I've had in a while.

I stare back at my reflection in the mirror after climbing out of the shower, my usually curly red hair now slick down my back, and my pale complexion is replaced with a dusting of pink across the freckles on my face from where the shower was probably too hot. My skin is red raw from the scrubbing I just gave it, so I grab some lotion and rub it all over myself, feeling better after. I climb into the fresh white sheets and snuggle down into the bed, excited to get to work when I make it home.

.....

The journey back took so much longer than I wanted it to, and I felt like I wanted to stick pins in my eyes from the number of idiot drivers on the roads due to the icy winter weather. But I make it back just in time to meet my new landlord. He's waiting at the front door of the bakery for me when I pull up, and honestly, I don't know how he carries on.

He's an older man, in his late 80's and walks with a cane, with grey hair that covers the sides of his head as the top has gone baled. His wrinkles around his eyes crease more when he smiles at me, and I beam back as I make the short walk from my car to him.

I hold my hand out to shake his cold one as his fingers wrap around mine. "Hi, you must be Mr Miller. I'm Rose, it's nice to finally meet you" "Ahh yes, I'm sorry I had to send an old friend out to you last time, I really do prefer to do these things in person, but my health isn't the greatest these days and I couldn't make it last time to show you around".

I shake my head a little, smiling at him, "It's really no bother. I'm just happy to have somewhere". We walk into the bakery, and it's just as I remembered it.

Cream walls line the shop, with a glass cabinet towards the front and a couple of small tables and chairs for people to sit in and eat. My fingers drift across the glass as I make my way around to the kitchen. It's small, but it works perfectly for what I need, and I can't wait to get started. I picked this area because the footfall is high, and there isn't a bakery for at least three blocks, so I know I don't have competition straight across the street.

Mr Miller hands the keys over, and after signing the final documents, I sit in one of the wooden chairs that take up space in *my* bakery. I have a pinch-me moment; it feels so good that I finally have somewhere to call my own. I run out to the car and grab a few of my bags, making my way upstairs with them so I can get settled in. It's only a small apartment, and I'm not entirely sure everything works properly, but it's something for now, at least.

Oak floorboards line the entire loft-style apartment, with a small kitchenette off to the right of the room. A sofa sits in the far left, which leaves a view in front of the large floor-length window that's allowing me to catch a glimpse of pink and red swirls from the evening sky as the sun sets. I drag my bag into my bedroom, placing it just outside of the small cupboard I now have for a wardrobe. The place is furnished, so for now I don't need to get anything, and the bathroom through my bedroom is quite small, just like the rest of the place, but clean either way. It's home, for now, and that's more than I had a week ago. I thought I might have to take up an offer of a spare room to stay, but this way I can have my business right at my fingertips.

I spend the rest of the evening unpacking my things, and order takeout, before settling in for the night in my new home.

2

Rose

Sleep didn't come as easy as I would have liked last night, the bed is a little lumpy, but I make a mental note to order a new mattress as I drag myself from it into the kitchen. Thankfully, I have a coffee machine up here; otherwise, I'd have to drive to the nearest coffee shop. I pour myself a cup, glad that I picked up coffee before I got in last night and make my way over to the sofa to enjoy the view with my drink.

The blossom tree-lined street will add a touch of colour to the neighbourhood when they begin to bloom in a few short months. A park sits across the road from the bakery, where dog walkers and parents with young children who don't like the indoors make their way around. I like it here, and to be honest, if Hallie said tomorrow that she was selling up the house we share then I wouldn't complain, I can live with this since it's just me.

We got the house just after leaving college, thanks to her dad getting us first refusal, it's actually Hallie's place but since it's a three bed, she insisted that I house share with her, only paying towards the bills and not the mortgage. I love living with her, and even with Grace for the short while she stayed with us, before moving in with her boyfriend Jaxx after the fire, it made sense for them to do that, as he was always at ours or she was at his. But, right now, I think I could get used to living by myself.

After finishing my coffee, I get a quick shower and get ready for the day, getting stuck in with the long list of things I need to do before opening. I called up a local sign place a couple of weeks ago when I secured the building, so that's being fitted today, along with an opening soon sign. The guys turn up to put the new sign up just after ten in the morning, and after an hour of them going up and down ladders, it's finally up. I step out into a crisp day, turning and seeing my dream come to life that little bit more.

Cake my day

A grin tugs at my lips as I look at the new sign. While the guys put the sign up, I spent the time cleaning up the inside, getting everything turned on, and checking that things worked. It all seems to be good enough, so I head over to the wholesalers to get all my supplies. It costs a small fortune to get everything, but I can't say I don't enjoy making my way around each aisle, picking up some unnecessary purchases as I go. It makes a massive dent in my savings when buying everything, but I got myself semi-decent mixers and supplies, so I'd call that a big win. I think about the girls and my dad and what they will think of me doing this without telling a soul, but I really hope they support me either way.

Dragging the countless bags into the bakery, I collapse onto one of the chairs, giving myself a little breather before I unpack and head over to Grace's for the evening. It doesn't take me too long, but by the time I'm finished, I'm ready for a drink, and by the time the evening rolls around, I'm more than happy to be going to Grace and Jaxx's place, having not seen her, or my other best friend Hallie in well over a month, I feel myself getting excited to spend some time with them.

I order an Uber, deciding not to drive if I'm going to drink so I don't have to mess about getting my car tomorrow and make the 10-minute journey to my friend's house. I knock on when I get there, expecting Grace or Jaxx to open the door, but to my surprise, as the door swings open, I come face to face with none other than Luca himself.

His gorgeous, almost symmetrical face lights up as he greets me like we're best friends, pulling me in for a hug. I briefly hug him back, feeling awkward around him for some unknown reason, *probably because you want to fuck him.* The little voice in my head tells me, but I push those thoughts to the back of my head as Luca's scent clouds my brain.

It's a mix of bergamot and orange with a hint of coffee somewhere in there, and it has me leaning into the hug just that little bit more. He pulls back from me too soon, though, smiling down at me as his brown hair flops over his face a little.

His chocolate-brown eyes bore into mine as he assesses my face. Clearly happy with what he sees, he gives me a quick nod, turning to walk us into the house, his hand coming to rest on my back as he does. He leans into me a little, his breath fanning the side of my face, sending tingles up my spine at the feeling.

"Good to see you, Red. I was beginning to think you wouldn't show tonight". His smooth voice vibrates through me, and I'd call him swoon-worthy, but his new name for me has my eyes shooting up to his as I scowl at him, my voice taking on a more annoyed tone as I reply, "Will you stop calling me that, it's really fucking irritating".

His free hand comes up to tug on one of the strands of my hair as he lets his fingers run through it, "Hmm, nah. I like it too much, call it my pet name for you". He slides me a wink, before pushing us both forward and into the living room where the rest of our friends are, and I wonder why he decided he should be the one to answer the door of his friends' house.

I spot Grace and Hallie instantly, making my way over to them and falling into them both on the couch across the room. They let out a squeal as they wrap both of their arms around me, smothering me with kisses and hugs. I giggle back at them, "Ahh, I've missed you like you wouldn't believe, Rose; I'm so glad you're back home again". I hug Grace back a little when Hallie speaks up, "Yeah, I know I'm not in town all the time at the minute, but I've missed seeing you when I am back; I'm happy you're home, too!"

I've been friends with the pair of them since we were just six years old, all trying to figure out life in the school playground, and we've been inseparable ever since. I love them both more than parts of my own family, not that it's hard with my mother, but these girls are my family.

Jaxx comes over to hand me a glass of wine, and I gladly take it from him, gulping down a mouthful straight away. He eyes me as he watches me down the drink, chuckling to himself when I polish the glass off in one go. "I know it's your birthday, but would you be a dear and refill me?" I smile up at him, wiggling my now-empty glass in front of me. Jaxx grins down at me, a curious expression on his face, "Why do I feel like you're going to cause trouble tonight, Miss Adler?"

My smile widens as he takes the glass and wanders back to the kitchen to refill my drink. I shout over to his retreating form, "And fill that baby right to the top, Jaxx. Don't mess about with giving me half a glass again". He barks out a laugh at my orders from the kitchen as I feel Grace's fingers pinch at my side a little, "You all right, Rose? I know you love a drink, but you normally at least have the first glass down in two goes rather than one". I chuckle at her comment, side-eyeing my friend as I spill my week onto her and Hallie.

"I had a shitty final week, the restaurant I was at was super stressful, but I've got some really good news that I have been keeping a little secret, so don't go mad at me for not telling you sooner". "You're not pregnant, are you?" Tristan asks from his spot on the floor. Four pairs of eyes find mine as my mouth drops open at his comment, "No I am not. I'm not even seeing anyone, so God knows where your brain went to come out with that".

He shrugs at me, as Jaxx makes his way back into the room, assessing me, as if he doesn't want to hand me the large glass of wine in his hand. I take it from him, having a healthy sip before continuing.

"Now we've cleared up that I'm definitely not pregnant, as I told Grace on the phone I've got somewhere to live, and it just so happens to be attached to my new bakery". The words leave my mouth, and I wait, holding my breath for everyone to realise what I just said. "Ahhhhh!" Grace and Hallie scream down my ear from either side of me, deafening me a little as they do. I wince at them, death dripping my glass as I'm sandwiched between the two of them as they hug me.

"This is the best freakin news ever, I can't believe you didn't say anything. When did you get it?" I glance over to Hallie, now unable to hide the massive grin that's taken over my face. "I actually decided to take it about a month ago, but I didn't want to say anything until I had the keys in my hand. It comes with an apartment above it, and I was going to use that as a bigger staffroom or storage area, but it's come in really handy since I didn't have anywhere to stay, I'll be opening at the beginning of next month". Grace blinks back at me from my other side, processing what I'm saying.

"Wait, that's like a week away, are you going to have everything ready in time?" I can't help but let out a dry laugh, tinged with irony, at her expression, she's looking at me like I'm the unorganised one of the three of us, and not in fact her.

"Yes, Grace, it will be ready in time. I only need to shop for the things that can't be bought ahead of time, and I can start baking". I grin at my friends, "Dibs having first order from you, I *need* my brownie fix" Hallie looks like she's about to start drooling on me, and I glance over to the boys, who seem happy with my new shop, too.

I chance a glimpse at Luca, who's watching me as him and Jaxx lounge on the sofa, his eyes are fixed on me as I talk to the girls about the shop. I have to look away from his intense stare before the blush I feel taking over my face gets too obvious, and down some more of the wine in my hand.

As the evening wears on, I try like hell not to let anyone spot me sneaking glances at Luca. He catches my eye the odd time, his lips tipping up on one side of his face each time he does, showing that perfect dimple he has on his cheek, his short stubble doing little to hide it.

I know I shouldn't keep watching him, but the more drunk I get, the more I see why every girl within a fifty-mile radius wants to be with him.

3

Luca

I wake up early, the first light of dawn peeking through the curtains of my bedroom, and let out a sigh, rubbing my face and wondering how I'm going to get through the day without thinking about Rose incessantly before I get to see her again later.

Determined to keep myself busy, I throw on my gym clothes and head to the small gym I set up in my garage. As the weights clank and sweat drips, I try to focus on each rep, each set, anything to keep my mind off her. After what feels like hours, I glance at the clock—only thirty minutes have passed, and I groan, pushing myself harder, determined to exhaust my body.

I manage to push myself to do a full hour, before eventually giving up and heading into the house to make a strong coffee, the caffeine doing little to help me as I flip through the morning news on my tablet, trying not to focus on the gossip sections that seem to chase me at every point in my life.

I work harder to keep out of them these days, but with my dad pushing me to meet someone and settle down, I find myself with a new date to events, even if I do leave them at the end of the night, no longer allowing anything to happen between me and them.

I've held the player title for far too long, and now, as I'm about to hit my thirty-fourth birthday in a few short months, I know that I should probably do what he says and settle down. If only the smart-mouthed redhead I keep picturing would entertain me with more than a few light-hearted comments here and there and let me take her out properly.

I make my way through the rest of the news, but every story seems mundane, every article a distraction that can't hold my attention. I switch tactics and decide to tackle some work, logging into my laptop and going through emails, reviewing contracts, and anything that requires focus.

By mid-morning, I feel the restlessness creeping in again and pick up my phone, half-tempted to text Rose and see if she's free for coffee like I have over the last couple of months, then think better of it, knowing she will most likely shoot me down like she always does. Instead, I put it back away and head into the office for a couple of hours to attempt to get some work down and flag down Brad as I step off the elevator; he's one of the guys on my team who I need to go over things with before we finish for Christmas. For a Saturday, the office always seems to be busy, even though no one needs to be here.

After a working lunch with him, I head back home. Still hours to kill before I can head over to Grace and Jaxx's for his birthday.

.....

I'm sat twitching in anticipation from 6 pm when I arrive at Jaxx and Grace's house incredibly early, using the excuse that I haven't seen my friend in a while, but the urge to see Rose again got the better of me.

Just over a month has passed since I last saw her, and for some reason, I just can't get the girl out of my head. Maybe it's her sassy attitude, or those freckles that cross over her dainty nose that points up a touch, or that unruly red hair of hers that dips just past her shoulders in big curls.

I stupidly suggested that she come stay at mine while her house gets fixed the last time I saw her, and she shot me down, and now hearing from Grace that she found a place to live has my mind going a mile a minute, as try to figure out how I can see her more than just the fleeting visits she gives us.

I know it's probably the worst idea with my dating history, she clearly thinks I'm a player. And well yeah, maybe I was a few months ago, but since the night I first met her, the other girls just don't seem to interest me.

I know I need to keep things friendly between us, so when the doorbell goes, I jump up from my spot in the living room, knowing full well who is at the door, "I'll get it", I say as I squeeze myself past Jaxx. He shoots me a dirty look because he knows what I think about her and doesn't want me anywhere near his girl's best friend, but my brain doesn't want to deal with logic now as I stride to the front door, swinging it wide open, and am greeted with the face that I can't get out of my head.

I beam at her, my grin so wide it hurts my face a little, and all sense leaves my head as I pull her into my arms, just so I can smell her sweet cherry scent once again.

I feel her tense under me as my grip tightens around her, so I pull back a touch, allowing her space to get her bearings. Taking a sweep over her face, her hazel eyes search mine back as she stands there, clearly waiting to be let in the house.

I slide my arm around her back, keeping my hand there so I have what little contact I can grasp from her as I walk her into where our friends are waiting. But not before leaning into her and reminding her of the name I know she hates.

"Good to see you, Red. I was beginning to think you wouldn't show tonight". Her eyes dart up to mine as they narrow in on me, "Will you stop calling me that. It's really fucking irritating". I can't help myself as I tug on a couple of loose strands of hair, running it through my fingers, "Hmm, nah. I like it too much; call it my pet name for you".

If looks could kill, I'd be a dead man from the death stare she's giving me as she glares at me before turning her head as I push us through to the living room, so much for being on her good side.

After hearing about her new bakery, on the inside I feel like a giddy child wanting to see the place, but I keep my expression neutral as she tells the girls about it opening up next week. Her brownies are to die for, and I've even begged Grace a time or two to get Rose to bake me some, but every time she's been working away, so I couldn't.

As the evening wears on, everyone becomes more drunk, I stayed sober tonight, after making the decision not to, knowing I have an early day tomorrow and have to go into the office first thing. The girls fall into conversation, catching up on whatever they didn't get to tell each other over their phone conversations, and I turn to Tristan, wanting to know how being a business owner is going for him.

"You know, it's not as bad as I thought it would be. The business has picked up already with whatever Grace and one of her admin friends have been doing. Apparently, it's some marketing for the business, which I have no clue about. I stay well away from that,". I grin at my friend, "Is that your way of saying you're getting old, Tris?" He glares at me, "Absolutely fucking not. I'm only Thirty- three don't even think about calling me old. I think you forget you're the same age sometimes".

Jaxx stifles a laugh beside us, nudging me a little, "You know I think he's onto something there, Luca" I roll my eyes at the pair of them, "You two just wish you looked as young as I still do, those little wrinkles aren't helping your youthful look Jaxx, and neither is complaining". I poke my finger at his face, and he laughs, pushing my arm away, "All right, don't start ganging up on me; he's the one who usually complains about everything". Jaxx motions in Tristan's direction, who's got a scowl on his face. He's possibly the grumpiest person I've ever met, and I don't recall a time when he's not had a look of pure annoyance on his face.

Apparently, that's just his face, and he's told me a time or two to get used to it, but I enjoy winding him up every now and again.

I've known the two of them since my dad moved us to Tennessee when my mom died at the age of thirteen, and just like the girls, we are closer than most families. Jaxx and Tristan knew each other from being young kids, but when I joined the pair of them in high school, they acted like I'd always been in their lives.

It's past midnight before everyone decides to call it a night. Rose and Hallie drunkenly fumble to grab their things, and I use that as my in to offer her a ride home just as she pulls her phone out.

"Rose, I'll give you a ride back to your place. You're not getting a ride share at this time of night". She looks up at me, her eyes glazed over from the alcohol she's had to drink, and I know I've made the right call offering her a ride, but she shakes her head at me anyway,

"I'm good, honestly". Her eyes slide over to Hallie as she says it, but Hallie shrugs back to her, "I'm getting a ride share with Tristan; I'm staying at the ranch whilst I'm back in town; you should go with Luca. It's safer". I grin in Hallie's direction as I stride over to Rose, plucking the phone out of her hand. Her reactions are too slow to stop me, proving my point that she should listen. I sneak a glance in Jaxx's direction, but he's too drunk to care what I'm doing for once as Grace battles to get him up from the couch.

She nods over to Rose and me, "He's right, just go with Luca, it's safer at this time of night" that earns everyone a scowl from Rose as she stomps her foot into the floor like a small child, clearly pissed that she's been outnumbered by her friends.

My grin widens as she glares up at me, fuming that she's not got a choice. I slide my arm around her, pulling her to me and out of the door, "Sorry, Red, looks like you're outnumbered tonight; let's go". She huffs her annoyance, but comes with me, stumbling a little as she does, and I can't help the relief I feel that she is getting a lift from me. I help her into my truck, reaching over as I fasten her in, "I can do that myself, Luca; I'm not that drunk".

I turn my face to hers, our eyes meeting and our noses inches apart. My eyes slide down to her lips briefly before coming up to meet with those hazel eyes I'm quickly becoming addicted to.

She's scowling at me again, and I can't help myself as I lift my thumb to her head, smoothing it over her brow to soften her features. "Stop scowling at me like that, Red; you'll ruin that pretty face of yours". Her eyes roll dramatically at me, but a ghost of a smile touches her lips as I glance back down, making sure her seatbelt is fastened.

I twist my head, my lips brushing her face as I do, and my voice strains as I murmur to her, “There, safe and sound”. I pat her leg with my free hand, my other resting on the door frame, as I pull back to get a look at her.

Her lips are parted just a touch as her eyes dart between mine, trying to get a gage on me; keep trying, sweetheart, 'cause*' I don't have a fucking clue what I'm doing either.*

I clear my throat, pulling myself out of the car, and round to the other side, trying to clear my head from the dirty thoughts that have surfaced as I go. I put her apartment into my nav and make the short drive over there. She’s silent the whole way, watching the few cars that are out tonight go by out of the window, and I keep sneaking glances at her, checking that she’s still okay.

As we pull up to her place, I realise I run this way most mornings, and my house is only a couple of blocks away, too. I jump out, beating her to the door before she gets it. She’s still too slow right now from the alcohol, and she gets frustrated when I open her door, grinning at her again.

“Luca, you’re being weird.” She gives me a pointed look as she says it before her head drops down to search for the key in her purse. After what seems like forever, she fishes it out and jumps down from the passenger side of my truck. I follow closely behind her, making sure she gets in okay and that she notices my movements, stopping and spinning on me.

The cold December night mixed with the alcohol turns her cheeks a rosy shade of pink.

Her breath comes out in little puffs into the winter air as she stares me down, confusion etched into her features because I'm following her. "What are you doing, Luca? I'm fine here, you can go now". A husky laugh slips from my lips as I shake my head at her, "No can-do, Red. I'm walking you to your door, so turn that fine ass around and show me where it is".

She huffs at me again, her sassy attitude taking over when she's had a drink, before turning and stomping over to the stairs that lead up the side of the bakery and to her place. She climbs the stairs quickly, like she's trying to run away from me, but I'm quicker, and catch up to her with ease.

I follow her right to the door, where she struggles to get the key in the lock from the low lighting. I pull my phone out to bring the torch up to help her, taking the keys off her as I do and sliding it into the lock. "You really need to get a light for out here when it's late". She grumbles her reply to me, acknowledging what I've said at least as she finally pushes the door open. She spins on me, standing so close that we're almost toe to toe.

I keep my gaze trained on her, jingling my keys in my hands as the silence stretches between us. Rose clears her throat, bringing my attention to her plush lips, "Do you want to come in for a drink since you followed me all the way up? I have coffee or water at the moment".

I want to say yes, but the small part of my brain that knows logic screams at me to go home. "I better get back, but thank you for the offer. I just wanted to make sure you got in safe since you haven't been here long".

I lean into her, pressing a light kiss to her cheek as I say my goodbyes. A small intake of breath comes from her as I do, and I hold my lips close to her for a moment longer than I should, not wanting the goodbye to end. She pulls back first though, stepping away from me a little and grabbing the door to keep herself from stumbling as a dust of pink spreads across her freckled cheeks. "Okay, well, thank you. Goodnight, Luca". My lips tip at the edges in a silent victory that I've got her flustered.

"Goodnight, Red, see you soon".

I stare at her door for a minute after she's closed it, wishing I had accepted her offer and gone in just to spend a little time with her alone. Still, I turn on my heel, forcing myself back down the steps and to my waiting truck, and as I make the drive home, I think up every way I possibly can see her again, the first starting with my run tomorrow.

4

Rose

The week leading up to opening goes by in a blur as I busy myself with the final touches on the shop. It's difficult to get everything done with it being the Christmas period, but Grace and Hallie called up multiple times, offering to come and help, and they've been doing a little running about for me and even offered to work the odd shift if I need them. But I managed to rope my cousin Paisley into working here for a month whilst I get adjusted and she waits to start her new job, so she's given them a break as she begins her first day.

She's a couple of years younger than me and just got back from travelling for a couple of months after college, ready for her interview as the new pt for the Silver Wolves ice hockey team, which, of course, she nailed and will be starting in a few weeks.

She was all too excited when I asked if she could help me out for a couple of weeks since I haven't seen her in so long, and I'm just as excited to see her when she waltzes into the bakery at 7 am on Tuesday.

Her bright blue eyes catch mine as soon as she enters the place, a huge grin taking over as she rushes over to me and pulls me into a hug. I squeeze her back as we jump around like giddy teenagers. Having not seen her for six months, I feel that it's nice to have her around, even if it is for a short while. Her dad and mine are brothers, so she's on the better side of my family, the one that I actually like and want to spend time with, compared to my mother's side, who haven't bothered with me since I was young.

She pulls back from me, assessing me, and I do the same to her. She hasn't changed one bit since we were in our early twenties, her bright blonde hair hangs around her waist, the sun from her time abroad leaving natural highlights.

Bright blue eyes and a button nose on a heart-shaped face that matches mine stare back at me as I take her in; her long, flowy dress floats around her lower calves even though we're still in the midst of winter. Aside from our difference in hair colour and her being a touch more tanned than me, we got mistaken for siblings all the time when we were younger, and we'd pretend that we were strangers just because we wanted to be.

"Rose, oh my god. I missed you so bloody much. Facetime isn't the same as seeing you in person" I grin back at her, "No, it's not, and I don't want to go that long without seeing you in person again".

We make our way over to the till, and I show her how to use that and the coffee machine I got in as she makes notes beside me. The glass display is packed to the brim with sweet treats that I spent hours baking yesterday. I spent two days during the week handing out flyers for the place and sticking them everywhere, hoping it wasn't all done in vain.

I'm not expecting anyone to walk in anytime soon after opening, but Grace and Hallie come bounding in not five minutes after I've flicked the lock, with huge grins on their faces to come and show me support.

"Girlll, this is amazing. I can't believe how quickly you got this up and running, I'm so bloody proud of you", Hallie comments as she stands with her hands on her hips looking around the place and I make my way around the counter to her and Grace, pulling them both into a hug. "This place is so nice, Rose. You've done really well here", Grace marvels at the space from my side. I pull them over to one of the seats near the front, grabbing them a coffee from the machine once they're settled. "What do you both want to eat?"

They make their choices, Grace taking a blueberry muffin and Hallie taking a slice of banana bread. I plate them up, taking the food and coffees over to them, and join the pair whilst the place is still quiet. "So how many people are you expecting in today?" Hallie asks through a mouthful of cake as she shoves it in across from me. For someone so slim she sure can put food away.

I shrug back to her, "I'm not really sure, to be honest; I know it's going to be slow, to begin with, but the more I post on socials, the more people will hopefully come in". She nods back to me, "Well, I've already put something on for you, so even if just one person comes from that, it will help".

My lips tip up into a smile as she continues shovelling cake into her mouth, and the door goes again, pulling my attention over to it. My mouth goes dry instantly as I take in the sight before me.

Luca has stepped into the bakery, clad in black shorts and a t-shirt even though it's close to freezing outside, a small sheen of sweat beads at the base of his neck in the dip between his collar bones, where his pulse beats rapidly there, he must have just come from his run, and I take great pleasure in giving him a once over before standing to greet him. A smile takes over his face when he spots me, bounding over to the counter where I've walked around it to make sure I keep my distance from him.

After last week, when he dropped me back at my place, he's all I've had in my head, wishing he had come in for a drink, but I know full well I'm not his type. The tall, slim, tanned and brunette models are a far cry from me, so I keep pushing those thoughts to the back of my head. He has yet to notice Grace and Hallie in the corner, watching his every move as he carefully decides what he wants.

"Mornin' Red. The place looks great, I think this could be a new local", I raise a brow at him as my fingers grip the sides of the counter, "Oh really, you come this way often, do you?"

He nods enthusiastically at me, "Yeah actually. My house is literally a block couple of blocks away, and I take this route when I run, so I'll be seeing you most mornings, you'll be sick of me in no time". I roll my eyes at him, my lips twitching at his comment.

It's sweet that he's come in on my first day open, but I don't think I'll see him as often as he says. I doubt he eats a lot of sweet treats when his body looks like it was carved from the gods. He glances up to me briefly before focusing his attention back on the glass casing in front of him.

"I'll take a pastry and one of those brownies, oh and a coffee to go to please". I make quick work of sorting his order, grabbing his food and placing it in a box. The girls stay quiet the whole time, weirdly not saying a word to him, as if they don't want him to know they're there. I hand him his things, and he drops a note onto the counter for me, giving me a wink as he turns to leave, "Keep the change Red, and I'll see you two nosy sods soon".

A burst of laughter spills out of him as he catches the girls gawping at our exchange, and I glance down to see he's left me a $100 bill.

"Luca, you've given me way too much, don't be ridiculous" he stops short as he reaches the door, one hand on the handle as he pushes it open. "Can't put a price on perfection", He shoots me a panty-dropping wink and is out the door before I can protest any further, leaving me staring at his ass as he crosses the street.

I blink back down to the bill on my countertop, my gaze shifting over to a curious Grace and Hallie, "What did he leave you?" I grab the note, pick it up and show them, "$100; looks like breakfast is on Luca for the pair of you".

Grace looks thoughtful as she sips on her coffee, "You know, I really think he might have a thing for you. I've never seen him this smitten around anyone before". I scoff at her, brushing off her comment, "Please, have you seen the women he dates. I highly doubt I will be one of them".

She shrugs back to me as she finishes up her coffee, the pair of them standing to leave. "Just don't shut the door on that, you never know". I barely hold my eye roll at Grace, "All right, I think that's enough of your matchmaking for today. I'll see you later". I wave the pair of them off, clearing away their plates and organising behind the counter a little.

The rest of the day goes by in a blur as more customers come through the door over the morning period and into early afternoon, my dad calls to congratulate me, and I'm a little bummed he isn't here for this, but he's away with work, so he's making me promise to meet him for dinner soon and that when he's home, this will be his first stop.

By the time the day is done, I'm sold out of most things, and after closing up and making my way upstairs, I flop down onto the sofa, throwing my head back and closing my eyes. I'm exhausted, and all I want to do is sleep, but when I drag myself into bed that night, the only thing I seem to think about is when I'll next be seeing Luca again.

5

Luca

"Jesus, how many times have you stalked Rose this week?"

I glare at Tristan from across the kitchen of his farmhouse. He spotted the green box from her bakery straight away as I made my way inside, placing it on the counter. "I'm not stalking her; she's just really fucking good at what she does".

He raises a brow at me, silently telling me I'm full of shit because, well, I am... kind of. I've decided I need to cut myself off and reduce my daily trips to a couple of times a week after today, or I'm going to get diabetes from the amount of sugar I've consumed in the past two weeks.

He passes me a coffee across the kitchen island, flipping the box open and helping himself to a cookie. I figured out that Rose comes downstairs to open up and start prepping for the day at around 5am, perfect timing for when I run past the shop and can catch a glimpse of her and then again when I'm on the way to the office at 7.30am when she's just opened up.

Ok, maybe I do sound like a stalker, but I will take any glimpse I can get of her recently. I'm trying to pluck up the courage to ask her to dinner, but every time I get even close to it, someone walks into the shop, and she diverts away from me so quickly like she knows what's coming and doesn't want to let me down.

Maybe she does, but that doesn't mean I'm going to stop trying. I lean over the counter, plucking out a brownie from the box and letting out a moan as I take the first bite of the sweet treat. Just as I do, Grace walks in, stopping short when she hears me, "Luca, get a room". Tristan's gruff laugh sounds through the kitchen at his sister as she comes in, helping herself to a treat, too.

"You know Luca, if I didn't know any better, I'd say you were trying to find every excuse you can to see Rose" Grace raises her brow at me, looking just like her brother, "Ha, I said that too. He's definitely taking this to stalker level".

I shoot him a look, but it doesn't deter him. "I told you to just give up. You don't have a chance with her, and you know it," Grace spins on her brother, "What do you mean he doesn't have a chance?" My eyes flit between the pair as they carry on their conversation like I'm not even in the room, "She would eat him alive. That girl does not take shit from anyone and doesn't even say she wouldn't because we both know the last guy she was seeing said he couldn't deal with her 'attitude' and did a runner".

He brings his fingers up in mock speech marks as he finishes his sentence. Grace just shrugs at her brother and brings her gaze back to me, clearly not convinced by his words.

"Well, I for one think Luca would be a good match for her", I smirk as I glance back over to Tristan. He's scowling at me like he always does, and my mind instantly goes back to Rose in my truck the other week.

If these two don't stop me, then I don't think anything will. "What are you doing here on a Saturday anyway?" I always love seeing Grace, since she's with one of my best friends, but usually she escapes work as much as she can. She glances back over to me, a triumphant smile on her face, "I've actually just finished meeting with the new vet for the horses, a couple of them need their annual vaccinations and then some more again in a few months, and one is a little ill at the moment, so we need someone who can be on hand".

She stares at me for a moment longer, before speaking again, "You know what's so weird, you and he look so alike, if I didn't already know you were an only child I'd be wondering if you were related".

I scrunch my face as she assesses me, "Are you sure you're not just thinking we look alike because we have dark hair or something?" She shakes her head at me, "No you had the same eye colour and everything, must be a coincidence", she shrugs her shoulder at me, continuing to make her way through the box of food, like she didn't just imply I have a relative in town.

I wrack my brain to think of who it could be but come up short. I put it down to coincidence too, pushing it to the back of my mind as Grace and

Tristan start bickering again and down the rest of my coffee. Listening to these two bickering for the rest of the afternoon will drive me crazy, the perk of being an only child is that I had no one to bicker or argue with. Some might say that it's better with a sibling, but I'm enough of an extrovert to make up for it. I could make a conversation with a rock if I needed to.

"Okay, I'll leave you two to it. Please try not to kill each other". They barely spare me a glance as I head out. I leave the rest of the treat-filled box on the island and head out to my truck. I don't need any more snacks today, or I'll end up making myself ill.

From Tristans, I make my way to the gym, needing to burn off some of these cakes I seem to be making my way through. I never realised until now how much of a sweet tooth I seem to have. That's what I keep telling myself anyway, not the fact that I get to see a particular redhead every time I go to the bakery for my breakfast.

She's caught on to me coming in all the time already, hovering around so I can speak to her just a little bit. To be honest, I'm surprised she hasn't put a ban on me coming into the shop altogether, but I'm happy she humours me all the same, and I get a little snippet of her life each time I do.

I push the weights until my body can't take anymore, and the sugar rush wears off, dragging my workout as long as I can before heading home for the evening.

I bought my place a couple of years ago and spent my time doing it up, only giving up my city apartment recently and moving towards the suburbs full time. It's nice here, but lonely. I bought it with the intention to one day start a family and settle down like my dad keeps demanding that I do, and I do want that; I just haven't found the right person to do it with until now, but she won't give me the time of day. I shake off the thoughts as I pull up to my home.

The craftsman-style house I bought had a full renovation, and now I actually do enjoy coming here. The living room is cut off and has been made into a cosy private room with a log fire, dark walls with artwork on them, and sofas that you can sink into after a long day, which is precisely where I head when I walk in.

It's the small amount of peace I get when I've been busy working by hiding in here, away from the world for just a few short hours, but sitting and doing nothing is the last thing I should be doing right now as my mind drifts back to Rose as it does more often than not lately.

She looked absolutely perfect today in her loose-fitting jeans, white t-shirt and her hair tied up in a loose bun, with tiny tendrils that come down beside her face. I wanted to reach out too many times to tuck those behind her ear but kept my hands to myself as much as possible.

She might not know how much I want her just yet, but that will change, and soon.

6

Rose

The incessant drip that's coming from my apartment into the kitchen is bugging the life out of me. I thought this place was great when I got it, and not even a month in, I'm already finding problems.

I grab a bucket to put under the drip, making a mental note to try the landlord again. I tried calling him twice yesterday but got no answer, and now I'm going to have to try again today. I wrack my brain to think if anyone I know can check it out for me, but short of calling Luca, I'm at a dead end. Not that I've seen him since last week, and I'm not sure if I'm happy or sad that I haven't seen him in that time either.

He seemed to become a regular every morning for his coffee and cake, and now, radio silence from him. I'm beginning to think he got bored of me running into the kitchen and away from him every chance I got.

I could tell he wanted to ask me something each time he was in from the hovering around he was doing when I'd already given him his order, but I'm worried that question would be for a date, something I'm not sure I'm ready to commit to right now.

Yes, he's unfairly gorgeous with a perfect body to match his face, but his player reputation overrides his looks and charm. A charm that I know gets every woman he wants swooning at his feet.

My train of thought is interrupted by Paisley as she pushes her way through the glass door and into the bakery. Her hair is piled on top of her head in a neat bun, and her face clear from makeup with red blotches surrounding her eyes and cheeks. She looks upset, but I can't quite figure out why.

My eyes follow her as she wanders into the kitchen, her shoulders slumped a little as she gets to work. "Coffee?" I call over to her, seeing if I can fix her mood with some caffeine. Her head shoots up to catch my gaze, "Um, no I'm good, thanks".

That's odd. Usually, she's two cups down before she's even started working. I follow her into the kitchen, resting my arms against the counter as I lean over it, pulling her attention to me, "Hey, are you okay? You don't seem like your usual self".

She glances in my direction, chewing on her lip as she tries to decide if she wants to tell me what's going on. After what seems like forever, she blows out a breath and turns to face me, propping her hip on the counter and scrubbing her hands across her face. "If I tell you, please promise not to tell anyone anything". Alarm bells ring in my head, and I usher her into the seats out front so she can tell me properly what's going on.

"Right, spill".

My tone is no-nonsense, the kind I need to be with her right now. She's like a little sister to me, and I need to help make things right, whatever it is. She plays with her hands in front of her for a moment before lifting her head to speak to me. "Okay, so you know how I was away? Well, I met this guy whilst I was there. He was super lovely, and even though we only spent a couple of weeks together, I genuinely thought that we would carry on seeing each other when we got back home, even though it would have been long distance". I nod, urging her to carry on as I try to figure out where she's going with this.

"Well, I got back, and he's pretty much ghosted me, apart from the one text message that I got from him after I last text". Oh, she's had her heart broken by a boy. "Well, what's meant to be will be; I'm sure if he was the right guy, he will either come back into your life or maybe it just wasn't meant to be at all".

She looks up at me, eyes swimming with tears. *Crap*, she must be pretty hung up on him. "Oh paise, don't cry. There are plenty more guys out there that I'm sure would want to date you".

She sniffs back the tears, shaking her head a little. "That's the problem". She pauses for a moment, blinking back the tears before continuing, "I just found out I'm pregnant, and when I tried to call him, the number said it had disconnected. I have no way to get hold of him and tell him I don't even know where he lives because he said he was moving".

I freeze, blinking back at her. Did she actually just tell me that? "Wait, hold on, you're pregnant?" She nods to me, the sobs coming out thick and fast now. I move around to the other side of the table to hold her. “It’s fine. I’ll be right here for anything you need, and I’m sure your mom and dad will be fine with it, and you are going to be the best mom ever”.

She cries harder into me as I brush my hand down her arm in reassuring strokes, “I just don’t want to do this alone. How can I raise a baby by myself?” That’s one question I don’t really have the answer for because I’ve never been in her position. “You have me and your mom and dad. You’re a part of my family, and nothing will ever change that”. She nods into me, the tears now subsiding as she pulls herself together. “Just so we’re clear, I am assuming you want to keep this baby?”

She laughs at me as if that’s the most absurd thing I could have asked, “Yes, of course I want to keep it. I just didn’t think I was going to be a single mom at twenty-five”.

I rub my hand up and down her arm as she visibly relaxes now that she’s told someone. “You have all of us to help you; even Hallie and Grace will help if you need them too. Are you sure you’re going to be okay?” She nods to me, and I feel myself relax a little and start getting a bit excited, too, now that I know there’s going to be a new baby in the family.

I may not show it to many people, but the idea of having babies and a family of my own is something that I’ve wanted for so long, but finding the right guy is exhausting. I’m beginning to think it might never happen for me. Luca pops into my mind as the thought of babies and a husband does, and he morphs into the dad I see holding my children, the house and the dog that goes along with the fairytale.

I could see him being a good dad, but not to my children because he isn't interested in me like that. I shake the thought away just as quickly as it came when the door goes, and as if I had summoned him with my thoughts, Luca walks through the door, his eyes finding mine instantly.

He grins at me like he does every time he comes in, his flawless smile with perfectly straight white teeth and the dimple on his right cheek making an appearance with it. His smile is quickly replaced with a frown as he takes in the scene in front of him, and Paisley and I quickly scramble to our feet as if we weren't just having a moment together. "Luca, just the man I'm after, I have a leak that needs looking at".

He quirks a brow at me, reading into everything I say as if it's dirty. I roll my eyes at him, turning and motioning him to follow me. "Stop looking at me like that; I think there's a leak coming from my bathroom. Can you have a look? It's in the kitchen".

Luca follows me through, and I point to the offending bucket in the middle of my kitchen floor. "It could be a pipe that's leaking. I'd have to take a look upstairs, but I'm not a plumber, Rose; I can have someone come out to look at it for you and fix it, though". I nod to him, "That would be great. I don't know anyone, and it's been like this since yesterday, and I can't hold off my landlord".

He pulls his phone out and taps away at it. A response comes through almost immediately, and he glances up at me before typing again. "He can't get out here until the end of next week. I'll push to see if he can come any sooner, but for now, I'll go have a look and see if I can stop the drip until he gets out to it".

"Okay, thank you, I'll show you upstairs". He follows me back out of the shop, and I call over to Paisley to say that I won't be there for long. I feel weird for some reason that I'm letting this man into my home. I know him well enough, but knowing how much I find him attractive and not acting on it just seems weird to me.

I show him the bathroom, assuming that is where the leak is coming from, "I'll be downstairs if you need anything". He nods, getting to work quickly for me; I watch him for a moment as he bends over to get a look at the issue, his jeans straining against his perfectly formed ass as they tighten.

A jolt of excitement runs through me, but I have to look away as that feeling quickly turns into arousal. There's just something about watching a man work that's a turn-on for me, and I know I should not be looking at said man the way I am. I make a dart for the bakery, busying myself in the kitchen until I hear the door go. Luca strides back in, not ten minutes after I left him, looking a little flushed.

"It's holding for now, although I don't know how much longer it will stay that way. I'm hoping I can get my guy out to you sooner, but if it gets worse, tell me". I make him his usual coffee and hand it to him, ignoring the heat that spreads through me when our fingers brush. "This one's on the house for that". He looks at the cup in my hand, pulling out cash from his pocket as he does. "I'm not taking anything you've made me for free".

I try to protest and refuse to take it, so instead of handing it to me, he shoves it in the tip jar to the side. "Luca, I don't take handouts". He winks at me, "Neither do I, Red. I have to get going to work, but thanks for the coffee".

I suddenly feel worse that he has made himself late for work on account of helping me, but he's out the door before I can say anything else. I catch Paisley smirking at me from the corner of my eye and turn to her, "What?"

She raises her brow at me knowingly, "You know what. I saw you watching him". Rolling my eyes at her, I busy myself with readjusting the pastries in the cabinet, "You know nothing. So what, he's good-looking, doesn't mean I'm going to act on it; we have nothing in common, and I'm certainly not his type".

She chuckles beside me, "Yeah, all right. You keep telling yourself that". I ignore the snippy little comments and get back to work, keeping myself busy with the steady roll of customers coming through the doors, putting Luca to the back of my mind once and for all.

7

Luca

I managed to avoid stopping in and checking on Rose for a whole week before giving in to temptation. Now, as I enter day four of the week following her leaky pipe situation, I can't help myself when I make the turn to go past her shop again on my morning run.

If I time it just right, I might be able to catch a glimpse of her heading in to set up for the day. I know I'm bordering on stalker level right now, but I can't help but want to see her any glimpse I can get. As I round the corner, I spot Rose sitting on the edge of the curb with her head in her hands. Panic claws up me as I up my pace to get to her a little faster, and as I near her, she must hear me because she jumps a little, taking a moment to realise who I am because it's still a little dark out.

"Hey, what's going on? Why are you sitting out here?" I barely get my words out as I try to steady my breathing. Her hand flies to her chest as she gulps in a breath. "Shit Luca, you scared the life out of me. It's five thirty in the morning. What are you doing here?"

I motion down to my clothing, brushing the small amount of sweat from my head. "I run this way sometimes. What's going on?" She lets out a huge sigh, and her hands come up to scrub over her face. "That pipe you kind of fixed the other day blew, along with two others. My whole place is flooded, and half of my bathroom along with part of my kitchen are missing upstairs. It's a mess inside".

Guilt consumes me, I thought I had fixed it enough that this wouldn't happen, and now her whole place is ruined, "Shit, I'm so sorry; I should have just found an emergency plumber to come out the same day for you. This is all my fault". Rose whips her head up, her eyes narrowing as she does, "Don't you dare put this on yourself. It's my fault for not making sure everything was up to scratch when I signed for the place".

I nod to her, completely ignoring that she said it's not my fault, "Have you spoken to your landlord? What can I do to help?" Her head shakes as she motions for me to follow her inside, and as we trudge through the small amount of water that now traces along the entire floor, another wave of guilt washes over me.

"He hasn't been answering my calls; I don't know what's going on. I know he said he hasn't been in the greatest of health recently, but surely a family member would have seen his tenant ringing his phone constantly. I don't know, but either way, I don't even know what to do. I can't stay in my flat; the bathroom is ruined along with the kitchen, and the downstairs kitchen is flooded too".

We stand in the front of her shop, thankfully this part isn't too bad, although the ceiling has seen better days, and only a tiny amount of water is here, but as I make my way into the kitchen, it looks like half of the appliances have been ruined from water damage. I glance up to the ceiling, where there is a massive hole now there, plaster hanging down from where it's come through.

I turn to Rose, her arms are wrapped around herself as she studies the place more, her lip is pulled between her teeth, and a small tear streaks down her face. The guilt amplifies, and I pull her into me and wrap my arms around her, "It will be all right. We'll get this sorted in no time at all". A sob breaks free from her as she buries her head in my chest. "I just don't know what to do. I poured my life savings into this place, and now I have nothing".

I pull her back, holding her at arm's length as my eyes search hers. "Listen to me, you're going to come stay with me, and I will get this all sorted for you, I have contacts that can fix this, I don't want you to worry about anything". Her eyes go wide, and she shakes her head at me again, stepping out of my hold just enough that I lose my grip on her. "No, I can't stay with you. I mean, thank you for the offer, but I'll be all right, I promise". I chuckle at her comment, like she thinks that will stop me fixing this.

Leaning into her space, I keep my voice low and firm as I level my gaze with hers, "I'm sorry if you misunderstood, but that wasn't a question. Get a bag packed. You're coming to stay with me". She pulls herself out of the trance she was in, staring me down.

"Luca, no. I'll go and stay with Grace or something". The rational part of my brain knows that I should agree with her and that she should go stay with her friend, but I'm not a rational man. "I caused this problem by not getting someone out for you when I saw the damage, so you're staying with me, pack a bag". She huffs at me but relents and makes her way towards the front of the shop.

I call up some guys to come clear all the damaged goods from the place and make a mental list of the things I need to sort in order for this to be fixed, hanging around whilst they make their way over, and start digging to find out who her landlord is and why he's been ignoring her this whole time.

It took hours for the team to clear up the mess the flooding had left, and almost everything was damaged. Rose had been a complete mess all afternoon. I tried to calm her down the best I could, but she would be fine one minute and then angry the next.

By the time we're done sorting everything out and saving what we could, it's gone 10pm in the evening. I had to shift my day around, but I was not about to leave her to deal with the mess herself, especially since it was my fault.

I grab her keys from the side, and after packing the last few bits of hers into her truck, she goes to jump in the driver's seat, but I put an arm out to stop her, resting it on the door frame. She stops abruptly, scowling at me, "Luca, seriously, I need to get in the car". I nod to her, "I know you do, and the passenger side is over there. No chance am I letting you drive after the day you've had".

Rose opens her mouth to protest, but I grab her shoulders and spin her around on the spot. "Get your ass in the car before I have to put you there myself". My comment earns me another scowl from over her shoulder as she makes her way around the car, and I grin back at her. I love winding her up, but more so when she's being a little brat and won't listen. I don't think I've ever met anyone so stubborn in my life.

I spend the whole drive over to my place gripping the steering wheel like my life depends on it, my knuckles turning white from the pressure I have on it. I make sure to avoid looking in Rose's direction, holding on to hope that she won't come to hate me for fucking her place up. By the time we pull up and I glance over to her, she's fallen asleep, her head resting against the door frame.

I let out a sigh, preparing myself for when she wakes up, as I look up to my house, knowing it's not just going to be me here anymore. My place isn't obnoxious like most people would think I'd have. I designed it myself and had it built a couple of years ago. I only actually moved into it at the beginning of last year, and it's pretty big for just me, so I'm sort of glad that I now have someone staying here to fill the empty space.

Timber frames surrounding the outside, giving it a farmhouse feel, but with big glass windows to allow as much light in as possible, it backs onto the other side of the large lake, the same one that Rose and her friends have their house, so my back yard looks out over it every morning too.

It's bigger than most on the street, but the space still feels warm and cosy inside, with a large modern kitchen out back, and a separate living space, with my office off to one side, allowing me to have the view of the lake from there as well as my kitchen. I do have a guest room downstairs, but I figure I'd rather have Rose close to me as I climb out and round the car to her side.

I open her door, and she doesn't even budge. I'm running out of mental energy for the evening, so I go with the easier option and quickly scoop her into my arms to save time. She lets out a squeal as the movement wakes her, but she's tiny, so she's easy to carry. "Luca put me down", she whines sleepily, "I can walk".

I stop, turning my head so our faces are so close that our lips almost touch. The thought of kissing her instantly fills my mind, but I push it back out just as fast. "I want to get to bed at some point tonight, so just let me do this, and we can get inside". She stares back blankly at me but nods her head, choosing to keep that pretty little mouth shut for once.

I walk us into the house, putting her down in the entrance hall and run back out to my truck to grab a few of her things, and when I get back, I stop short, watching her for a minute as she looks around.

Her eyes are wide as she takes in the space, the tall, vaulted ceilings allowing extra light in the place during the daytime, but the entry hall is dark right now, since it's late. Rose will be the first woman to stay here, and I can't lie, I'm a little nervous about sharing my space with someone else.

She was pissed at me all day for demanding that she come stay with me, but I couldn't have left her back there, not knowing where she would end up, so she'll just have to suck it up and get used to our new living arrangements.

I take her bags up to the spare room across the hall from mine, having her follow me up. "Shit Luca, this place is really something, although I pegged you more of an apartment in the city kind of guy". I put her bags in the wardrobe, turning to look at her as my lips tip up into a smirk. "I did have one in the city too, but I just sold it to live here permanently, and one day I'll hopefully start a family here".

She looks at me a little shocked, turning her head as she takes in the queen size bed in front of her as I walk over to the bathroom, flicking the light on for her, "This is the biggest guest room, you have a full bathroom and wardrobe in here, so you'll feel right at home, I'm just across the hall if you need anything, but this is your home now, until yours is fixed anyway, so just do what you usually do, the kitchen is fully stocked so grab anything you want, and add whatever you like to the shopping list on the fridge if you want anything picking up".

"Thanks Luca, I really appreciate this, and um.. I'm sorry about my mood all day, I know that you were only trying to help". She looks over to me as she says it, her teeth pulling at her lip as she stands there. I nod to her and quickly make my way over to the door but stop to turn and look at her one last time as I reach the doorway, "Don't worry about it. Sleep tight Red, see you in the morning".

I rap my knuckles on the door frame before closing it and almost running to my room, taking a long shower as I try to reign in my thoughts about Rose. She's got such a sexy little body. I felt how petite she was when I held her tonight, all because in the back of my mind, I wanted any excuse to touch her, but now I know how she feels, I can't get the touch of her out of my head, and my dick is hard as a rock.

I fist it, bracing my free hand on the wall as I squeeze the base, my head filled with thoughts of her, imagining it was her mouth around me instead of my hand. The water runs down my back as I move my hand up and down my cock, bringing myself to my release and watching as it washes down the shower drain.

I need to get a grip of myself if I'm going to have to live with this woman for the next few weeks at least. I quickly finish up in the shower and make my way out to the bedroom.

Hearing Roses' door open and her soft footsteps pad down the hallway, presumably going to get herself a drink. I go to open my door and check on her but think better of it and head straight to my bed, climbing in and close my eyes, trying like hell to get to sleep, but all night my thoughts are filled with the image of Rose's pink lips, parted and staring back at me.

8

Rose

The feeling of silky soft sheets float over my skin as I come around from one of the best sleeps I've had in a while. Somehow, even after the events of yesterday, I grabbed myself a shower and ran downstairs, hoping to avoid bumping into Luca again as I got myself a drink from the kitchen and climbed into bed, eventually drifting off into a peaceful sleep.

I peel my eyes open, the room still dark with the curtains drawn, and grab my phone to check the time. It's still relatively early, given how late I crawled into bed, so I just lay there for a while thinking about my poor shop and how lucky I was that Luca happened to be in the area.

I'm glad he helped me and brought me back to his place, even though I kicked off and had sworn to myself I wouldn't ever accept his offer to stay, but this house is pure luxury, and I can't think of a single reason right now why I even said no in the first place.

I swing my legs out of bed, heading into the bathroom to brush my teeth, and have a nosey around it whilst I do. I didn't get much chance with it being so late last night. It's a nice size and has everything I need, with a panelled glass partition for the shower;

all of the fixtures are black apart from the toilet, and the walls are a deep grey tile, sitting flush from floor to ceiling.

A soaker tub sits against the frosted window, with a single vanity with a light-up mirror sitting above it on the opposite side. It's allowing a warm glow to flow through the bathroom from the golden light it gives off. It's giving me hotel vibes from the way everything is placed so strategically. After spending far too much time examining everything in the bathroom, I make my way downstairs, not knowing if Luca is up already or not.

When I reach the kitchen in search of hot coffee, I stop short, seeing a half-naked Luca standing over the coffee machine while talking into his phone. His back is to me, and he's so engrossed in his conversation that he hasn't noticed me come downstairs, so I take the time to soak him in. The ridged muscles in his back as he moves around the kitchen, his hair is wet and mused from his shower that drips a little down the back of his neck, and grey sweatpants that are hanging just a little too low on his hips.

He's slim but tall, and strong. Really strong because he somehow managed to carry me last night like I weighed nothing. He turns slightly, giving me a view of his side as his muscles flex, showing the outline of his abs. He must work out a lot, surely, because no one looks that good without working for it.

I hear a throat clearing, and my eyes snap up to meet his chocolate ones, crinkling a little at the sides of them. A smirk is tracing his lips as he watches me. Heat creeps up my throat as the embarrassment of being caught takes over, and I immediately avert my gaze to the coffee machine beside him, trying not to show how desperately I am checking him out.

Trying to think of something that doesn't make me sound stupid around this man, I quickly remember the reason I came downstairs in the first place, "I, um, came down for some coffee", I point to the machine next to his body and shift my gaze back to his momentarily, catching him as his eyes rake up and down my body in return, my eyes drop to what I'm wearing. I cringe, realising I'm wearing an oversized t-shirt that's hiding my shorts underneath.

I quickly tug at the hem of my shirt, embarrassed knowing he thinks I'm prancing around his house half-naked.

"I have shorts on! Sorry, I will try to remember that I'm not by myself anymore", I let out a nervous chuckle as I mumble the words. His eyes lazily come back to mine, his smirk now turning into a full-blown grin, "You wear whatever you like, Red. You'll be here by yourself most of the time anyway. I'm going back to Florida tomorrow for a week. A housekeeper will be in later today to keep things tidy, so you'll have her around if you need anything".

I hide the disappointment that springs out of nowhere at the thought of him leaving so soon, but I know it's better that we don't get in each other's way. I shake my head a little to clear my thoughts and head over to the coffee machine to pour myself a cup.

It's full of random buttons and way too high-tech for me, so I spare a glance in Luca's direction. He's watching me still, but amusement is clear on his face when he sees I can't figure this dam thing out. I turn back to it, trying to figure it out on my own.

"Need some help there?" I still slightly as his voice comes from a little too close to me, and I realise that he's right behind me when his chest brushes against my back, sending a shiver through me. One of his arms come around to the front of me, whilst the other rests against the countertop. I peek down at his long fingers and the veins that run along his hand, wondering what they would feel like against my skin.

He cages me in as he presses a few buttons on the machine, showing me as he goes, and I try my best to concentrate on what he's showing me instead of drinking in his fresh scent. Coffee begins pouring out of the machine, and the smell hits my nostrils, making me release the breath I didn't know I was holding.

He leans into me a little more as the cup finishes filling up, his breath fanning my bare neck and sending goosebumps over me. "There you go, you think you can remember that, or do you want me to write it down for you?"

My mind fogs as I inhale his scent, and for a moment forget he actually asked me a question. The beep from the coffee machine pulls me out of my

Luca-induced haze as I remember what he said to me, "Um, yeah, it's fine. I'll remember it, thank you". Luca's hand lightly grazes over my hip as he pulls back, and I'm not sure if he realises how much he's having an effect on me, but if he does, he doesn't say anything as he walks back over to grab his own mug from the side, taking a sip from it as he watches me again.

He's quiet for a minute as he thinks of what to say, his fingers playing with the top of his mug whilst he does. "I just got off the phone with my team. They're going to start sorting work on your place, and I'm still working on getting hold of your landlord, but let me worry about that. You can use the kitchen in the meantime for any orders you've got". I smile over to him, so grateful for everything he's doing to help me. "Thank you, Luca, you really didn't need to do that for me".

"It's the least I could have done for you. I feel responsible for this, so I needed to sort it". I shake my head at him, "Luca, this wasn't your fault, please don't blame yourself". His jaw clenches as he watches me, "No, it is my fault. I should have called someone out as soon as I saw how bad the pipes were, and I didn't. So let me just do what I need to do, you don't have to worry about a thing". I let out a sigh, feeling a little more at ease about the situation but equally hating the fact that he's blaming himself for this and won't let up.

He pauses for a moment, a worried expression crossing his face. "Are you sure you're okay with me going away and leaving you? I know we're not best friends or anything, but I feel kinda bad leaving tomorrow when you just had your whole life turned upside down". I wave him off, feeling a little better that he doesn't actually want to leave me by myself so soon. "Don't worry about me; I've got a load of orders I need to fill so I can keep myself busy, and I'll pop around to see Grace and Jaxx if I need anything".

His eyes sweep over my face one last time before giving me a quick nod, "All right, well I have to head to the office for a little while and won't be back until later this evening, so just sort yourself out for dinner, if I don't see you tonight then I'll catch you when I'm back".

I nod to him in thanks, and he turns to walk out of the room, stopping and turning slightly when he remembers something else, "Oh, I have the housekeeper do the food shopping, so don't worry about having to go get it".

My eyes bug out of my head at his comment, but I move myself around so he can't see my expression. I knew he had money, but I feel like that's just another level, I turn my back placing my mug down on the counter, "Mmm hmm, yep, that's fine, I'll remember to write what I need". With that, he takes his leave upstairs, and I melt onto one of the nearby chairs, sinking into it as I feel another wave of embarrassment rush over me.

My family don't struggle, my dad runs his own law firm, but I never saw the side of money my mom does, because she spends it all. And I mean every last penny he makes. I sometimes wonder why he lets her do what she does to him, but she clearly has some sort of hold on him, for him to allow her to do what she does. My mind moves on as I give way to the thoughts in my head and let myself study the huge kitchen whilst I sit finishing the rest of my coffee.

It's such a beautiful house, the back of it overlooking a serene lake, the same one ours backs onto, with floor-to-ceiling windows that spread along the back wall of the kitchen, allowing natural light to flood the space.

The modern oak countertops complement the navy blue cupboards perfectly, while a dark navy splashback adds a touch of elegance along the walls. An archway to the right of the kitchen leads to a spacious dining room, furnished with a large wooden table and matching chairs, perfect for hosting dinner parties or family gatherings.

It suits Luca to a tee. I vaguely remember Grace mentioning that he designed the entire house himself, and now it makes sense seeing it in person. Every detail has a personal touch, merging modernity with the warmth of a family home. The open-plan layout in the back creates a seamless flow between the rooms, making the house feel even bigger than it already is.

My mind drifts back to last night and him saying he bought this with having a family in mind, but I still find it odd that he sleeps about so much knowing that he was going to settle down eventually, maybe he hasn't found the one yet. *God, I hope he doesn't bring any of the girls back here.* I let out a groan as the thought comes to my head, I don't think I'd be able to deal with him having a different girl here every week.

I eventually push the thought to the side, finishing up my coffee, hunting out the dishwasher to put my cup away, and heading back upstairs to enjoy a hot bath in the huge tub I've got in my bathroom. I stay there until I'm wrinkly and the bubbles have all disappeared. I drag myself out, wrapping myself in the towel hanging on the door, and grab my phone to call Hallie.

She answers quickly, "Hey girl, how's the bakery treating you? I'll call over tomorrow when I'm back in town". She's not got a clue about what went on yesterday.

I sit up a little taller as I delve into the story of what happened, "Hallie, you wouldn't believe it, but a few pipes burst and the whole place flooded, everything is ruined, and I was having a mini meltdown at first but then Luca turned up and saved the day. He's organised everything getting fixed on the place, although I feel awful. He's blaming himself for it because I asked him to look at a pipe a few days ago, and now this has happened".

I blow out a breath after finishing my sentence; I tend to ramble when I need to get things out. Hallie gasps down the phone, "I'm sorry, what? Are you okay? I can't even believe that happened. Wait, where are you staying if your place is flooded?"

I chuckle down the phone at my friend's confusion, "So, the funny thing is because he's so adamant that this is his fault, Luca demanded I come back to his place. So, I'm currently sitting in my new bedroom. His house is fucking huge".

"How big are we talking? I might have to come round one night". I snort a laugh down the phone, Hallie doesn't shy away, she's just like me, most of the time. The shyness and embarrassment seem to have only developed when I'm around Luca. "He's actually going to Florida for a week from tomorrow, so please come round this week so I'm not by myself, I'm sure he won't mind".

"I don't care if he minds or not. I'll come see my girl either way". The tone in her voice is light, letting me know she's joking as she says it, but I find it funny, imagining Hallie telling Luca off.

"Okay, deal. Well, I'll let you get back to your day, but I'll see you this week, and I'll message Grace too".

"Yeah, sounds good, see you soon, love you".

She goes off the phone, and I throw mine onto the bed beside me. I lay there for a short while, a million different things going through my head, as I go from thinking about last night, to then this morning.

Luca seems to be the forefront of each and every single thought that I seem to have right now, and that can't be a good thing. Yeah he's hot, but I seriously need to watch myself and not get too tempted by his good looks or charm.

I eventually push the thoughts aside, getting up to explore the house a little more as I wander down the hall, peaking into the other rooms. There are two other rooms upstairs, one with another bed in it seemingly a second guest bedroom, and the other with a few boxes, I guess he mustn't have gotten round to fully unpacking yet. They're smaller than my room, Luca seems to have put me in the biggest one aside from his. I pull the door shut and find the most enormous bathroom I think I've ever seen. I thought the one in my room was big, but the huge claw tub sitting in front of the large windows has me staring in awe. I glance over, noticing the double shower too, and wonder what the bathroom in his room is like, if this is so big. I pull myself back, shutting that door and wander downstairs to check out the rest of the house.

The living room is cosy, with a huge plush corner couch that you could definitely sink into and two large armchairs opposite it, they all look like you could fall asleep on them, and I spot a few blankets rolled up near the large fireplace, hmm Luca likes to cosy up clearly. Theres another guest room down here too, but I close the door on it, and turn and head into the kitchen to grab a glass of juice, checking in the freezer to see if he has any ice cream in.

I'm disappointed to find it bare of sweet treats, so I grab the pen that's stuck to the fridge, writing out cookie dough ice cream on the list that's there.

Happy with what I've written, I go to put the pen back when I hear Luca's deep, smooth voice from behind me, "Hmm, ice cream, yeah, I could definitely do with some of that stocked". I freeze up, not realising he had snuck in on me. Spinning on my heel I turn to face him, not realising my towel has loosened as I go.

I feel like everything happens in slow motion as I spin around, feeling the towel drop from where it was tucked and onto the floor, leaving me standing butt-naked in front of Luca.

His mouth drops open at the sight of me, eyes wide as saucers, clearly not thinking to divert his eyes from me. I feel the heat take over my body, turning my skin a shade of rosy red. My hands come up to cover myself, and it's then he realises he's been gawping at me. His eyes snap up to meet mine, his brows shooting right to his hairline. God, this is so fucking embarrassing.

"Fuck Red, I didn't think I was gonna get a strip show from you this morning. Is this your way of apologising for being a brat yesterday?" I scowl at his shit joke, my voice coming out a little snappy as I reply, "Don't fucking sneak up on me! My towel must have come loose, and you startled me; I wasn't stripping for you".

A sexy smirk takes over his face as he tries and fails not to look down at my naked body, he's close enough to me though, that he bends down, reaching out to grab the towel off the floor, keeping his eyes on mine the whole time.

He pulls it open, wrapping it around me as he leans in close and murmurs in my ear, "Sorry I made you jump, Red, but I'm not sorry I got to see you like that". He pulls back, the slight smile still playing on his lips as my fingers try to grab hold of the towel again before he lets go. Just as quickly as he came in here, he turns on his heel and begins to walk out of the door, shouting over his shoulder as he leaves, "Came back to grab something, but I'll make sure to announce my entrance loudly next time. See you soon Red".

I stand speechless as his body retreats out of the room away from me, and I try to wrap my head around how I'm going to get through the next few weeks living with him and not fucking him.

9

Luca

Fucking hell. What did I just walk into then? I wanted to stay a lot longer than I did, but the sensible part of my brain kicked in and made me move my ass to another room. Far, far away from Rose and her perfect tits.

I rush to my office, shutting the door and taking a breather. Allowing the view out of the back of the house to help remove the filthy thoughts from my head that are now stuck there, along with the picture-perfect image of a very naked Rose. I move around my oak desk and grab the paperwork from the bottom drawer, silently cursing myself for allowing my eyes to wander down her tight little body.

All 5ft 4 of her naked, just asking for me to touch her skin. She probably would have punched me if I actually did, but the thought of doing it was enough for me, the worst kind of torture for someone who's trying to behave themselves and be a gentleman. I definitely wasn't being today, nor have I been any other time I've been in her presence, but I tried at least.

I move around the room, grabbing everything I might need so I don't have to come back today, and make my way to my truck, making sure I keep my head firmly on the direction I'm headed in and don't even chance a look into the kitchen where she very well could still be.

I don't want to fuck up any more than I already have, and with any luck, she might not move out after our little slip-up. I need to get her out of my head, and fast. It's bad enough that I practically forced her to live in my house, but I really shouldn't rock the boat and do anything stupid until I can somehow convince her to date me.

My mind is somewhere else as I make the twenty-minute drive to work, and I take the longest route I can go, stopping off at the drive-thru for coffee on the way. By the time I pull up, I struggle even to remember half of the drive. I park my car and head into the large glass building that's held my dad's firm for the past ten years, enjoying the peace and quiet on a Sunday and knowing that the office will be dead. Hopefully, it means I'm able to get some work done.

I figured I'd get more done today without my dad nagging me every five minutes, or my assistant trying to hit on me every time she comes into my office, having too many excuses to 'need to see me in person'.

I really should do as my dad says and hire a guy, but other than her walking around with her shirt a little too low and her skirt far too tight, she's actually done nothing that warrants me firing her.

I dump the files I grabbed onto my desk and make myself my third coffee of the morning to hopefully keep me going. I had possibly the worst night's sleep. I spent a good portion of it with my thoughts filled with Rose, wanting to protect her and fuck her all at once, and then remembering all over again how much of a stupid fucking idea this whole thing was, inviting a woman I can't get out of my head to live with me.

I bury myself in work for the next couple of hours, trying to do as much as I can so the day drags on, just so I can avoid having to go home to sit and make small talk with the woman I need to keep out of my mind. Instead of doing the work I came in the office to do, though, I spend the time ignoring the new blueprints I really need to look at and go back and forth in my head for way too long, procrastinating when I shouldn't be over whether I should make moves on Rose or not. The last thing she needs is me hitting on her after I gave her a place to stay, and in the back of my head, I know I really should leave her alone.

By mid-afternoon, I figure I'm not getting anything productive done like I set out to do and get changed into my workout clothes, heading to the gym we have on the top floor of the office.

The steady hum of the air conditioning and the rhythmic thud of my shoes against the treadmill are the only sounds filling the space. I run hard, each footfall a steady beat against the belt, each breath sharp and controlled. I run for what feels like hours, sweat trickles down my back as I push myself further and further, forcing my legs to keep moving, as if I can outrun my own thoughts.

Minutes blur into an hour. Then another. By the time I finally stop, my body is trembling with exertion, my muscles burning from the relentless pace I've kept. My shirt is drenched, clinging to me uncomfortably, and my lungs ache with the effort of keeping up. I wipe my face with a towel, breathing heavily as I finally admit defeat. There's no running from her, not really.

Giving in, I head downstairs to my car, deciding to shower at home instead of here. My brain reminds me that I still need to pack before my flight tomorrow, but my stomach has other priorities. A loud growl echoes through the car, a pointed reminder that all I've had today is coffee. I pull out my phone and order some Italian to pick up on the way home, making sure to get a little extra. Just in case Rose hasn't eaten.

I weirdly feel myself getting excited as I approach my house, knowing I have someone here to greet me at home, which surprises me because I usually hate having people over who aren't my closest friends. As I pull up to the house I spot her car on the drive, but disappointment fills me when I look up to see the lights are all out. Maybe she went to bed, it's only half eight so she could also be out, she does have a social life and friends after all.

I trudge into the house, plating out some food and decide to head into the living room to eat whilst catching up on the ice hockey, but stop short when I spot Rose, curled up and fast asleep on the couch with a book resting on her arm as her wild curls splay across the couch cushions.

I feel like I'm intruding on her privacy, watching her sleep, but I can't help myself. I stay in the doorway, watching her for a couple seconds more, then head back into the kitchen to eat my food, not wanting to wake her.

I finish my food in what feels like record time, knowing I should probably just go upstairs myself, but I start thinking about Rose instead, tapping my fingers on the kitchen counter as I get carried away with my thoughts and whether I should take her upstairs or wake her.

The urge to hold her and spend what little time I can with her before I go away pushes its way to the front of my mind, as I grab my plate, shove it in the dishwasher and go as quietly as I can into the living room, scooping her up into my arms.

She doesn't even move an inch as I carry her, and I'd be worried she was in a worse condition if I didn't hear her light snoring when I poked my head in earlier. I place her on the bed, pulling the covers up and over her to tuck her in, and she finally moves about a little, readjusting to get more comfortable.

I realise I should probably leave her alone, and I'm about to move away from her, but I see her lashes flutter and her eyes open as she peeks up at me.

She blinks a couple of times, and her eyes move around the room trying to figure out how she got there and what I'm doing staring at her. My hand reaches out instinctively, brushing the hair off her face. “Hey, you fell asleep on the couch. I tried not to wake you”, I say in a hushed voice, trying not to startle her any more than I have, and she nods sleepily at me. There’s some food in the kitchen if you get hungry, but I’m gonna head to my room and pack for my trip, so I’ll see you when I’m back, yeah?”

Her voice comes out a little croaky when she responds to me, “Okay, thank you, see you soon”. Her eyes close again almost instantly as she falls back asleep, instead of just getting up and walking out like I should do, I lean down and press a kiss to her head, brushing the hairs from her face as I do, before standing from the bed making a swift exit for the door.

I don’t look back. I can’t, or the urge to climb in with her will be too much for me, and I’ll do something I regret, so I focus on what I should be doing and head to my wardrobe, mindlessly throwing a few pairs of jeans and shirts into my bag.

I’m not a guy for suits, never have been. I prefer to wear my boots, Jeans and a shirt, and I don’t mind if any of the staff in the office keep it more causal too, we’re on and off building sites all of the time, so the last thing anyone wants to be doing is getting an expensive suit filthy.

My dad loves a suit, and it shows in the way he speaks to me and other people sometimes, but I just want people to see me as an equal, not always as a boss. They know where they stand with me and not to push it, but what’s the point in having people that fear you, like some people fear my father.

I pack my bag quickly, shoving the rest of the bits I need into it and jump in the shower, knowing I need to be up early for a flight. I figure I'll probably end up sleeping on the plane at this point.

.....

All sleep evades me yet again. I spent the night tossing and turning, making me sleep through my alarm, and when I woke up late, I was grumpy with everyone, and unfortunately, that included my assistant, who was tagging along on the trip.

I told her she could dress down a little more since we are over in Florida and that she doesn't need to be so formal in the office all the time and certainly not when travelling, but when I board the plane and take my seat, she appears not five minutes later, wearing what looks like the most uncomfortable dress.

I sigh looking over to her, "Cora, you really didn't need to dress so formally, I've told you so many times, you must be uncomfortable". She shakes her head at me, even though I can see in her face and the way she's moving about, she really isn't comfy at all. "I'm used to this. Honestly, I'm fine, don't worry about me".

She takes her seat next to mine, and I can't help but wonder if she always wears things like this. Her blonde hair is pulled back into a tight bun, her face not too thick with makeup, but enough you can tell she's made the effort, and she's squeezed herself into a tight black dress that looks like it could suffocate her. She's a pretty girl, but not my type. *Neither is Rose, but you want her.*

I ignore the voice in my head and grunt my response, returning back to the work I've brought on the plane with me, the beauty of traveling business means I get the space to do my job without worrying about bashing the person next to me, and thankfully Cora gets the hint that we need to work and pulls out her own laptop.

The majority of the flight is spent working and I barely hear a peep out of her, and by some miracle we actually manage to work in comfortable silence for the most part. By the time we land and get to the office where our meeting is, it's only just gone past lunch. The car waiting takes us straight to the office, and as soon as we're in I grab my phone again, replying to emails as Cora gets me up to date on the meeting ahead and other events I need to respond to.

"Whilst you're here, you need to attend the dinner that has been book by your father. He's asking if you will be attending with the date he's got in mind". I try and fail to hide my irritation as I glance up from my phone at her, "You have got to be kidding me, this is a business dinner, and he wants me to attend with a date".

She looks down at her tablet, before nodding and looking back up to me. "Yep, that's what he's requested. He expressed the need for you to find a wife multiple times, so I'm not sure why this surprises you".

Her bluntness has me whipping my head around, "And what exactly does that have to do with the dinner?" She blinks back at me, biting her lip like she does every time I seem to ask her something she doesn't want to answer.

"I um. I'm not entirely sure Luca. But this isn't the first time he has requested it. I can find someone on short notice for you in replacement for who he has". I scoff, shaking my head at her. "No, I won't be attending anything with a date whilst I'm here. He can just deal with it".

She nods, clearly not happy with my answer, and mumbles something about me taking her, but I choose to ignore her and push forward with the rest of the day's agenda, making a mental note to have her moved to another floor and hire myself a male assistant when we get back home, because fuck me this is going to be a long week.

10

Rose

The first few days in the house without Luca seem to go by without any problems, and after our little mishap the other day, I make sure to wear some form of clothing each and every time I leave my room.

The housekeeper must have been around as well, as the house looks like it's had a thorough cleaning, with the scent of fresh linen lingering in the air and the floors gleaming as though newly polished. The fresh towels in my bathroom were another pleasant surprise, neatly folded and arranged with a small lavender sachet, adding a soothing fragrance to the room.

On Monday afternoon, after a long day of making deliveries around town, I poked my head in the fridge, which had been stocked with all my favourite foods, including some fresh fruits, vegetables, and even a variety of cheeses I hadn't tried before.

The added edition of extra ice cream in the freezer was the cherry on top. It felt like a small treat after a tiring day. I took my time to organise everything, smiling at the thoughtfulness behind these small gestures.

By the time Friday rolls around though, I'm ready for the weekend to arrive. I decided to stop orders early after such a busy week, along with some wine that was nicely stocked in the fridge for me whilst I wait for the girls to arrive for our wine night that's now moved to here.

I stopped by the bakery this morning, surprised at how quickly they had the place cleared out and ready to get fixed up. I dump my bag by the door, toeing my shoes off and head into the kitchen to grab myself a glass of wine and stop short when I see a box on the kitchen island with a sticky note attached to it.

Rose,
A little gift for you.
Luca

I stare at the note and the shiny new mixer boxed up in front of me. I'm not sure what I did to deserve all this nice treatment I'm getting from him, when I've done absolutely nothing but take up space in his house and cause him problems. I grab my phone from my bag, texting him to thank him for the purchase.

ME*: Thank you for the mixer, although I'm not sure what I've done to deserve it.*

I sit staring at my phone, weirdly hoping that he will reply but nothing comes through, so I grab my laptop and head into the living room to do some accounts and admin while waiting for the girls. I'm working for a few hours when a message comes back through from Luca,

***LUCA**: Not a problem. I know you needed one, so I saved you the trouble. Just accept the gift, and don't overthink it.*

I should probably send a nice reply back to him, but I know that will do me no good as I'll just end up coming out with some sarky comment, so I go with the next best stupid option my brain picks out for me by googling him instead.

It's probably the worst thing I could have done for my ego when a recent picture pops up on the screen of him escorting a beautiful brunette into a restaurant. I'm instantly deflated. I mean, the text message he sent literally said don't overthink it, and here I am pretending I don't know the guy isn't the hottest thing around with every girl after him. I let out a sigh, pushing my laptop to the side and going in search of some more wine.

I don't even know why I let my mind get carried away over thinking these situations and this weird crush I seemed to have developed for him. Luca is a player, and the sooner I remember that, the better. I'm just his lodger. There will be no playing house while I'm here.

I settle back onto the couch, waiting for Hallie and Grace to arrive so we can finally order some food. We'd agreed that tonight would be the best night as Hallie is back from her brothers for the weekend, and Jaxx is working the night shift, so Grace doesn't want to be alone.

They finally arrive and I'm so hungry we get food ordered straight away before falling into our usual conversation, catching up on everything. Hallie takes the opportunity to give herself a tour around the place. Grace has already been here a few times with Jaxx, so she's used to it by now.

Hallie comes wandering back into the living room after doing her full tour, wide eyes shifting around everywhere as she spots something new. "Damm, this guy has got some taste. I mean I know what nice houses look like, my brother's houses are all gorgeous, but this is not what I expected from him". I hum in agreement. Hallie's three brothers all play ice hockey, two for the Silver Wolves here in Tennessee, the team my cousin just became a PT for, and the other for the Red Bears in New York, so she's not short on the limelight side of things, or the big fancy houses.

I wave my hand around the room, "Yeah, it is pretty nice, but I definitely thought he'd have gone for something a bit flashier. I'm just wondering how many girls he's had here". I sit back into the cushions, my brain taking over with intrusive thoughts of Luca having sex on the couch.

Grace lets out a little chuckle, shaking her head at me from across the seat, "You think he's brought girls here? No way, that was reserved for the apartment downtown. He's never had a girl here". She sits smirking at me and begins tapping her finger on the chin, "Come to think of it, you're actually the first girl I think he's had to stay from what I know". I sit glaring back at my friend, knowing full well she said that to wind me up, but it does have me thinking maybe Luca isn't who I had him pegged as since he told me he's just sold it.

"Well shit. I wouldn't have thought that. He can still be an asshole sometimes, although he did have a new mixer sent to the house for me to help with work, and the fridge is fully stocked with wine and ice cream, so I guess that's something that may redeem him slightly". The girls share a look, and I wonder if they think I'm really into him, so I quickly move the topic along to other subjects, like how long this house is going to take to be ready.

"Have you got any news on when the house will be complete yet, Hallie?" She sighs shaking her head, "No, they're dragging their feet to be honest, but I did try to push it a bit further along. I love my brother but he's driving me insane". I couldn't agree more with her. As much as it's nice here, I know my time is limited, and I don't want to get myself too comfy knowing I'll be leaving here soon. "Hmm yeah, I know what you mean, hopefully it won't be too much longer, and we can finally move back in".

She gives me a funny look, like she's confused as to why I'd want to move out of here, "Surely it can't be that bad living with Luca, I mean he's nice to look at, surely that's something".

I shrug a little, “Yeah, I can’t say I’m not enjoying him in his gym clothes on a daily basis. I don’t think I ever really looked at him like that before I guess”.

The girls share a look, “What?” They look back at me, Grace biting her lip while she figures her words out. “I think Luca might actually be trying to change his ways, maybe you should test the waters with him, see if he is actually interested in you”, I blink back at the girls, my head trying to get a grasp on what their saying. “I don’t think I’d be his type even if I did test the waters”, Hallie blows out a small laugh beside me, “Have you seen the way that man looks at you. I’d definitely be testing all kinds of things with him, never mind the water”.

I throw her a dirty look as I sit back in the chair, my thoughts racing. If that’s the case, no wonder he’s been so nice to me lately. I mean, maybe she’s got the wrong end of the stick, and he is just genuinely being nice, but part of me wants to test the theory.

I’m pulled from my thoughts when the doorbell goes with the food delivery. I jump up to grab the food and make my way into the kitchen, the girls trailing behind me as they dig into the bags for what they requested, which we plate up, staying in there so we don’t make any mess in the living room, moving the conversation on to other topics. I push Luca out of my head for the rest of the night, knowing I really shouldn’t be thinking of him the way I am.

11

Luca

The week I spend away seems to drag. Cora got on my nerves so much on the trip, making small comments here and there that hinted at her wanting to be more than just my assistant. I might have been a man whore at one point in my life, but I'm not a fucking idiot.

As much as everyone thinks I sleep with every assistant I've had, it's not completely true. I ended up giving her other tasks that required her to be nowhere near me for the rest of the trip because of her brazen attempts at flirting with me and causing myself more work in the process. I then spent the next five days not concentrating on the meetings I had and instead trying to find a replacement for her.

Rose never replied to my text the other day either and I know I told her not to read into me giving her a gift, and she shouldn't because then I would too, and we would end up in a bigger mess than I seem to have gotten myself into, but I couldn't help but feel a little gutted that she didn't reply to me after that, maybe even a little pissed off too.

I know I shouldn't, but the jealous part of me wants to know who gets to enjoy her in her downtime, knowing it isn't me. The little spout of jealousy that's just crept up out of nowhere has me pissing myself off even more, I knew I shouldn't have offered up my place to her, but my mind drags me back to the image of her sitting on the curb in tears because I fucked up and ruined her shop. She couldn't stay where she was and the demand for her to stay with me came out of my mouth before I could stop it, and I couldn't think of a reason at the time as to why it was a bad idea.

But that bad idea comes to bite me in the ass when I walk in the door at 10pm on Saturday evening. The house is dimly lit, the glow of the TV flickering across the walls, and there—sprawled on the living room floor- is Rose. She's surrounded by the remnants of a lazy night in. A half-eaten pizza sits open beside her, a forgotten slice resting in the box, its cheese congealing under the warmth of the room. On the coffee table, a half-drunk bottle of wine leans dangerously close to the edge, the deep red liquid casting lazy shadows in the dim light with a half-filled glass next to it.

She's so utterly engrossed in whatever's playing on the TV that she doesn't notice me at first. Which is just as well, because I take the opportunity to watch her—like the creep I seem to have become when it comes to this woman.

Her hair is piled into the messiest excuse for a bun I've ever seen, stray tendrils slipping loose at the nape of her neck, curling slightly as they brush her skin. She's wearing the flimsiest pyjamas imaginable, the thin fabric draping over her in a way that clearly doesn't cover much at all. From where I'm standing, I can't quite see her face, but I can picture it perfectly bare of makeup, her freckles dusting her cheeks and nose in a way that makes her look younger, softer.

Then, as if she can sense me, her head lifts, and hazel eyes lock onto mine from across the room. Her hand flies to her chest as she sucks in a sharp breath of air, clearly caught off guard. "Jesus Luca, you scared the fucking life out of me. I didn't think you would be back so soon". I frown at her, remembering I said a week, but maybe the time had gotten away with her. I lean against the door, a small smile beginning to tug at my lips as I watch her.

"I was gone a week, Red. Sorry if I scared you". Her face pulls into a scowl as she eyes me, "Yeah, and a week is Monday dipshit, hence me not expecting you", she says, pointing a finger at me, "And stop fucking calling me that, it's pissing me off". I bark out a laugh at her comment, choosing to ignore it and nod over to where she's sitting, motioning to the bottle of wine.

"Mind if I grab a glass and join you?" Her eyes flit to the side of where her bottle is resting. She looks like she wants to say no but instead nods her head to me. I spin on my heel, not waiting for her to change her mind and turn me down as I grab a glass from the kitchen and come back to join her, opting to sit on the couch instead of the floor next to her where I would rather be, but I know this is the safer option.

She pulls the wine off the side, tipping it into my glass for me, and I sit back, enjoying the slight burn of the merlot going down my throat. I lean down to where she is seated, examining her little set-up. "Why are you sitting on the floor instead of the sofa?" She looks around briefly before bringing her eyes up to meet mine as she shrugs her shoulder at me, a haze over her eyes from the alcohol. "I didn't want to get pizza on your nice couch. It looks like it's brand new".

I let out a laugh at her comment, shaking my head as I try to figure out her logic. "Get up here and eat your pizza in comfort. If you spill anything on the couch, it can be cleaned".

Indecision crosses her face as she goes back and forth as to whether she should get up, so I take the decision out of her hands, grabbing the box off the floor and resting it on my leg. I reach down to her, taking her hand in mine as I motion for her to get up. She relents, coming to join me on the sofa, and I steal a slice from the box, her eyes move from the pizza to my mouth as I take a bite, watching her back as her tongue comes out and swipes across her lips.

We sit in comfortable silence, eating and watching the show she's got on for a while, and when it ends, she hands me the remote. I glance down at it and then back up to her, raising my brow in question as she shoves it in my direction again. "I didn't come to sit here to take over the TV, watch what you want".

She shakes her head at me as she shuffles to the edge of the couch. "I'm done watching it, and there's nothing else on tonight I want to watch so you can have it". I panic thinking she might get up and leave, and my hand comes up as I slide the remote out of her hand, our fingers brushing each other as I take it, pressing the off button. Her head flits back in my direction, confusion on her face. "Why don't we just sit and talk for a little while? I barely know you and I feel like we should probably get to know each other a little if we're going to live together".

Rose nods thoughtfully, humming her response to me as she turns herself and fully faces me. Her legs come up as she bends them at the knee, wrapping her arms around herself to keep them in place. She takes a long sip of her wine, watching me as she does, waiting for me to go first. I bring my drink to my lips, sipping it before I begin.

"How come you wanted to set up the bakery?" She pauses at my question, taking her time to answer as she skims the rim of her wine glass with her fingertips.

"I used to enjoy going to all of the different places all the time, visiting the new cities, because I got to spend a few months on end at each of them. But honestly, I'm bored with that now and the bakery has always been a dream of mine, and I want to find someone, settle down, and maybe start... Um, yeah, but anyway…" Her response piques my interest, and I sit up in my seat, leaning in and edging a little closer to her as I do.

"Start what? A Family?" She blinks at me a couple of times before realising what she said, shaking her head a little, "Well, maybe one day, yeah. For now, I need to focus on getting the place back up to scratch".

I nod to her, “Oh, I haven’t had a chance to tell you; your landlord has been in hospital, and I have spoken to a family member, telling them about the problems with the shop. It’s all getting sorted, so you don’t need to worry, but there was more damage than we originally thought. It’s going to have to have a full rip out and be done from scratch”.

What I don’t tell her is that I spoke to him in person after requesting a meeting with him, he wanted to retire soon and wasn’t aware of the damage to the shop, so after a long afternoon of negotiations, I persuaded him to sell me his place and I’m now the owner of the shop until I get chance to fix some finer details. It didn’t need a full refit, but since I was taking over, I figured she would enjoy getting to completely renovate it.

She lets out a sigh shaking her head, “I can’t afford for all of that to get done. The insurance wouldn’t cover it all”. I place my hand over her bare skin, squeezing slightly to bring her attention to me and attempting to ignore the tingles under my fingertips as they brush over her, “Hey, I said you don’t need to worry about it, so don’t. This was my fault that the pipe went and now it’s all in hand. It’s all covered so just enjoy the fact you’re getting a full renovation”.

Her lips part slightly, and her eyes search mine like she wants to say something more. The urge to pull her into me only intensifies the longer I sit holding onto her.

My phone has other ideas though, blaring loudly through the silence and breaking our moment. She jumps, startled by the sudden intrusion of noise and her arm slips free from my hold as I reach into my pocket, fishing out my phone. My dad's name glares on the screen in the darkened room, and I stifle a groan as I answer, trying to figure out why he's ringing so late.

"Hey, Dad, is everything okay?" He huffs out a breath before snapping down the phone at me, "What the hell are you playing at Luca? I specifically told you to stop messing around with countless women. Your face is all over the local magazine from last week".

I finally release a sigh as I realise what picture he's talking about. "Dad, that's not what it looks like. She's a client, and you are the one who said I needed a date to dinner the other week". I feel Rose stiffen beside me, knowing my comment could have got to her.

He huffs down the phone at me, ignoring that he did, in fact, say that. "Luca, I get that, but you know full well what this will do to the company if you don't settle down". I let out a sigh, "Yeah, Dad, I know".

"I don't think you do. Come meet me in the office tomorrow at 8am. I need to speak with you face to face about something". I can't imagine what must be so important that he needs to see me in person that he can't say over the phone, but I indulge him anyway and agree.

"All right, I'll see you in the morning". I hang up and toss my phone to the side, letting my head fall into my hands, forgetting Rose was still in the room to witness that. "Rough day?" My eyes slide to my side momentarily, where she has moved back to sitting on the floor. I breathe out a laugh, shaking my head at the irony of the whole situation. "Like you wouldn't believe. My dad thinks this client I took to dinner is a new girl I've been sleeping with".

"And you're not?" Her question comes out so fast and blunt that it has my head spinning in her direction. "Is that really what everyone thinks of me? That I just fuck my way through America?" Her shoulder lifts a touch as she mulls over my question, "Well, you're not exactly this mysterious broody man that never gets in the limelight when people see you have a different girl on your arm each week. I'd say it makes it pretty obvious what you get up to".

Shit she has a point. I sit back in my seat, thinking about what she just said to me, "I need to find a way to get my dad off my back. He's not happy. I've not been great in the past, but he won't let this drop until I find a solution to all his problems. And just for the record, I haven't been with anyone in months".

I don't miss the way she scoffs at my comment, rolling her eyes at me as she gets to her feet, "Well, good luck with that. I'm going to bed now, so I'll see you tomorrow, maybe?" She grabs the pizza box from where it has been discarded, squeezing past me as she does, and I hum my response, not daring to lift my eyes to meet hers, opting to watch her bare feet instead as she pads out of the living room and upstairs.

I grab my wine glass once I know she's gone, gulping down the rest of the drink and re-filling the glass. I need to figure out a plan for speaking to my dad tomorrow, and I don't have a fucking clue where to start.

……

I crack my eyes open, letting out a groan as the alarm blares on my phone in the quiet room. My head throbs, a dull ache that pulses through me as I squint against the harsh light filtering through the curtains.

The room spins slightly as I sit up, the remnants of last night's alcohol still coursing through my veins. I'm not prepared for today in the slightest, and the amount of alcohol I consumed after Rose left me by myself was not ok.

I finished off the bottle of red, switching to the whiskey I keep in the corner of the room and finishing off that bottle too. My mouth feels like sandpaper, and the bitter taste of regret lingers on my tongue as I swing my legs over the side of the bed, my muscles protesting the movement.

Taking a deep breath, I reach for my phone, silencing the alarm and rubbing my temples in a futile attempt to alleviate the pounding in my skull. The room is a mess, clothes strewn across the floor, the empty whiskey bottle sitting ominously on the table. I drag myself to my feet, every step feeling like I'm wading through treacle, and make my way to the bathroom, hoping that a hot shower will wash away some of the haze clouding my mind.

choosing not to look at the sorry state of myself in the mirror, I drown my head under the hot shower. It burns my flesh but wakes me up enough that I can go downstairs, make myself a strong coffee and take some painkillers before facing my dad.

The drive to the office is bleak, with the sun not even bothering to make an appearance in the early morning with the sky shrouded in heavy, grey clouds, mirroring my thoughts. It feels fitting, given my mood right now, as I pull my car into the space and grab another coffee from the shop across the street, trying to prolong the inevitable as much as I can.

It’s short-lived though, when the elevator pings and my dad is standing at the door to his office, arms folded over his chest and a scowl marking his features.

He looks like an older version of me. Slightly greying hair with streaks of dark brown still going through it, a deeper olive skin tone to me from all the vacationing he’s been doing recently, chocolate brown eyes that match mine, and a height that just cuts under me at 6 ft 1.

He spins on his heel, walking into his office knowing full well I’ll follow. And I do. Making my way down the long corridor, I’m thankful no one else is in this office to witness me be berated by my own father for not being a goody to shoes.

I make my way into his office as he rounds the large oak desk that takes centre stage in his room, taking a seat across from me in the large, winged-back leather office chair as he leans forward, clasping his hands together in front of him. I sit in one of the leather executive chairs across from him, matching his stare and schooling my expression so he doesn't see how much he intimidates me.

"Son, this situation has gotten out of control recently. I know you enjoy living the high life when you are away, but you are going to destroy this company's reputation if I let you take over, so I won't be letting that happen until you can prove to me that you are serious about this role".

I squeeze my jaw, certain that I've just cracked a tooth, as I reel in the anger I feel bubbling towards the surface. I go to speak, to defend myself, but he holds up his hand, stopping me. "I have spoken to a few members of the board, and they have suggested that you either find a wife or stay out of the limelight altogether, and potentially take a step back from the company in the meantime".

My hands clench into fists, and I swear I feel a vein pop from squeezing my jaw so much as I stare him down, "This isn't the 50's dad, and I'm not having you decide who I be with". He looks at me like I'm causing him such an inconvenience right now, sighing before continuing and clearly ignoring what I have to say.

"I have spoken to an old friend of mine who has a daughter a similar age to you, she's unmarried also, and it wouldn't hurt for you to get to know her a little more, maybe forge a relationship with her, for the sake of your future at the company".

Anger spills out of me as I shoot to my feet and begin pacing his office, "You have got to be fucking kidding me. I am not going to marry some random woman just because you have decided you think I'm not fit to run this company. I don't see why I should even be married yet, I'm almost thirty-four, not forty".

"The reputation of this company sits on your shoulders now, and I don't want you to squander it just because you won't settle down", he's attempting to stay calm, but I can see in the way his eyes burn into mine that he is trying not to be even more pissed at me for ignoring his requests than I am at what he is suggesting.

I have to stand there, seething, trying not to lash out any further, but before I can respond again he continues "You know the girl, Elise Mathers, her father owns the contracting firm in Florida and…"

I finally cut him off, I've had enough with his bullshit today, "Absolutely fucking not. She is poisonous and only after one thing and that's financial security, and I find it a little convenient that you are choosing someone for me whose father has a similar business that would benefit yours". I spit the words at him, done with this conversation as I rake my hands through my hair, but he isn't finished.

"You will meet her and at least try to have a relationship that isn't just based on sex. I won't have this company ruined because you can't keep it in your pants. I've tried setting you up on dates that I believe are marriage material for you, and each time you ignore me".

I spin on my heel, glaring at him. He has no fucking clue what he's talking about or the fact that I've actually slept with Elise, and she hung onto me for weeks trying to leech what she could from me. That and the fact I've been making an effort to behave recently and stay out of the gossip columns.

My phone pings, and I use it as a distraction from this god-awful conversation as I pull it from my pocket, instantly feeling my anger dissipate as I spot Rose's name on my phone.

Red*: I'm cooking dinner tonight as a thank you for everything, be home for 6pm.*

"Jesus Luca, can you not have a fucking conversation without being distracted for once". My dad's words have my head shooting up, my eyes meeting his as the world's most stupid idea forms in my head, and before I even know it, the words are spewing from my mouth.

"I'm already seeing someone. She's actually just moved in with me and we've just got engaged". I already know it was a bad idea the moment the words leave my lips, but what I said throws my dad slightly. "Well, this is news to me, I find it a little hard to believe since you never mentioned it before, and I've never seen this girl".

I think fast, covering my lie with more lies that won't stop coming as they spill out of my mouth. "It's moved quickly. She was a friend of a friend, and we have been spending a lot of time together. I didn't want to mention anything as I wanted to make sure everything was perfect, but you trying to force me down the aisle has pushed me to tell you sooner than I wanted to. But Rose is going to be my wife, so I need you to accept that".

Rose is going to fucking kill me when she finds out what I've done, but I'd rather ask for forgiveness rather than permission at this point, so I roll with it, hoping she will get on board and help me.

"I want to meet her. There's a charity event coming up next week and you will attend with her". *Shit, shit, shit.* There's no fucking getting out of this right now, I need to come up with a plan that benefits Rose as much as it does me so that she agrees to this thing. I stay calm on the outside as I keep my expression neutral, looking my father in the eye and agreeing with him.

"All right, that's fine. I'll bring her to the event, and you better be fucking nice to her. She is nothing like anyone I've been with before, and for good reason too. I have things I need to sort today, so I'll see you this week at some point". I spin on my heel, storming towards the elevator before he gets another word in.

I need to figure out a way out of this company and away from being in the shadow of my father for the rest of my life. But now I have a bigger problem.

One that means I need to come up with a plan on how the fuck I'm meant to get Rose on board with this elaborate scheme to keep my place in the company until I figure things out.

12

Rose

Sunday is a day of rest. That's what my grandma told me every week when we would visit her when I was a child. We'd go to hers for a Sunday dinner, and each time, my grandpa would slide me a dollar, telling me to 'not spend it all at once' with a wink from him.

I'd taken that very seriously by making sure to spend my Sundays enjoying doing something I love. And that is baking.

I'd text Luca this morning, telling him I'd cook him something as a thank you tonight, but I can't do dinner without dessert, because well… That's the best bit. I heard him sneak out of the door at around half seven this morning, trying to be quiet but failing, when he went off to meet his dad.

I could hear the conversation over the phone, but I didn't want Luca to know how nosey I was and pretended not to know what was said.

I stayed awake for hours last night after I'd ditched him, going over what he said about the shop being sorted, and I can't help but feel the relief that I have someone helping me fix the issue, even if he does think it's his fault. I know he's good at what he does so it doesn't worry me in the slightest that he's taken over getting the shop up to scratch.

I could hear him up for a while before he came up to bed last night too, the glass bottle holding whiskey clinking each time he tipped himself another glass, all too much of a giveaway that he was drinking by himself.

I didn't believe him for one minute when he said that he's not slept with anyone in so long, I wanted to, but that small part that niggles at me had me holding back, so I hightailed it out of there, hiding in my room for the rest of the night.

I almost went back down to sit with him, but I'd already had a few too many to drink last night and I know nothing good could have come from drinking with Luca Wilde.

He would have said something charming like he usually does, and my panties would have been down in no time. Me and alcohol should never mix when in his presence.

I'm baking away when Luca strolls into the kitchen from his day. He looks tired, and maybe slightly stressed, but I think better than to comment on it as I give him a small smile. He looks around the space like he's trying to figure out what the hell I'm doing, as he props his hands on his hips, watching me. "Need any help?"

I badly want to say yes, just so I can spend some time watching him, and seeing if he can cook. I carry on stirring the brownie mixture, keeping my eyes firmly fixed on the bowl and shake my head at him. "No thanks, this needs to go in the oven in a minute and then we can have dinner. You just do what you need to".

He doesn't say anything as he moves around the kitchen, grabbing knives and forks to set the island for dinner, even though I just told him not to bother. I ignore him the best I can as I put the brownie mixture into the oven, before moving back over to the stove to finish dinner.

I'm surprised he even came home and joined me for dinner, to be honest, after receiving a one-word answer this morning by text, "Sure". Maybe I pissed him off last night when I flat-out rejected his offer and then practically ran off to my room.

But he's here now, looking mighty fine in his jeans that fit just snug around his thighs and a corded quarter zip jumper. His hair is slightly mussed like he's been running his fingers through it all day, and I get the urge to do just that, but I keep my hands busy, so I don't do exactly what my thoughts want right now.

He sits at one of the seats in the kitchen after he's finished messing, looking grumpy for a Sunday evening, and I examine his face looking for any signs I should leave the conversation alone. His stubble growing that little bit longer than usual, and tired eyes. I can't help but wonder if his dad said something that pissed him off, and the urge to be nosey overtakes as I turn around, gripping the sides of the countertop and blurt out, "How did the chat with your dad go?"

His head shoots up, and I realise I caught him off guard with my question. His hand comes to his face, scrubbing over it as he seems to think of what to say back to me. Letting out a sigh, he eventually drops his hands, placing them out in front of himself, and I can't help but notice how his arms flex when he clenches his hands into fists and back to normal again. *Focus Rose.*

"It was a rough morning, one I'm not ready to talk about until I've got a drink and some food in me. Shall we eat, and we can discuss it after dinner? I wouldn't want to ruin a lovely meal talking about my dad".

My mouth snaps shut. I clearly overstepped asking about his conversation today. His *private* conversation. One that he obviously doesn't want to talk to me about. I clear my throat and move back towards the stove, trying to make it less awkward than it already is, stirring the food I've prepared for a few moments more before speaking, "I hope you like salmon, I made a risotto", I say trying to move the conversation along.

"I think I'd like just about anything you cook Red". I'm caught off guard as his voice comes from close behind me, and I tense when I feel him brush past me as he makes his way to the fridge, feeling tingles run up my spine at the small touch from him.

I seriously need to get a grip of myself or get laid, but that's something that will have to be put on the back burner for now. I peek over at him, where he has his head stuck in the fridge looking for a wine for the evening, "A chardonnay will go nicely with dinner tonight", he nods his approval, pulling a bottle out that I left chilling for a few hours. He looks it up and down, seemingly happy with my choice.

"This is a nice wine, you have good taste", he reads the bottle, turning it in his hands. I force myself to look away from him, not wanting to get distracted anymore and reach to get the dishes from the cupboard. I'm too short to reach the ones I want though, and struggle as I come up on the tips of my toes trying to grab them.

I feel the heat from his body as he presses up against me, reaching above my head to get the bowls I need for dinner. My mind can't focus on much else as my ass seems to grind against his legs when he reaches past me.

"Sorry, I didn't think about you not being able to get things, I'll sort that". I wave him off, not wanting to be any more of a nuisance than I already seem to be, "Don't worry about it. So long as I can get my coffee mug in the morning, I'm good", I smile stiffly to him, as he moves around the kitchen, grabbing glasses for us and pouring the drinks whilst I plate up the food.

We sit in awkward silence as we eat, and I try not to watch as he shovels food into his mouth like he hasn't eaten for days. Clearly, he's trying to avoid conversation with me as much as he can, and I can't help but regret suggesting he eat with me. He's a grown-ass man who I'm sure has plenty of better things to be doing with his time than sitting with me.

Luca eats his food in record time, gulping back a glass of wine when he's finished. I feel like I need to say something, to apologise maybe for forcing my time on him. I set my fork down, adjusting myself in my seat as I turn my head to him, "I'm sorry if you feel like you had to eat with me tonight. I shouldn't have assumed you would want to".

He stares at me for a moment, a crease forming between his brows. Eventually, he turns in his seat so he's facing me head on, pulling me around to face him too. I spin in the chair as my legs come around, bumping into his a little as his arms come up to either side of my legs, holding on to my thighs as if I'm going to escape. My body heats to his touch, like it's overly aware he has his hands on me.

"Don't ever apologise for asking me to eat with you. It was nice coming home to a cooked meal for a change. I shouldn't have brought my bad mood home, but there is something I need to talk to you about. Why don't we finish up dinner and we can go sit in the living room to talk".

I instantly panic, thinking he's going to ask me to move back out, and he senses it, giving me a stern look, and moving in just a little closer to me. "Get that idea out of your head right now Red. You're not going anywhere".

I feel myself relax at his words, nodding to him as I turn myself back around and finish my dinner. He re-fills our wines as I grab the brownie from the oven, plating it up with some ice cream for us both, and when I turn back around, he's finally smiling as he eyes up the food in my hands.

"Have you made brownies? You know they're my favourite, don't you". My shoulders lift as I shrug them, pretending like I didn't in fact know that he loves them, and was begging Grace to ask me to make some the last time he saw her before I came home, and since opening the shop he's been in far too many times to buy one or two.

He takes the dessert from me, eating up every ounce of it, and I giggle as I watch him eat with such determination. My eyes fixate on his lips every time he puts the spoon in his mouth and gives an exaggerated moan when he pops it back out.

We finish up dessert, keeping the conversation light, as I try not to show my nerves for this conversation he's taking forever to get around to, and when I go to grab the plates and clean up, he puts his arm out stopping me, "You take your drink and go get comfy, I'll be in there in a minute".

I nod to him, not trusting my mouth right now as I grab my glass and make my way into the living room and plop down on the couch with a deflated sigh. I'm fully on edge, wondering what the hell he has to talk to me about, maybe it's something his dad has said to him today.

He comes in a couple of minutes later, carrying his own drink, and takes a seat on the couch with me, sitting close to me but not close enough that we're touching. My legs are tucked under my ass, and

I have my body facing him, ready to give him my full attention for the conversation.

He takes a sip from his drink, placing it on the coffee table then turns to me, propping his arm up on the back of the couch, the other in his lap. The way he's looking so calm right now has me thinking that it must just be the way he offloads in the evening. I mean, it's not like I spend time with him constantly, so who am I to know how he unwinds at night.

I can't help but watch him as he gets himself comfy, his tongue darting out to swipe across his lips, or the way his foot tucks under his other leg, causing his jeans to strain a little when he turns towards me some more.

Luca clears his throat, bringing my attention up to his face, where he has a small awkward smile playing on his lips. "I um.. I had a bit of a heated discussion today with my dad, about my image and the company. We went back and forth for a while but basically, he won't let me take over the company until I prove that I will settle down and marry someone".

His words have my heart sinking, he must want to find someone and have her move in, and whoever she is, she won't want me living here. I nod along, not allowing myself to speak as my brain tries to scramble through every possibility as to how quickly I can find somewhere new to live until either the shop or Hallie's is ready. Maybe I have a few more weeks; the house or shop could be done by then, and I could get out of his hair.

My train of thought is interrupted when Luca continues, “My dad suggested I marry someone that he knows, and well… See, the thing is Red…” I cut him off, not needing to hear anymore, as I hold my hand up stopping him. His mouth snaps shut, waiting for me to speak, “It’s fine, Luca. I’ll find somewhere else to live, and you won’t have to worry. I won’t invade your space. I assume whoever she is will be moving in here”.

He looks at me dumbfounded for a moment, his brow scrunching together as my words process, before quickly shaking his head at me. His hands come to my thighs, stopping me in my tracks, and my eyes flit down to watch them as his fingers grip the bare skin on my legs. “You’re getting carried away, I didn’t agree to it”.

My brows scrunch together as I scowl at him, trying to figure out where he’s going with this when one of his hands comes up to smooth over the skin between my brows, “Stop scowling at me, Red. Just keep that pretty mouth shut for a minute and let me get my words out, all right?” I smother a laugh as I nod to him, allowing him to speak instead of getting ahead of myself and butting in.

His hand drops and he lets out a long breath, preparing himself for whatever he’s going to tell me. When he brings his eyes up to meet mine, the deep chocolate pools flit between my eyes as he searches for some sort of answer in them. “Please don’t go mad at me when I tell you this either, but I kinda, sort of.. Well, I told my dad that me and you were engaged”.

I rear back like I’ve been slapped, my eyes going wide as I take in the absolute bomb he’s just dropped on me. My mouth drops open from shock, and I see the look of regret wash over his face as he watches me. “You had better be joking right now Luca, that isn’t even funny. Please tell me this is just a joke”.

I jump up from the couch and begin pacing the living room floor. My teeth dig into my lip as I chew furiously on it. He sits watching me, looking like he wants to reach out and stop me, but he knows better right now. “I wish I were joking right now, but you texted me right as he was going in on me about it.. And I just panicked and said I was marrying you”.

I stop short, spinning on my heel to face him. The look on his face right now making him look like a naughty child, and if I didn’t think it would ruin his gorgeous face, I’d want to punch him in it right now too!

I jab a finger in his direction, the anger bubbling inside me as I spit my words at him, “That is not a fucking excuse to lie and say I’m your fiancé Luca. I can’t fucking believe you would lie like that”. I throw my arms up in the air as I pace some more, trying to think, shaking my head at this ridiculous idea.

I eventually come to a stop, bringing my arms across my chest as I give him my only way of a solution, “You’re just going to have to man up and tell him that you panicked and lied. I can't pretend to be your fiancé. I'm literally the farthest thing from your type. You couldn't possibly expect a single person to believe that we would even be together, let alone getting married".

Luca stands abruptly, coming around the coffee table to stop in front of me, his hands come up, grasping at my arms as he tries to calm me from his idiocy, and I feel his fingers flex over my skin as they grip me.

I force myself to focus on his throat as his Adam's apple bobs when he swallows, not allowing myself to look into his eyes. "I think a lot of people would believe it, you might not see it, but I think we could actually make a good couple, and I know I'm an idiot for saying what I said, but I'm not above begging right now when I say I need you. I need you to help me out and I will just about do anything right now to get you to agree to this. Please". There's a level of vulnerability in his voice as he pleads with me to go along with his plan.

I finally drag my eyes up as I stare back at him, trying to take in what he's just said to me, eventually pulling away from him, as I move across to the other side of the room to put some space between us.

I'm afraid if I let him too close to me right now, I might stupidly agree with his plan. "You're not even attracted to me, Luca. We have nothing in common. I don't see how we could convince anyone this is even remotely a thing". He frowns at me, putting his hands on his hips as he watches me from across the space that feels all too small right now.

"Who the fuck said I wasn't attracted to you? I've been trying to be a gentleman for once in my life, and clearly that's getting me nowhere". He makes quick steps to reach me, crowding me with his body and causing me to breathe him in. Bergamot and orange filters into my nose as I try to focus. I realise all too late that he's walked me back into the wall when his arms come up to cage me in.

I try like hell not to look up to him, but his hand comes up, grasping at my chin as he pulls my face to look at him, my breath hitches as I search his eyes.

"Tell me who said I don't want you? Because I've been trying to keep my distance from you for months, and I don't think that's working out for me anymore Red. I asked you to move in, convincing myself it was for your benefit and not mine, and now I seem to make these constant mistakes involving you because I can't get you out of my mind".

His breath fans my face as he moves impossibly closer to me, the feeling sends heat straight to my core.

"Look, I'm sorry that this has happened, and I wish I could take back what I've said, but I can't now, and I will do whatever I can to make it up to you. But I really need you to help me out with this. It will get me out of the shit with my dad, and we don't have to keep up the act for too long, just enough so he's convinced I can settle down, and then we will break up once I know he trusts that I won't ruin the business. Please don't just dismiss this so quickly and at least think on it for a little while".

I blow out a small breath, leaning into his touch that little bit more as he speaks, his scent distracting me from the colossal fuck up he's made today. I pull back from him just enough to look him in the eye, brushing over the fact he said he's attracted to me because he must just be saying that to get me to agree. He's so desperate right now I think he'd say anything.

"You could have said anyone else in the world to pick to be your fake fiancé Luca. Why would you bring me into this knowing full well this is a bad idea. This is going to go horribly wrong if we do this, I can feel it". He smiles back down at me, "Only if we let that happen".

My fingers dig into his shirt, crumpling it between them as I push against him slightly, needing the space to think, his proximity is all too much, overwhelming me. But much to my surprise, he allows it, stepping back and allowing me to gather my thoughts.

As much as I feel like it will be a bad idea, I also know that this could be the chance Grace and Hallie were telling me to take. He must sense my inner turmoil, speaking up to fill the silence, "Don't overthink it, but also please think about it, I really wouldn't ask you to help me if I wasn't desperate".

I blink up at him, trying to figure out what the hell to do. I wait too long to speak though so he continues, “I know this all seems like a lot to take in right now, and I don’t want you to make a decision too quickly, but my dad is asking to meet you and soon, so it really would mean a lot to me if you would, but if you really don’t think you can do this then tell me and I’ll figure something else out”.

I want to say no right here and now, to just forget this entire thing even happened this evening and go hide in my room, but the small part of me that has a soft spot for him wants to help. I need more answers before I agree though, so I steel myself, ready to be shot down if he doesn’t agree.

“If we do this and you want people to believe this is real, then you need to act like you’re in a proper relationship, with only me. And that means no sex or seeing any other women. I can’t be dragged into something if it’s going to make me look like an idiot in the end”.

Luca freezes, his eyes wide and full of hope as they meet mine and he nods along eagerly, “Of course, I wouldn’t go behind your back like that. Wait, does that mean sex is on the cards for me and you?” He wiggles his brows at me, motioning between the two of us, clearly trying to lighten the mood, and it suddenly has me thinking of what it would actually be like to sleep with him.

I hold up my hands to stop him from getting carried away, “Can we just focus on one thing at a time here, please?” I take a breather, briefly closing my eyes before I continue. “I’ll play the role you need me to, but we aren’t compatible in the real world,

Luca, so I don't think mixing feelings or sleeping together would help us here. This is a means to an end for you so we should stick to the plan".

His shoulders sag, not a lot, but enough that I can see the disappointment in his body language like that wasn't what he wanted to hear, and I let out a sigh as I continue, "I'm not your type, I never will be, and I can't let myself get caught up in this little fantasy where we play house to the outside world and then that changes when we get home. It's easier this way for the both of us, I'm just someone that you need something from, and I don't want us to get confused over what this is".

He's disappointed in what I've said to him, I can tell by the way he's looking like I've just kicked his puppy, but he nods anyway. I assume he'll leave me to think about my decision, but he speaks again.

"Take some time. I know this is a big decision, and we would have to potentially lie to our friends, too. It would need to be convincing enough, and I don't want you going into this thinking this is a one-sided thing. I want you to benefit from this agreement also. If people think we are together, it will bring good publicity for the bakery, and you can probably take it a lot further. But, um, yeah... Just sleep on it. I'm going to head up to bed and give you some space. I'll see you tomorrow, yeah?"

I nod to him, unable to look up and see the disappointment that I'm not agreeing immediately. I hear his feet shuffle around and eventually hear him going up the stairs. I flop down onto the sofa, letting out a groan. How the fuck have I gotten myself into this situation already. This was supposed to be easy, just somewhere to live whilst the shop gets sorted. Drama free.

Maybe I could play this role for Luca's sake. He is putting me up in his house free of charge and offering to sort the bakery for me, I don't like asking for help, but the offer was just too tempting. And maybe even the man himself is just that little bit tempting, too.

13

Luca

What the fuck was I thinking?

I march up the stairs, pacing my bedroom floor for a good ten minutes, going over whatever the hell just happened downstairs. Why the fuck did I think that she would even consider this stupid arrangement. I should just go back downstairs now and tell her it was a bad idea and to forget this ever even happened.

I won't lie and say it didn't hurt my ego a little when she almost flat-out refused me, but that's what I get when I act like a dick half of my life, then spend the last few weeks winding her up, to then ask her to be my fake fiancé.

What if she actually agrees, though? This could be my perfect way to convince her that I am someone she could see herself with, that maybe we aren't as opposite as she thinks.

The first time I saw her when she walked into the bar with her friends all those months ago has yet to leave my mind, and every fucking meeting I've had with her since has tortured me.

I have to pretend I'm not desperate just to get to know her that little bit more each time she graces me with her company. It's like she has some magical fucking powers that draw me to her the more I see her.

I can't even have sex with another woman without her popping into my head. I gave up trying after the second time; it's just awkward and embarrassing for me and them when I can't get that smart-mouthed little redhead out of my mind.

I undress, jumping into the shower to try and calm myself down, but all I do is the same thing I've done every night since the first time I thought about having her perfect little body. My hand finds my dick and I fist myself, almost suffocating it as I jerk off to more thoughts of Rose.

I stand under the hot rush of water in the shower, wanting to punish myself for even thinking I might have a chance with her or thinking she would agree to anything.

I must be there for a while because my fingers start to wrinkle slightly, like they're telling me I need to get a grip on myself and get out of the bathroom. I eventually drag myself out, wrapping a towel around myself and wander into my bedroom to mope about some more.

A big part of me hopes that she will come through tonight, telling me she will agree to help me out, but the little part in my brain that tries to remind me that none of this is a good fucking idea pushes forward, keeping me very aware that she will most likely say no.

I know there's nothing I can do now, so I climb into bed and stare at the ceiling for what feels like an eternity as I wait for her to come upstairs. I hear the soft click of her door, knowing that she has gone into her room for the night, and as much as I want to go in there, demanding an answer from her, I know I should leave it alone. So, I close my eyes and hope sleep takes over, and quickly.

.....

Three days. Three torturously long days.

That's how long she's been avoiding me, and I'm starting to feel the stress from this whole situation weighing heavy on me. The little twitch in my eye has come back, that I thought I had finally managed to stop, and the mood I'm in does no one any favours when I go into the office on Wednesday morning. I should have just worked from home, but I still need to start looking for a new assistant, because I'm not sure if I can deal with Cora a minute longer.

Speaking of the devil herself, she taps on my door as she wanders into my office like she didn't piss me off when we were away in Florida, placing a coffee on my desk like she has done every morning since she started eight months ago.

I'm impressed I didn't let her go sooner, to be honest, but other than the shameful flirting she's begun recently, she is good at her job. Maybe I didn't mind it before, or I didn't notice because my mind wasn't stuck on that mouthy little redhead that's taken over my house.

I keep trying every morning to catch Rose, but she seems to get up at the crack of dawn so she can escape me and I've been working at home as much as I could to try and have a conversation with her, but each time she comes within breathing distance of my office, I end up in a two-hour long meeting.

I'm pulled from my thoughts by Cora, who stands there waiting patiently for me to go over my day with her like she does every day, except today, she's got a look on her face that says she has something on her mind. I clear my throat, ignoring the look as best as I can, and motion for her to begin.

Her eyes flit to the side slightly like she's nervous about something, and she should be because she is getting replaced, whether she is good at her job or not.

I lean forward in my seat, placing my arms out in front of me on my desk as a frown tugs at my brow, I'm getting impatient waiting for her to start. "What is it, Cora? You look like you have something you want to say this morning". Her eyes widen as she realises she can't hide her feelings, and she stutters a little, going red in the face, "I um... It's nothing"

My eyes narrow in on her as she chews on her lip. She looks fidgety the way she's standing like she can't wait to get out of the room quick enough for a change. "No, go ahead. You look like you have something on your mind, and I know you don't shy away from telling everything that's on your mind lately, so what's going on?".

She fidgets some more on the spot as she messes with her hands in front of her, eventually looking up to me, and for a moment, I see what looks like tears in her eyes, but then her brows pull together as she levels her gaze with mine, "I just wanted to apologise for whatever I had done to upset you in Florida. I love this job, and it wasn't my intention to upset you if I did or said anything that was not to your liking".

The shock must be evident on my face as she has acknowledged that she has done something wrong, and I feel like I may have been just a little too harsh on her in the first place by practically forcing her to work for anyone other than me in the offices in Florida.

I let out a sigh, bringing my hands in front of me on the desk, "You just can't act the way you are with me, Cora. We have to keep things professional, I'm your boss, and you treat me like I'm a friend, if not more sometimes, and with my reputation, as I'm sure by now you must know about, people will start talking and the last thing I need is people thinking I'm fucking my assistant".

Her eyes widen again at my brazen response as she bobs her head up and down quickly.

"Understood, Luca, I'm sorry, and it won't happen again". Huh, maybe I can keep her for a little while longer then. "Thank you for apologising. Let's get back to the day then". She nods, pulling out her calendar as she sits across from me and going through the day like the professional I know she can be, our little mishap now forgotten.

"Today's meeting at 1pm got pushed back to next week, and the Thornley project got pushed back to begin work from the start of March instead of next week". She reels off more information to me as I start getting my emails up.

"Okay, that's fine; send an email to the head of the job for the Thornley project and get him to contact me; I want to find out what's going on and why it has been pushed back another three weeks". She nods, turning to leave and closes the door behind her with a soft click.

I let out a sigh as my head falls into my hands, relief washes over me knowing I don't have to fire Cora, for now. The other problem in my life still sits at home ignoring me, and I know I need to speak to Rose as soon as possible and get an answer from her so I can figure out what we're doing going forward. I grab my phone sending her a message.

ME: Any more thoughts on that proposal?

The irony in the message I've sent isn't lost on me as I wait for what feels like forever for her to respond to me, and when she does, it just pisses me off more.

Red: Nope sorry. Not had a spare minute. I'll let you know by the end of the week.

You have got to be fucking kidding me. I stare down at the text message on my phone, getting more and more impatient the longer I look at it. I don't know why I expected this to go smoothly with her, she's as stubborn as they come, and I know full well I'm not in for an easy ride if I'm going to pull this off.

She isn't going to make this easy for me, so instead of waiting for her to come to me, I make the decision to go to her and catch her when she least expects me to.

Grabbing my things, I tell Cora I will be working from home for the rest of the day as I make my way down the office and to the elevators. It's rammed with staff from other floors, but I stand hiding in the corner, ignoring people as much as I can, rushing out to my truck as soon as the door pings open. Someone tries to call for me as I make my way through the busy foyer, but I wave them off, not wanting to wait for another fucking day to talk to Rose.

The traffic is a nightmare the whole drive home, and I curse myself for not living closer to the city on a more permanent basis, but then, if I did that, I definitely wouldn't have a hot new roommate, and my life would probably be a lot simpler too, but I push my thoughts aside, remembering that I picked the hard life all by myself, and now I have to beg Rose to join me so I don't drown in this pool of lies.

Music blares through the speakers in the house as I walk through the entry hall, some 90s R&B on the playlist she has blasting. I wander into the kitchen, spotting her straight away. She's baking something, her hands deftly moving between the ingredients and utensils, though it's clear she's not entirely confident with this particular recipe. She keeps going back to her laptop, which is precariously balanced on the counter, to check the recipe she has up on the screen, her brow furrowed in concentration.

Her back is to me, so she doesn't see me come in. I stand in the doorway, silently watching her for a moment, a small smile playing on my lips. She's in her element, completely absorbed in her task, the flour dusting her fingers and a smudge of chocolate on her cheek. The scent of vanilla and freshly melted butter fills the air, mingling with the music as she bobs her head to the beat. I know full well she will kill me if I scare her again, but the temptation to watch her like this is too strong to resist.

Her hair is piled on top of her head in a messy bun as always, and she has an oversized shirt on, a pair of loose-fitting jeans, and her perfect feet bare of any socks or shoes. I'm not usually a foot man, but hers could fill a kink any day.

She looks so natural and in her element, like she belongs in my kitchen, in my home. She reaches up to grab something from one of the top cupboards and I silently curse myself for not moving everything down a shelf yet when she lets out a little huff because she can't reach the bowls.

I move quickly, coming behind her to reach up and get what she needs, forgetting that she doesn't have a clue I'm home.

A small screech leaves her mouth as I reach over her, causing her to jab me with her elbow in the ribs. I let out a grunt as she winds me, falling back onto the counter as I try to catch my breath. She spins around to face me, a mix of shock and surprise on her face that quickly morphs into anger. "Luca, how many fucking times do I need to tell you? Stop sneaking up on me".

I nod to her, unable to form words because she has one hell of a swing, and that anger quickly changes again into worry as her eyes go wide, and she panics a little, looking at the state of me, "Oh fuck, did I hurt you? Here sit down".

She runs around the counter as quickly as she can and grabs a chair for me to sit on. It takes me a minute, but I finally catch my breath enough to speak, "Jesus, at least I know you are safe here by yourself with a jab like that". I chuckle as I say it, but I wince at the pain that now pulses in my ribs and wonder how hard she actually just hit me.

Rose folds her arms in front of her as she raises her brow at me, completely unimpressed by what I just said. "I saw you wince then, and as much as I hope you're all right, it serves you right for sneaking up on me. You can't do that. What if I seriously hurt you?"

I motion to the area she just jabbed, "You did fucking hurt me. Do you even realise your own strength, woman?" She shakes her head, laughing at me as she turns back to what she was doing, but I'm not done with our conversation yet; in fact, it's just beginning.

I come up behind her again, reaching up to grab the bowl, and as my body brushes against hers, I watch as the hairs on her forearms stand up on end at the simple touch from me, and smile to myself as I take it off the shelf and place it down next to her, ignoring the pain that's still in my side. She mumbles her thanks to me but doesn't look up.

"Back to ignoring me now, are you?" It's a petty comment, I know it is, but it gets me her attention either way as she scowls up at me. "No, in case you didn't notice when you were busy sneaking up on me, I'm working on a new recipe". She goes back to working on her baking, but I hover over her like the annoying fucker I've turned into just so she gives me her attention.

She stops after a minute, turning to face me and lets out a little huff as she removes the flour from her fingers before folding her hands across her chest again and propping her hip against the side. I mimic her actions as we stare at each other down. "What do you need, Luca? I know you aren't hovering around to watch me work, so what is it?"

I raise a brow at her, trying to figure out her mood. It's probably not the best time to be bringing it up when she's trying to work, but I'm too impatient to wait any longer.

"Do you have an answer for me yet? I'm an impatient man, and it's killing me not knowing if you are going to agree to this or not". Rose huffs at me, rolling her eyes as she turns herself back to her workstation. "I've told you I'll talk to you about it at the weekend Luca. I don't see why you need to know right away".

Ah fuck, she's going to kill me when I tell her the next bit, but it really can't wait. "I need to know soon, because I am supposed to be attending a charity event this Saturday. With you". Her hands freeze as she stops what she's doing, the utensils clanking loudly in the bowl and making me wince at the noise as it pierces my ears. Her head spins in my direction, and I want to crawl in on myself from the death stare she's giving me right now. Her movements are slow as she turns on the spot.

"Luca, I'm going to give you one chance to take that statement back and tell me you were joking because I swear to god you better had be. Otherwise, I'll be attending that event by myself, and you will be dead". I step back slightly from her; she's a little scary when she's mad, and I won't lie and say it doesn't turn me the fuck on at the same time.

I feel my dick twitch at the thought of an angry Rose but reign it in, and I hold up my hands in surrender, "Okay, don't kill me just yet". I let out a sigh as my hands drop to my hips and my eyes find a spot on the ceiling.

"I'm sorry, okay. I just agreed to it on the spot when my dad asked to meet you, and I really didn't think it would be an issue". My eyes finally meet hers as she stares daggers at me.

Her voice is low and controlled when she speaks again, "How the fuck did you think any of this wouldn't be an issue, Luca? You lied about being in a relationship with me and then lied some more to me about the whole situation. When were you even going to tell me about this event, Luca? When we were on the way there?"

By the time she's done, she's shaking with anger, and I reach out to her to attempt to calm her down, but she pulls back, her voice now raised.

"Don't fucking touch me right now! Do you realise how much of a shit show this is, Luca? Because I sure as shit don't think you do. I think you just assume that I'm going to roll over and do exactly what you ask of me because you are helping me out by sorting the bakery or me living here, I won't do it. I won't be pushed into something just because it's you, so you can look at me with those puppy dog eyes all you like, Luca, but you're not taking liberties. I decide on my own time if and when I want to do this". Tears well up in her eyes as she speaks to me, and I know I've pushed her too far.

I lower my gaze to meet hers and step closer, encroaching on her space again and teetering on the edge of danger, knowing full well she could clock me again, and to be honest, I would let her.

"I'm sorry. I'm really fucking sorry for putting this on you. I know I didn't think it through when I said what I did, and if I could take the words back, then, I would, but the reality of it is I fucked up. And I know that it's not on you to fix anything; it's on me. I know I'm putting pressure on you right now, and it's really not my intention to do that. I just wanted to know if you had an answer for me".

My eyes bounce between hers as she listens to me, the anger slowly leaving her as I feed her the shit that's leaving my mouth, hoping beyond hope that one day she will forgive me for putting her through this.

Her eyes don't shift from the spot she is fixated on against the wall behind my head, and I know what I need to do, "I will call my dad and tell him that I fucked up and we split up or something, and just hope that he takes pity on my stupidity, and I'll agree to be with whoever he sets me up with".

She takes a small step back, pulling herself together as she glares at me one last time before turning away to continue her work. I glance down at her, waiting for her to give me some more shit that I deserve for being the world's biggest dick, but she doesn't say anything, and I know I've really fucked up with her.

"I'll leave you to finish your work, and I'll be in my office if you need me". She just nods to me, completely shutting me out now, and I turn to walk away to my office, dragging my feet as I go in the hope that she'll call out to me, but she doesn't. I know I'm an idiot for even thinking this would be a good idea or that she'd even consider it, but I had to try, and now I know my answer. –

I sit staring at my computer for what feels like an eternity, but in reality, only an hour has passed. A long torturous hour that I spent trying to get work done and failing, but I don't dare leave the office knowing she's just in the other room. I give up trying to work as I prop my elbows on the desk, digging the heel of my hands into my eyes and sit with my thoughts for a few more minutes before I know I need to get up.

A soft knock comes to my door, interrupting me from my quiet, and a couple of seconds pass before it creaks open. Rose is standing there holding up some cakes.

"Thought you might want to try one. I need a guinea pig, and well, you're the closest thing". I eye the sweet treats in her hand, and my stomach chooses that moment to let out a small growl, reminding me I've yet to eat. The noise earns me a small smile from Rose as she comes over, handing me one of the cakes.

"You haven't poisoned it, have you? To get me back for being a dick?" I keep my tone light so she knows I'm joking. She shrugs her shoulders a little, keeping her expression neutral, "Guess you'll just have to try it and find out".

I snort a small laugh as I take a bite of the cake, and a moan slips free as the sugary treat hits my tastebuds. "Oh my god, why are you so good at this. Can you just marry me so I get these for the rest of my life". I realise my mistake as it comes out of my mouth, and my eyes shoot up to hers, waiting for her to berate me again. But instead, all I see is a tug of her lip as she watches me.

I carry on eating, opting to keep my mouth full so I don't say anything else stupid, as she wanders around the room looking at all the certificates I have on the wall, stopping and reading each one fully. "You've done a lot in a short space of time". I nod to her, not wanting to say anything that might piss her off since she's in a good enough mood to talk to me again.

She makes her way around everything I have up in the room, briefly taking in the view of the lake from the window before eventually flopping down on the leather sofa in the corner, crossing her legs under her as she lets out a sigh and finally tells me what she's thinking.

"I got my back up a bit before. I don't like being pressured into making decisions. I've had to do it most of my life, trying to be the perfect daughter to my mother, but it got me nowhere, and I don't want to agree to this and let you down". She takes another breathe as she prepares herself for whatever else she has to say, "But I will agree to it anyway because for some stupid reason, I like you enough not to see you have to be part of some arranged marriage just so that your dad allows you to stay apart of the company".

Hope fills me as she speaks, but she holds her hand up, silently telling me she's not done yet. "Until you can prove to him that he can trust you to run the business, I'll do what you need me to, and then when the time comes, we say I've left you, and then there is no blame on you, and you will get what you need". She takes another breath as she keeps her gaze locked on me. I break out into the biggest fucking smile, "Thank you so much for this, Red; I promise that you won't forget it. God, I could kiss you right now".

The laugh that spills out of her is almost angelic, and I silently vow to do everything I can to make sure I hear that as often as I can. "Luca, we both know you aren't coming anywhere near my lips until you stop talking shit".

I huff a quiet laugh as I push myself up and out of my office chair, "Can I hug you at least?" She allows me that, standing herself as I make my way around the desk to get to her. I pull her into me, breathing in her intoxicating scent and press a kiss to her head.

"I mean it. I'll do whatever I can to make this up to you, and that starts with the bakery; you can do whatever you want with the refurb, and we will get it up and running again soon. This food is too good not to have everyone enjoy it every day". She lightly shakes her head at me, "I'm not doing this to get more out of you Luca. I'm doing this because we are friends, and I don't want to see you miserable unless an arranged marriage is what you want?"

I nod back down to her, squeezing her just that little bit more, not wanting the moment to end too soon. "Fuck no. I am helping you because I want to, you agreeing to this is just an added bonus, and I'd help you even if you turned me down, plus you make a pretty good fake fiancé".

She pulls back from me just enough so she can look up at me with wide eyes, and I bring my hand up, running it over her soft skin, "I mean it. I want you to do whatever makes you happy, and if that means I spend every waking hour for the next month getting your bakery sorted then that's what I'll do".

She looks like she's about to protest but I stop her, placing my finger over her mouth. Her brows scrunch together as I do, and I can't help the smile that creeps up on my lips. "I mean it. Don't fight me on it".

She breathes a sigh, nodding to me, "What about our friends? What are we going to tell them? They will see it as soon as this hits any form of news". I think about her question. Really, we shouldn't tell anyone, and I don't want it to get into the wrong hands that this is all fake, "Then we tell them when the time comes, but if they see pictures of us at the event together, then we can just say I took you as my date. I'd say that's believable since we are living together".

"And what if they catch on to us being *engaged?*" She exaggerates the word, and I inwardly cringe, knowing how much she hates this. "We really need to keep the act up as much as we can, so we say that we were secretly seeing each other or something. We can figure it out as we go along". She chuckles a little, "Well, that shouldn't be a problem. I think the girls think you have a thing for me anyway".

Warmth fills me that the girls have already planted the seed that I want her, but I go along with it, playing dumb. "What do you mean?" She sighs into my chest, "Just Grace and Hallie being their usual selves, nothing for you to worry about; they just seem to think you have a thing for me, but I brushed it off because it's not true, is it".

She says it like a statement rather than a question, but before I get a chance to correct her, she continues. "I really hope that we don't have to lie to them too much about this". I nod back to her, unsure of how else I can reassure her right now, "Don't worry about it. We will figure it out and thank you again, Rose".

Her hazel eyes widen a little as she looks up to me, "You actually used my name for once". I let out a small chuckle as I lean in closer to her, "I'm just being extra nice, don't get used to it, *Red*". Her expression slowly changes into something else I can't quite put my finger on.

The urge rises in me to lean in and kiss her, and I'm so close to her that I lean in a touch more. Her lips part ever so slightly, and her breathing quickens. I inch towards her, about to press my lips to hers, when my phone begins ringing behind us, making her jump and pull away from the little moment we were having.

"I... Um. I should go". She spins on her heel, leaving me standing in my office as the reality of what we are about to do hits.

14

Rose

I avoid Luca as much as I can for the rest of the week following our discussion, I can tell I'm pissing him off by doing so, but if I spend too much time in that man's proximity, I'll do more than be his fake fiancé. Every time he comes near me, my skin breaks out in goosebumps. I can't help it; his voice is smooth and deep, and if I have to listen to it too much, I swear I'll end up with a little damp patch in my panties.

He's being awfully nice to me, too. I came into the kitchen the other day and found he'd moved literally everything from the higher shelves that he thought I might need quickly, and he put some steps in the kitchen so I can get to the bits that very rarely get used, and my coffee cup is always set to go under the machine in the mornings, allowing me to just press a button and it's all done for me.

I'm trying not to be too much of a bitch with him since I am already avoiding him and making him dinner every night, but running off to my room before he gets in, sending him a text to let him know not to bring anything home. Before I moved in, he would live off takeout of some sort, though it wasn't unhealthy, but I have to say it's an absolute shame that this kitchen would go to waste, and I felt like I needed to do something to thank him for his generosity, so the offer of food each night seems the best way forward.

I think I would have agreed to be his fake fiancé even without everything he's done for me. From the look in his eyes, I could tell that he was desperate for me to help him, and I won't lie and say that it isn't just a little bit appealing to pretend to be with him. I mean c'mon give me a little credit, I may give off that he irritates me a little, but I'm not blind.

The guy is hot. And I don't just mean, typical works out a lot hot, although his muscular body is an added bonus. I mean, he has that sexy smoulder that would make any woman swoon at his feet, a sharp jawline, a little dimple that sits just below the stubble on his right cheek, hair cropped but that flops in front of his eyes on occasion, the type that makes you want to run your fingers through it, and a slight crease above his left brow from him raising it all the time.

No wonder he has spent so long being a bachelor. He can when he looks like that, and I can't say I wasn't a little disappointed that our moment got interrupted the other day when his phone rang.

The temptation was so strong to go back into his office and kiss his face off, and it took everything in me to keep myself in my room and away from him all night. I find myself thinking about him and those perfectly kissable lips all too often recently, and I wonder just how much more it's going to take before I give in to his charm. –

Tonight is the charity event that he asked me to attend with him, and I can't help that I'm freaking out a little bit. He will actually have to touch me and pretend to be in love with me all night, and I'm not sure how I'm going to handle that. I didn't bother Grace or Hallie with my mini meltdown because, well, I just can't face questions I don't have the answers for yet. I need more time to prepare myself for the confusion of me attending an event with someone who I pretend not to be attracted to.

I'd just stepped out of the shower, having a slow afternoon of getting ready, when there is a knock at my bedroom door. I swing it open, assuming it will be Luca needing something, but instead, I find two women I have never seen before smiling brightly back at me.

"Umm, can I help you?" I ask unable to hide my confusion. "I'm assuming you are Rose. I'm Melody, and this is Lena. Luca has sent us up to get you ready for this evening". I blink back at the pair, unable to figure out what the hell is going on.

"Excuse me one moment". Squeezing past them, I make a run towards the stairs, "We will just get set up in your room". Melody calls back, and I give them both an awkward smile before turning again and hunting out Luca. He's in the kitchen sipping on a coffee and reading through some documents where he has taken a seat at the island as I come storming into the room. I must take him by surprise because his eyes are wide and a little panicked when he looks up at me. “Woah, where’s the fire? Do you not like the girls I sent up?”

I roll my eyes at him as I cross my arms over my chest, “I don’t need someone to come and dress me Luca. I’m perfectly capable of getting myself ready”. I blow a piece of hair out of my face as I huff out a breath. His lips twitch a little as he watches my outburst, before taking another sip from his coffee like I didn’t just say anything.

I wait for a moment longer before growing bored with waiting for him to respond, but as I turn to stomp back up the stairs he speaks, “I know you don’t need them, but I got them in so you can relax a little before tonight, I put a bottle of champagne in your room whilst you were in the shower, it’s on your dresser on ice with a glass. Just humour me and let them do their job, please”. I stare back at him open mouthed before realising what he just said.

My shock turns to a scowl as I regard him, “You came into my room when I was in the shower. Naked”. His lips twitch again and form into a small smirk, and it takes everything in me not to stomp over there and punch him.

God, I need to chill out, this man makes me think stupid things.

“Yeah, I did. Given that you didn’t even know I’d been in your room though, I’d say that you’re safe and I didn’t see you. Although the length of that towel you’ve got wrapped around you right now, I could just give that a small tug, and we can have a repeat of the other week".

Heat creeps up my throat as the memory of me standing in this very kitchen naked comes to the front of my mind again, and Luca just sits there lapping it up. I glare at him when his smirk turns into a full-blown grin, "Fuck you, Luca".

I turn to storm off back to my room and hear him shout behind me, "Oh there's a few new dresses I had delivered too, just in case you decided you wanted something different, they're in your wardrobe". I don't allow him to see the shock on my face as I continue up the stairs and to my room, where Melody and Lena are patiently waiting for me.

Feeling a little embarrassed that they probably heard that, I quickly poke my head into my dressing room, and sure enough, there is a rail of five dresses hanging in my closet, with shoes to match them.

I want to be so pissed at him right now, but as I turn around, Lena has poured me a glass of champagne and holds it out to me with a smile, "Come take a seat and relax, and we will do all of the hard work. Luca said you were a little stressed about tonight, so we're here to take that away".

A small part of me is relieved that I don't have to think about anything for the next two hours, apart from maybe how I can kill Luca without causing suspicion.

The girls get to work straight away, Melody grooming my hair to perfection and Lena doing my makeup for me. They take about an hour to work their magic on me, and when I take a look at myself in the bathroom mirror, I'm stunned to see how good I look. I love a bit of makeup on myself, but I'm certainly not this talented. I peer closer at myself, admiring Lena's handy work.

My hazel eyes pop from the golden tones she has used, with the smoky winged liner giving me a more cat-eye look. She's kept my face relatively light, with a deeper nude on my lips.

Shit I look good. Melody pinned my hair up into a messy-looking bun at the back of my head, the kind that you can only do with precision, leaving a few tendrils dangling down and my bangs framing my face. I smile back at my reflection and go out to thank the girls, before heading into my dressing room to see what Luca has brought in for me.

I have a few of my own that I could have worn tonight, but since he's going all out, I decide to indulge a little a see what my options are. I spend the time taking each dress off the rail and seeing it up against myself in the mirror before eventually settling on a dark, emerald green satin dress with a deep low cut back, and I'm so thankful right now for having small boobs because I certainly couldn't wear a bra with this dress.

The cut at the front doesn't show off too much, with spaghetti straps keeping everything held together, and it has a long slit going up the front of my left leg stopping just below my panty line. I slide myself into it enjoying having something new for a change instead of my usual rotation.

Grabbing the strappy gold heels from the floor, I go down the stairs to where Luca is adjusting his bow tie in the mirror, and my mouth goes dry at the sight.

He's wearing a black tux that hugs every inch of his body perfectly, his hair messy as usual, making him appear a little younger than he is, and I'm thankful right now that I'm wearing panties because heat pools at my core at the sight of him.

His eyes catch mine in the mirror, and a sexy smile spreads across his face, revealing that small dimple on his right cheek. I bite my lip as I watch him watching me, and as he turns his eyes roam up and down my body in appreciation as he lets out a low whistle.

"Damm, I lucked out with this arrangement. You look sexy as fuck in that dress Red, I'm a little gutted you aren't mine for real right now". I roll my eyes as I pad towards him, a small smile tugging at my lips, "You're just saying that because you are on a spout of abstinence right now, I'm sure if you were fucking someone, then you would change your mind". He shakes his head at me, letting out a low chuckle. "Trust me, I'd go forever without sex if it meant I could look at you like that".

I blush at his words; maybe I should reconsider his offer to have sex because the sexual tension between us can't just be in my head, surely? I shake the thought away and turn to put my shoes on, but his hand reaches out to grab hold of my wrist. Tingles run up my arms at the sensation, and I turn on the spot to look at him once more.

"I need to give you something before we go out tonight" he reaches into his pocket, pulling out a small box, "I picked this up today; since I told my dad we were engaged, it would be a little suspicious if you weren't wearing a ring". He opens the box to reveal an oval cut, almost golden stone, with tiny diamonds on either side cut into little triangles that trail around the band, giving it an earthy look, not too big either, so it doesn't overpower my small fingers. It's exactly the type of thing I would have picked out myself.

My eyes meet his as I try to find the words, and his hand comes up to take mine as he slips it onto my finger in a perfect fit.

"This is beautiful Luca. I.." my voice trails off. The effort he's gone into to get this flaws me. He could have picked any old ring for me to wear. "It matches your eyes, that's why I picked it, as soon as I told my dad, I went out and had it all arranged. It was only finished this morning; that's why I haven't been able to give it to you sooner, but I put a rush on it so you'd have it for tonight". His hands go back into his pockets, seemingly becoming a little shy as he tells me the effort he's gone to for this.

I study the ring again, taking in its beauty and trying to figure out why he'd put so much effort into picking something that is for a fake engagement. I blink up to him, studying his features, "You got this before I even agreed. Why?" His lips turn up ever so slightly at the corners as he mulls over his answer.

"I think even if you said no, I'd have still given it to you anyway, as maybe a way of apologising for the absolute fuck up of this whole situation that I've dragged you into". I grin up to him, "Well then, I guess I'll have to keep this firmly in my possession. I won't lie, I'm a little scared I might lose it". He lets out a chuckle, "Don't worry about that, it's insured in case anything happens, but I think you'd know if it slipped off your finger".

I glance down one last time before realising I need to put my shoes on still. "Oh shoot", I prop myself on the sofa to put my shoes on quickly before we're late, but the straps are fiddly, and I fumble with them a little, cursing when they won't go together.

"Here, let me" Luca takes a seat on the coffee table in front of me, lifting my foot into his lap. His callused hand grips my calve as he does, and I have to grip the sofa, to keep me from giving into the tingles running through my body and straight to my core.

He works quickly, sliding the tiny buckle into the clasp with ease before placing it down and picking my other foot up.

The split in my dress slides open more as my foot comes up to rest on his thigh, revealing a little too much leg to Luca, and possibly even a hint of the lacy black panties I have on underneath. His eyes flit up momentarily and I watch as his throat works to swallow.

Taking what enjoyment I can from the situation, I lean back on my hands just enough that there's no denying he's not seen what I'm wearing, teasing him, and testing the waters where I can, just like Grace told me to.

He finishes his handy work, sliding his fingers up the back of my leg in one smooth motion and bringing them to a stop just below my knee. I focus on them as they grip the back of my leg a little on the firmer side, and I can't quite figure out why he's gripping me so hard until my eyes meet his.

His chocolate brown orbs swirl with lust as he leans forward and into me, just enough that I can smell him but not enough that I can taste.

For a moment I think he's going to kiss me, but instead, he pushes my knee into a bend, exposing my core to him more, my underwear not doing much to cover me up right now. I gasp at the sudden movement, and he glances down at my now damp panties, before pulling my leg to the side a little more and leaning impossibly closer into me.

His eyes meet mine as his smooth voice hits my ears, the words vibrating through me, and sending shivers up my spine. "I want you to enjoy yourself tonight, but I also want you to remember that the sight of your panties is for my eyes only because as far as everyone else will be concerned, you're mine".

I nod to him, choosing to keep my mouth shut for once as I realise that maybe I do have an effect on him after all. He gives me a firm nod back, happy with my agreement and places my foot back on the ground before standing and offering me his hand, "Shall we?" I look up at him, a soft smile teasing his lips. I nod once more, placing my hand in his as he pulls me to stand with him.

I follow him, as he leads me out to the waiting town car he's hired for the evening, and he opens my door for me, waiting patiently for me to climb in before closing it behind me. I slide in, watching as he rounds the car to his side and holding my breath when he climbs in, and his thigh touches mine. I don't let him see the effect he seems to be having on me. *This is just for show*, I keep reminding myself as we make the drive to the event.

The flashing lights from the cameras glare into the car from photographers, trying to catch a glimpse of anyone they can as we pull up to the imposing building. Little do they realise I'm just a baker that's hanging off the arm of Luca tonight.

I'm lost in my own world, watching as the people line up for their photos, when my door clicks open, and a hand appears at my face. I blink up and peek through my lashes as Luca looks down to me smiling, holding his hand out when he does, and he reaches in to pull me out of the car. I place my hand in his, feeling myself wobble on my heels a little from the nerves.

Luca snakes an arm around my waist, steadying me as he does, and to anyone else the moment would look intimate, but I know he's just doing it to keep up appearances.

I peek up at him and spot a small frown tugging at his brow as he watches me. He leans into me, his lips brushing my cheek, and speaks low enough so no one but us can hear our conversation, "Are you sure you're going to be ok doing this? If not, we can turn back and go home now. I'll say you weren't feeling well or something".

My eyes flit down to my dress, then back up to him, "What, and waste such a pretty dress? I think we should stay for at least a drink, don't you?" I bat my lashes at him, waiting for him to give me a response. His eyes flit between mine for a moment, before he decides he's ok with my answer.

Giving me a firm nod and gripping my hip a little tighter, we make our way up the stairs, and he makes sure to swiftly make his way past the photographers, guiding us into the lavishly decorated hall.

The dinner hall is an epitome of luxury, with its high, arched ceilings adorned with intricate chandeliers that cast a warm, golden glow across the room. The walls are draped in rich, velvet curtains, their deep red hues complementing the polished mahogany furniture. An opulent marble floor stretches out beneath our feet, reflecting the grandeur of the surroundings. Long, elegantly dressed tables are set with fine China, crystal glasses, and gleaming silverware, each place marked by a delicately handwritten name card.

The air is filled with the soft strains of a live jazz band, adding an air of sophistication to the atmosphere. Decorative floral arrangements, composed of rare blooms and greenery, are strategically placed, adding a touch of natural beauty to the lavish setting.

A waiter carrying drinks walks past, and Luca grabs two glasses of champagne as he does. I take a healthy gulp from mine, whilst also trying to look ladylike, but I know full well I'm not. I glance over to see Luca smirking at me, and bring my glass away from my lips, running my tongue along the seam of them from the moisture my drink has left.

His eyes follow the movement before coming back up to meet mine, raising his brow at me. I shrug, looking out over to the crowd now forming in the dinner hall as people take their seats. "I needed a little liquid courage for tonight".

He nods again, a man of little words tonight. He's clearly choosing to ignore the fact I'm probably drinking way too much and showing him up. We make our way to find our seats, but Luca is pulled from side to side as people greet him on the short journey to the table.

The dinner drags on, and for the most part, I'm relieved that I haven't yet met his dad. I'm introduced to a few people at the table, making polite conversation with the woman next to me. Leila, who is on a date with a friend of Luca's rattles on about something I'm not quite paying attention to as I feel like my ears are bleeding from the shrill noise that's coming out of her mouth.

"So anyway, how did you end up snagging a date with Luca?" Her question catches me off guard, and I open and close my mouth, trying to come up with something to say to her.

A warm hand rests on my thigh, gripping it just enough that I feel the pinch, and I turn my head, glancing at Luca. He must have heard what she's said to me, and I'm reminded from the subtle squeeze on my exposed skin that we're supposed to be in a relationship. The feeling of his hands on me sends heat straight to my core, and I have to push past the tingles his touch is sending up my thigh as he allows it to move just a touch too far to be appropriate for friends.

I quickly bring my eyes back to meet Leila's, offering her a soft smile, that I've somehow managed to force onto my face. "Oh, we've actually just got engaged". The lie slips from my lips a little too easily, and I'm rewarded with another gentle squeeze from Luca for keeping up appearances. Leila blinks back at me, stunned into silence for the first time this evening as she looks back and forth between Luca and me.

"Oh, wow, I um… I didn't expect Luca to be seeing anyone. He seemed like the eternal bachelor". I try to hide my annoyance at her as I continue smiling, wrapping my hand around Luca's lower arm and leaning back into him a little, allowing the ring on my finger to catch and sparkle in the light. "Well, lucky me that I snagged him then I guess".

My words come out a little harsher than I intended them to, but I can't help it as I feel the need to protect him from whatever harsh words she might spew back, but thankfully the end of dinner is called, and people begin getting up from their seats, making their way around the room to meet people. Luca uses that as his opportunity to save me from the world's most pointless conversation as he leans into us, cutting it short.

"Sorry ladies, but I need to steal my fiancé away for a moment. I'm sure she will find you again later". Leila must still be reeling in the shock of our little admission as she just blinks back at us, before nodding quickly.

We stand and make our way over to the other side of the room, with Luca stopping to say hello to the odd person as we go. "We need to say a quick hello to my dad and then I will have to go speak to a couple of people, but then we can leave if you like?" I look over at him, and he's got a worried expression on his face like he's scared his dad might say something, but I'm a tough girl, and I can handle someone not liking me; I've done it most of my life.

I nod as we reach an older man; he looks to be an older version of Luca, with the same chocolate brown eyes and matching builds, his hair more on the greying side, though. "Dad this is Rose, my fiancé. Rose, my dad Alistar".

Hearing the words leave his mouth still surprises me, even though I've been going over this same scenario for the past four days in my head. Alistar turns to me, his chocolate eyes that match Luca's narrow in on me just enough that I notice, but he quickly smooths his features as he assesses me like he's really not sure about me. "You're not the type of girl Luca normally dates". I'm not sure if that was a question or a statement from him, but either way, I give him my best smile.

Luca shakes his head in my periphery at his dad's short tone with me, but I jump in before he can say anything. "No, I guess I'm not, but I wouldn't say that's necessarily a bad thing given his dating history". It's a low blow in Luca's direction, but I'm not about to be torn apart by his dad.

He eyes me up and down once more, "So, Rose, what do you do for a job. That's assuming you have one anyway". "Dad", Luca warns from my side, his tone firm, but I grit my teeth and continue smiling at him. He probably thinks I'm a little psychotic with the way I'm looking at him, but I'm not going down without a fight.

"I actually own my own bakery, it's having a small refurb at the moment, but I'm sure I could whip something up for you in the meantime. Sorry to disappoint if you had a different view of me, but it's something I'm very passionate about". His brows hit his hairline at my job title, and if he thinks less of me for what I do, then that's his problem.

"Oh, you bake. I'm sorry I wasn't aware of anything you did, my son only informed me you were even seeing each other last week, seems he's kept you a little secret. This isn't something that should be gone into lightly young lady, I hope you know that marrying my son comes with pressures of having to attend things like this more often if you're to be apart of this family".

"Fucks sake dad, let up a little will you", Luca grumbles by my side, but I'm a big girl, I can handle him.

I keep the practiced smile plastered on my face, not giving anything away as I reply to him.

"Oh yes I'm sorry about that, we have been keeping things on the downlow, what with Luca being more in the limelight than me, I didn't want everyone to know, I'm sorry for that. But I can assure you Mr Wilde, Luca and I have something that you wouldn't find every day, and if I can manage him, then I'm sure I can manage the *pressures* of joining this family".

Luca squeezes my side a little in reassurance, speaking up to allow me a reprieve from any more lies I might have to dish out. "Rose is a really good baker dad. I'm overseeing the renovation work that's being done on it at the moment, and whatever you think of her, like I told you last week, she isn't like anyone else I've ever been with. Give yourself time to get to know her like I have, and you might find you like her more than you thought".

His dad nods along approvingly, seemingly changing his tune when he realises I'm not some gold digger hanging off the arm of his beloved son. "Well, that's just lovely then. And yes, I wouldn't mind if you did actually, it would be nice to get to know my future daughter in law a little better by sampling some of your work".

I bring my attention back to him nodding in agreement, "Of course, I'll whip something up and have Luca bring it to the office".

Alistar seems satisfied enough with us for the time being as he nods along, before being pulled into conversation by someone else. We use that as our escape, as we wander around the room some more.

"I'm sorry about him, I think he's just a little sceptical after it being so sudden". I turn to face him, his annoyingly perfect face is scrunched up as he talks about his dad. "It's fine, I'd be worried if he wasn't bothered who his son is marrying. At least he seemed happy enough with me". I smile at Luca as I say the words, feeling relieved that his dad semi accepted me. "Well, lucky for us that we don't have to do these things very often".

He grins back at me before getting pulled into another conversation and I find my way to the bar to get myself a drink after the most nerve wrecking meet of my life.

I'm not sure if I'd be cut out for this life, having to be nice to people and talk to everyone all the time. I order a cocktail from the bar, and sit enjoying sipping the fruity drink, but my moment of peace is interrupted by someone taking a seat next to me, speaking up to the bartender.

"I'll have whatever she's having". I bring my eyes up to meet cold blue ones. The man sitting next to me I recognise as someone who is in competition with Luca from what I've read online. He brings his hand up to shake mine, introducing himself as he does.

"I'm Gregory Hamilton, but I'm sure you already know that". His cockiness pisses me off as if I should know who he is, and I roll my eyes at him, choosing to ignore his outstretched hand. I play along with my own game, not wanting to boost his ego anymore. "Actually, I'm not sure I have heard of you. I keep my circle small, so I don't think I've met any boneheads recently".

He lets out an awkward laugh, pulling his hand back a little and smoothing it over his jacket sleeve like I've not just rejected him. I glance around, looking to see if anyone can save me, but I don't immediately spot someone.

He shifts in his seat, bringing himself closer to me, and I want to get up and move away but my position at the bar has me unable to escape. "And who left a pretty little thing like you all alone at the bar tonight then, hmm?" His hand comes up as he trails his spindly fingers down my arm, and it takes everything in me not to recoil from his touch. I'm about to tell him to leave me alone when Luca's angry voice speaks from behind us.

"She's with me, and I'll break your fingers if you don't get them off her right now". My head snaps in his direction as he reaches over, pushing Gregory out of the way to get to me. His fingers wrap around my arm as he pulls me to stand, and I have to steady myself as my head spins a little from how quickly I've moved when I'm pulled into Luca's strong hold.

"Now now, no need to get worked up. I was merely keeping her company whilst you were off having fun". The smirk on this guy's face clearly pisses Luca off as he moves me out of the space with him and brings me behind him like he needs to protect me. "I was doing my job, something you should try sometime. I mean it. Stay the fuck away from her".

The grip on my arm tightens as he turns us to leave, dragging me along with him. "Luca, let go of me. You don't need to manhandle me", I huff out as he pulls us into a deserted corridor. He stops as he lets go of me, spinning us so that I'm backed up against the wall as he gets in my space.

"You let him touch you. I don't like people touching what doesn't belong to them". I roll my eyes blowing out a laugh at him, "Luca, I think you're forgetting, I'm not actually yours, and if you had waited a minute more before barging in there, you would have seen me tell him to fuck off".

Luca crowds me, bringing his hand up to cup my jaw as he turns me to face him, his face full of anger and frustration at the situation that didn't need to escalate the way it did. He leans into me and speaks lowly in my ear, his voice firm and controlled, "I'll think you'll find whilst that ring is on your finger, you are mine, Red. And I'm not having some asshole touching you when he shouldn't be".

I want to protest, but as his breath fans my face, goosebumps spill out all over my body. He pulls his face back, allowing his nose to brush against mine as our bodies mould into one, his lips so close I can almost taste the alcohol on his breath. My heart is going a mile a minute at his closeness, and I feel my chest rising and sinking rapidly.

His eyes flit between mine for a moment and all sanity leaves me as I lean into him just enough that I can press a kiss to his lips. He freezes, and so do I as I realise my mistake. I try to pull back from him, to relinquish him of guilt that he feels he needs to carry on with me, but his hand moves quickly, wrapping around the back of my head to keep me in place as he deepens the kiss.

A low growl leaves his throat as he leans into me more, pressing his hips between my legs and holding me in place. His other hand trails down my body as he continues to kiss me and wraps around my waist. My mind is solely focused on him, and I let out a little moan, parting my lips and allowing him more access.

His tongue teases mine as we grope each other, my hands grip onto his shirt for dear life as I try to keep this moment that I've thought about for so long, going. I want to carry this on and explore his beautiful body, but our kiss is broken by a couple of people tumbling out of the room, interrupting our moment. Luca pulls back, pressing his forehead to mine as his breath comes out choppy. "Fuck, I really don't think we should carry that on here, or I'll get carried away".

I try to hide the disappointment that sinks deep inside me as he takes a step back, breaking the contact between us. His eyes scan over me, examining me as he watches me for a moment before taking my hand in his. "C'mon, let's get out of here, I've seen who I need to for this evening". I nod along numbly, knowing my moment of stupidity was in vain, as he places a hand on my bare back, causing my stupid body to react to him by sending tingles through my spine. I wish he didn't feel so good.

He's not interested in me. I don't know why I thought he would be, but I follow him out to the waiting car anyway, not wanting him to see the inner turmoil I feel at his rejection as he opens the car door for me, and I climb inside. I feel like an idiot for making the first move. Clearly, I've had too much to drink tonight, further proving my point that I shouldn't drink around this intoxicating man.

15

Luca

The car journey feels like the longest I've ever been on when in reality, it's only a 30-minute drive back to our house. *Our house,* why do I like the sound of that so much? Maybe because my dick has been straining against my zipper since Rose put her soft, pillowy lips on mine, and I've had to readjust myself several times since we walked out of the event.

I dragged Rose out of there so fast, I'm not surprised she's ignoring me now. Clearly, she thought I wasn't enjoying myself, but I had to stop, or I would have ended up sliding my hands right in between that too-high slit up her left thigh, where I'd been itching to touch again and again all night.

My fingers itch to reach over and touch her, but she's giving me the cold shoulder, and I'm not sure what I should be saying in this situation to make her aware that I very much want to carry on what we started.

I'm not used to having to work for it so much or to be given this kind of treatment after I just had my tongue in someone's mouth, but it's made me realise how much I expected women to fall at my feet. Instead of bulldozing straight to the point but still wanting to be close to her, I reach out, lightly brushing the skin on her exposed creamy thigh.

"Hey, are you okay? You've gone quiet on me". She freezes up momentarily, her shoulders hunch up, and her eyes flicker down to where my hand rests on her leg. My fingers pulse, wanting to squeeze the flesh there to allow her to feel what she can have if she gives into me, but I try to keep as calm as I can in this car, which feels incredibly hot right now.

Rose subtly shakes her head, not wanting to look me in the eye, "Yeah, I'm sorry I did that then, it was the alcohol talking. I shouldn't have kissed you".

I feel my heart sink at her words, but I don't let her see that. Instead, I push forward, leaning in closer to her and murmur to her, "I'm not sorry, and if you didn't kiss me first, then I don't think it would have taken long before I made a move to kiss you. You look too good not to want to touch every inch of your skin in that dress".

A small shiver runs through her body as my fingers trail a little higher up the slit along her bare skin. "Do you feel like you wish you hadn't kissed me, Red?"

Her eyes shoot up to mine, and I'm glad that I finally have her attention on me. She sucks her bottom lip between her teeth, and I swear she could pierce it if she bites any harder. My eyes bounce between hers, waiting for an answer.

I'm not one to give up easily, and if I have to wait for something more from her, then I will, but right now, I'll take whatever I can get. "I… I don't know, Luca. I think it was just a spur-of-the-moment thing, and I didn't think about anything else at the moment other than kissing you".

My dick begs for attention as it strains impossibly harder against my zipper while I think of her thoughts solely being on me, and if it were up to me, I'm going to be the last man that touches those perfect lips.

I lean over the seat, getting as close as possible to her. My fingers tighten around the apex of her thigh, and her breath hitches at the movement. I can't help the small twitch of my lips at the sound coming from her.

She smells heavenly, her cherry scent invading my nostrils as I inch closer to her. The alcohol has sent my head into a spin, and all it's making me want to do is claim her in this car as my own like some fucking animal. I press my lips to her ear, my voice husky and a little strained, just like my dick still is in my pants, "What if I want to kiss you again, *Rose?* Would you let me?"

I watch as her eyes pop, the hazel flecks swimming with the desire that she keeps fighting. Her tongue darts out across her bottom lip, and I keep my focus solely on her face as her eyes switch between my eyes and lips. She's trying to decide if this is a good idea or not, and right now, I can't think of any reason why we shouldn't. We're attracted to each other, and technically, we're engaged right now, fake or not, I'm adding that to the list of pros for taking things further tonight.

I graze my thumb over her thigh, feeling the goosebumps rise on her skin as I do. Her eyes flick down to the exposed flesh on her leg once more, where my hand is firmly in place, and her breathing gets heavier the longer she watches the movement of my thumb caressing her skin.

"Hey", I say as I reach over and take her chin in my hand, pulling her gaze towards me. "Don't overthink this. I won't think any worse of you either way, but I do want you to know that I don't regret a single moment of what happened in the hallway. My only regret is that we didn't continue what we were doing".

She nods to me, and a few stands fall loose from her hair, falling in her face from the motion. My instant reaction is to tuck the loose strand behind her ear.

I keep my eyes on hers the whole time and watch as they dilate. Her lips part ever so slightly when my fingertips caress the back of her ear, and I stroke my fingers down the side of her neck.

I lean in once more, getting impossibly closer as my lips brush hers, silently requesting permission from her to give me the go-ahead to kiss her again when we are pulled from our moment by the car coming to a stop. "We've arrived home, Sir", the driver announces from the front of the car. Rose blinks a couple of times before coming back to her senses and pulling away from me.

She's flustered but attempts to regain her composure, clearing her throat as she turns to bolt for the door. I want to stop her, but I also need her to come to me by herself. I don't want to force this on her and then she regrets it tomorrow or the day after, and I don't want her to regret a single moment of us.

I follow her inside the house and up the stairs, where she bolts away from me again and makes a hasty exit for her bedroom. *Alright, guess we aren't going to talk about what just happened then.*

Her sudden dismissal of me hurts my ego a little too much. I stop midway up the stairs, retreating back down them and storm into the living room to make myself a drink, pouring 2 fingers of whiskey into my glass and swilling the amber liquid around before downing it in one go.

I instantly fill it again, needing to calm the intense feeling of frustration that's swilling through my brain from what just happened. Because nothing happened, and all I can think is, what the fuck did I do wrong just then.

I make my way into the kitchen, my drink in one hand and the other tucked into my pocket as I look out of the back of the house over the lake, the moonlight glistening on the water as it ripples under the wind that's out tonight.

The crystal tumbler weighs heavy in my hand as I talk myself out of making a third drink in the space of five minutes, before dropping my glass onto the unit and staring at it whilst I decide what I should do.

Maybe if I took a shower, it would take the edge off. Give me some time to sort through my own emotions about the situation. God knows I need to do that. My therapist would be proud of me.

I'd been going to therapy for the last seven years, trying to work through the minefield in my head and the small amount of hatred towards my father, which I can't seem to shift.

He does his best to show me the love that I need, but he's never been as close as I want him to be, and well, that hurts more than I care to admit that I was pushed aside as a child, knowing he was too focused on his company and not our family until my mother was ill and dying.

My mom passed away from cancer when I was thirteen, and my dad promptly moved us from California to Tennessee so I could be closer to my grandparents whilst he built his fortunes more. I spent most of my summers there before that but never met anyone.

That was until I met Jaxx and Tristan in the first trimester of ninth grade. They took me under their wing, knowing I was the new kid and admittedly a little shy around new people.

Years of being told to keep quiet and just be polite had rubbed off by the time I hit high school, and it took me going to college and coming into my own for me to get out of my funk.

I slept my way through college, using my charm and good looks to get each and every girl I wanted. It helped coming from money because that's all the girls were interested in, what I could offer them, and every single one of them was disappointed when they learned that they weren't going to be the next Mrs Wilde.

I knew I wouldn't commit to anyone in my early twenties, and that has slowly slid into my early thirties. But something switched in me the night I met Rose. Something that made me want to do better. I started going to therapy again over the last few months, and I genuinely feel like I'm becoming a better person.

My only downfall is that I had to drag Rose into the shitty lie to keep my dad from forcing some woman on me and down the aisle. For some reason, I don't regret doing it because she's living in my house and wearing my ring, and I feel like I'm slowly breaking down her walls, bringing her closer to me. Well, at least I thought I was.

With a sigh, I decide to call it a night, knowing that the alcohol isn't going to fix my problems, and I'm at an age now where my hangovers are worse and worse these days. I trudge up the stairs to my room and make my way into the bathroom to strip off and drown my sorrows in my shower.

My head is still swimming with thoughts of Rose and her perfect creamy skin the whole time as I once again stroke myself, imagining it's her down on her knees in front of me, her beautiful, sassy mouth wrapped around my cock, taking each inch of me like I know she can. My hand braces the wall as I close my eyes, picturing her with each stroke I make, my grip tightens on my dick as I imagine her taking it deep into her mouth and sucking me dry.

A strangled groan slips free from my lips as I release all over the tiled floor of my shower. It's not helped the situation anymore, because this is a temporary fix. It is every time I do it, and I know full well that as soon as I see her perfect heart-shaped face in front of me again, I'll have blue balls.

I soap myself up, wanting to get out of the shower and into bed as quickly as I can now I've just made my mood worse by thinking of her again, and towel off before wrapping it round myself as I make my way into my room.

There's a small knock at my bedroom door as I come out of the bathroom. It's that quiet I almost miss it. But I walk over, swinging it open and come face to face with Rose. She's changed out of her dress and heels and swapped them for a little tank top and shorts. Her cheeks are flushed, and her mouth pops open as she stares at me, her eyes moving up and down my body, and I momentarily forget that I'm standing in just a towel.

I fold my arms across my chest and prop myself against the door frame whilst she blatantly checks me out, giving my ego the boost it definitely needs, and I cock an eyebrow at her when she finally brings those gorgeous hazel eyes to meet mine.

"You having a good look there, Red?" Her face morphs from surprise to that scowl I've become accustomed to. Her favourite facial expression that I swear is reserved just for me. She folds her arms in front of her, my ring sitting perfectly on her finger, she must wear it to bed.

She mimics my actions, and it pushes her breasts up, forcing me to bring my eyes back up to hers. She clears her throat, preparing herself for what she needs to say, "I'm sorry for doing what I did tonight. And I mean the whole night. I shouldn't have kissed you in the first place because it would just confuse things further, and I feel bad for just walking off when we got back into the house. I just... I needed to collect my thoughts before I said anything else to you".

She puffs out a breath once she is finished, but I need to know what more could have happened had she not pulled away from me in the car.

My alcohol-induced thoughts take a sharp turn as I reach out, wrap an arm around her slender little waist and pull her flush against me. Her eyes widen in surprise at my sudden movement, and her breath catches slightly, too.

I wrap my other hand around the back of her head, making sure she can't go anywhere as I tilt it up and lean in, my lips brushing against her delicate skin for the second time this evening, and murmur to her, "Just remember as you asked of me, whilst we are in this arrangement you are mine and only mine. If you want anything, and I mean anything at all, Red. You come to me, and I'll be more than happy to give you what you need".

I press a kiss to her cheek, pulling away just enough so I can watch her chest move up and down, her breathing quickens as she pulls back slightly and I let my eyes wander up to her face, her mouth is open as she attempts to calm herself, and those perfect lips are all too tempting.

She watches me, too, for a moment, trying to figure out what to say to me, and I take that time to study her every movement as her tongue comes out, swiping across her lips before she speaks, "And what exactly would I need to come to you for Luca? I'm going to need you to be more specific, you know, so I don't get it wrong".

She's playing a dangerous game here if she thinks I won't do just what I want right now. I told myself I wouldn't make the first move but fuck that. I need her.

I get close enough that my lips brush hers lightly as I move to rest my forehead against hers, making sure she's following what I am doing, "I think you know exactly what you need to come to me for, and I think you want the same as me. That kiss we shared, I know you want it again".

She doesn't pull back from me, and so I press my lips against hers, pulling her into the kiss as my hand comes around to trail my fingers across the base of her jaw so I can have her exactly where I want her. I'm rewarded with a perfect little moan from her as she deepens the kiss herself, allowing me entrance.

The moment becomes more intimate when her hand that's wedged between us moves slightly, and I move just enough, allowing her to brush her delicate fingers across my bare chest, her fingers brushing through the smattering of hair there.

A groan bubbles up my throat, the feeling of her bare skin against mine has my dick going impossibly hard, and it takes all my restraint not to rip those flimsy little shorts off her body. She takes over the kiss, seemingly getting more confident the more our lips move together, her hands coming up to lock behind my neck. I should do the smart thing and pull away right now, but I clearly make no smart decisions where this woman is involved.

I move us across the room, enough to push her against the wall, as I allow my hands to trail down her body, skimming over her ass and lifting her so she's closer to my height. Her 5ft 4 frame is all too easy to carry as her legs wrap around me on instinct, and she moans a little more.

My mouth moves from her lips down to the collum of her throat, and I'm finding it all too easy to get carried away with her. "I meant what I said. We can use this agreement to our advantage. You can't tell me we wouldn't be good together, and there's no harm in having some fun with the situation".

I breathe the words against her throat, wanting her to agree so badly, and she nods into me, those little moans coming from her doing everything to me. "You want this too, Red? Want to enjoy this arrangement and use it to its full potential?"

A light chuckle slips free from her lips, and I'm not sure if she's just fucking with me right now, enjoying what she's doing to me. My dick is lapping up all the attention she's giving me, and I'll be mighty fucking surprised if she can't feel it pressing in between her ass cheeks right now.

She pulls back slightly, her hazel eyes bright and wide as she looks straight into my eyes, a small smile adding to the angelic look on her face. "I think you'll just have to wait and see Luca, but if you play your cards right, then I might let you end that little stint of abstinence you've begun a little sooner". My lips tip up into a smile as I watch her, thinking she has one over on me.

"You tell yourself you don't want this, but I can feel how well your body responds to me". I brush my lips against her jaw, teasing her as much as possible. My hands move to grab at her ass, squeezing it as I press her pussy against me, pushing us further into the wall. I could take this so much further tonight, but I want her begging for it, and I know she'll come to me when she's ready, so I pull back from her, my fingers caressing the crease in her ass, so close to her opening I could just slide those shorts to the side right now.

Her breathe catches as I tease my fingers right near her entrance, her wide eyes meet mine when I tell her, "I want you to think of me tonight when you climb into bed and when your fingers find their way into those flimsy little shorts and you stroke yourself, I want you to imagine it's me between those pretty thighs. Because it will be. Very soon".

Her eyes search mine, the hazy look in them gives me all the confirmation I need, that she's going to go back into her room and do just what I've told her. I reluctantly let go of her, slowly dragging my hands over her body as I lower her back on the ground and give her a tap on the ass as she walks back into her room. The smile she's giving me over her shoulder is the last thing I see when I close my door, and I don't mind the fact that she's the reason I'm not sleeping for a change.

16

Rose

I'm playing a dangerous game with Luca. One where I enjoy the torment I'm giving him but doing just that to myself at the same time.

I shut my door, pinning myself against it as I try to reel in what the hell just happened. I keep telling myself that I'm not attracted to him, that I don't want him, but the guy is just so God dam good looking that I can't resist him. I have to push past the urge to go storming back into his room and demand he give me the orgasm I so desperately need.

His fingers played a little too close to where I needed them tonight, both at the event and when I had my legs wrapped around him not five minutes ago, and I could feel his dick pressing against my ass like he was just begging to slide it inside me. I bet he fucks like some sort of God too.

"Ughh", I let the loud groan slip out of me and don't even care too much if Luca hears it. Maybe he will come help me with my problem after all. The mental debate I go through in my head continues as I drag myself over to bed, crawling in and trying to get some sleep. But with the alcohol from this evening mixing with the thoughts of him, I find myself restless, knowing the only way I can fix this situation and get myself off to sleep is to sort the problem at hand- literally.

I close my eyes, slipping my hand into my shorts, and allow my fingers to play of their own accord whilst my brain pictures Luca above me instead. I'm so wet from the way he had me up against the wall mere moments ago, that I slide the slickness through my folds, toying with my clit as I rub in slow circles.

My other hand comes up to pinch at my nipple as I feel myself getting closer and closer to the edge. I keep the motion going, bringing myself to the high, and wanting so badly to call out to Luca and ask him to come finish the job he started by getting me in this situation, but I work my fingers faster, pressing a little harder until I feel myself fall right over the edge. My legs shake as my orgasm takes over me, and I ride it out until I feel myself come back to reality.

It feels nowhere near as good as what I'm picturing the real thing to be, but until I either tell him what I really want, or he takes it, I guess I'll never know.

.....

I didn't sleep a wink last night, and I bet if Luca found out I got myself off to thoughts of him, his head wouldn't be able to fit through the door. I don't want him to know the effect he has on me has become so much in such a short space of time, and I don't want to get too close to him either, knowing that this could all very well blow up in my face, and most likely will knowing the luck I have with men. I've dated in the past, and had one guy stay for longer than a few months, but he said I was too much, ultimately leaving me, better than the others who ghosted me or were absolute nutjobs I suppose.

I thought… Well hoped Luca would have left by the time I came downstairs in the morning, but my hope is squashed when I catch him in his workout clothes standing by the coffee machine after what's clearly been a good gym session for him and right now I really wish I didn't love coffee so much, just so I could avoid him that little bit longer.

I clear my throat, making him aware I've come into the room and make my way around the counter to the machine, I expect him to move along a little bit, but he just stands there as if he's not even noticed I've come in.

I'm about to ask him if I can get to the machine when he turns his body slightly and holds out a freshly brewed cup of coffee, cream already in it. I look up at him as I take the cup from his hands, and lord, he looks good in the mornings, black t-shirt that clings to him like a second skin, shorts that hang just a little on the low side, that allow me a peek of the tanned skin underneath when he reaches for something and a small amount of sweat dripping down his front that should put anyone off, but dam it makes him look so fucking hot.

I bite my lip as I try not to let him see me checking him out so much, but the smirk on his face says otherwise.

"Good morning, sunshine. Did you sleep well? I know I did". *Fuck did he hear me last night?* I frown at him, choosing to fain ignorance at the fact that I slept like shit, and he can probably tell. His hand comes up on instinct, smoothing over my brow like it does every time I'm in close proximity to him.

I want to punch his stupidly gorgeous face, but the guy did make me coffee, so I can't complain too much about him. I jut my chin out slightly, giving him my brightest smile as I lift my coffee cup to my lips, "I slept just peachy thank you", I squeak out just before sipping the warm molten liquid in my cup. My eyes shut on instinct, and a little moan slips out as I do. God, that stuff is good.

I crack my eyes open, realising my mistake when Luca is all too close to me, watching me intently with that smirk still plastered on his face. He leans against the counter, propping himself up with his elbow, and brings his cup to his lips, speaking just before he takes a long drink, "If that's the noises you make just from my coffee, imagine what you'll do when I finally give you the orgasm you so badly want".

I shoot him a dirty look as he sips on his drink, but he's not done, "Don't think I didn't hear little noises coming from that pretty little mouth from across the hall last night. You're a noisy one, I like it". His dimple comes out as he grins at me and I choke on my coffee as his words register in my head, spluttering everywhere as I cough and try to get a handle on myself.

Luca panics when he sees my coughing fit, putting his cup down and quickly rushing behind me to pat me firmly on the back, whilst taking my cup from me at the same time.

"Jesus, Red, I wasn't trying to kill you". I manage a small laugh, as I eventually calm down enough to stop coughing. His hand stays put on my back, as he rubs it in soothing circles, not realising I don't need him to carry on. "I'm good now Luca, thanks". I gesture to his hand, but he makes no move to take it away, leaning in instead and bringing his lips close to my ear, instantly prickling at my skin from his breath.

"If you want something to choke on, I can find a way to make that happen". The filth coming from this man's mouth this morning has my head spinning.

I pivot, leaning back against the counter so he's now standing in front of me. "Luca, I don't remember agreeing to be your fuck buddy last night". I fold my arms across my chest as I make my statement, and it doesn't go unnoticed when his eyes flit down to where my breasts are pushed together. "Jesus, do you think about anything other than sex?"

He brings his attention back to me, lifting a brow as he leans into me, his arms coming on either side of me and caging me in. "I do usually, but all I've been able to think about since you came to live here is all the things I could do to your body". My eyes roll of their own accord, like a tik when someone says something that's most definitely not true but also trying not to show how much his words affect me and that I do, in fact, want him to do everything he's thinking.

I bring my hands up, pressing them against his chest as I try to put some distance between us, but the arrogant fucker flexes, and all I feel is the muscles ripple under my hands. "I think we need to take a step back here. You want this arrangement to work then we need to set some ground rules".

He looks down at me, schooling his features so I have no clue what he's thinking and moves to grab his coffee, taking a seat at the island as he does. He clasps his hands in front of himself, turning into the businessman he is. "All right, shoot. What ground rules would you like in place?"

I clear my throat and stand a little taller, giving me the extra boost of confidence I need to get through this. "We can't have a sexual relationship. I catch feelings way too easily, and it won't do me any favours when you decide you no longer need or want me for this arrangement".

A slight frown tugs at his brow, but somehow, he manages not to flinch like I hoped he might, further proving my point that I made the right decision. He shrugs his shoulders slightly, and I'd think he wasn't bothered, but then he opens his mouth, "All right if that's what you want. I can't say I agree, but this needs to benefit you just as much as it does me".

My hands find my hips as I stare him down. I don't think I've ever been so confused by someone in my life. "What's that supposed to mean? You don't agree with me because you can't handle keeping it in your pants for a bit longer than usual. You went all caveman last night, and now you're being a dick, Luca".

He holds up his hand, stopping me from carrying on, "First of all, I never said that I wasn't in the wrong here, I am fully aware of what I did last night, as well as what you did. But let me make one thing clear. The only reason I'm saying I don't agree with you is because you think I'm going to drop you when you no longer need to help me and fulfil the obligation I'm asking of you. I never said anything of the sort, you are coming to that conclusion by yourself".

He points a finger at me as he says it, and my mouth snaps shut. I don't even know what to say to that… Because, well, he's right. He's never actually said that this is purely an agreement, but then he didn't say it wasn't either.

He watches me a moment longer before standing and making long, measured steps toward me until he's in my space again, bringing his fingers up to brush against my jaw and pulling my gaze to him as he continues, "I meant what I said last night, I do want this agreement to benefit the both of us. What happened last night, me losing my shit with that guy, was jealousy on my part, and I'm not afraid to admit it. I don't want to see any other man touching you. We clearly need to figure things out between us, because I can't have a repeat of that".

"Luca I... I don't know if I can do this". My breath is shaky as his eyes roam my face, a small smile forms in the corner of his mouth, and I know from here on out, I'm going to struggle to say no to anything this man says.

"Yes, you can. We're in this together, and I know you're a strong person, but right now, we don't have to pretend to be anything. Just you and me here together. Just don't think about anything right now".

His hand slides around to the back of my neck, pulling me closer to him. He watches me with every move he makes, silently checking that I'm really okay with it, and when I give him the smallest of nods, his lips come down to meet mine, brushing against my own and I give him the access he wants to me.

My brain turns to mush when his tongue meets with mine as he skilfully kisses me, and all the self-control I had in this situation goes out of the window. What was I even just saying about boundaries? My hands move of their own accord, as they slide up the sides of his body and around his neck. The extra foot of height he has on me has me pulling at him to bring him closer as I get lost in the moment.

In one swoop, my feet are off the ground as Luca grabs my legs to hoist me up, and I let out an involuntary shiver as my ass touches the cold countertops when he props me down, making it easier for us both to have the access we want. Our kisses become breathless and more hurried as we fight against each other, each of us trying to have more dominance. My fingers tug at his shirt as I hastily pull it above his head, needing to touch him again.

Luca's hands come down grabbing at my waist as he toys with the sides of my top. His fingers graze the skin where it has risen and brush the underside of my breasts, making my nipples harden under his touch as his fingers drift higher, allowing his thumbs to caress them.

A moan slips out at the sensation of his hands on me as my eyes close, and I prop my hands behind me on the counter to keep myself steady so I can enjoy the feeling of him on me. He leans into me, feathering kisses along my jaw, coaxing me to continue, I don't want him to stop, but I'm pulled from my thoughts by my phone ringing upstairs. I try to ignore it, but it cuts off and instantly starts back up again.

I let out a groan, leaning forward as I rest my head against his hard chest. He chuckles at me as he presses a kiss to my head. "Saved by the phone, I guess. Here, let me help you" he lifts me from the counter and sets me back down on the floor, "You go take that. I'll be in my office". Pressing another quick kiss to my head, he turns and makes his way out of the kitchen.

I'm left stunned from what just happened as I watch his back disappear out of the kitchen, and my phone blares loudly again. "For fucks sake" I grumble to myself as I shake off thoughts of Luca and make my way to my room.

My phone is on the fifth ring as I reach it and answer just in time before it cuts off again, seeing it's Hallie calling me. "Is there an emergency or something? Why are you calling so much?" I snap into the phone, but my friend quickly cuts me off.

"Don't give me your shit today Rose. Do you want to explain why Luca has his arm wrapped around your waist and is looking at you like you hung the fucking moon at a charity event last night, and the comments say he has attended with his FIANCE?" She screeches the last word to me, causing me to pull my phone away from my ear to avoid the shrill tone of her voice when she's mad.

Fuck maybe I should have told the girls first. I mull over my answer carefully, not wanting to out the lie that we have created, "Look, I need to explain what's happened, I'll meet you at the café in half an hour, okay?" "Fine, Grace is with me too, see you shortly".

She hangs up, leaving me reeling with thoughts on how the hell I am supposed to lie to the pair of them. I quickly throw on some clothes and run downstairs to hunt out Luca. He's in his office with his head buried deep in some blueprints, and I burst into the room, catching him off guard as I enter.

"What's wrong?" His brows pull together as he studies my face, trying to figure out what's going on with my frantic state. "Hallie just rang, and she's seen some article last night of us and Grace knows too and I'm panicking I don't know what to do and I'm meeting them in half an hour".

I suck in a breath after blurting everything out in one go. Luca comes around his desk, standing so close to me that I feel dizzy, a mix of his too-close proximity and having spewed so many words without taking a breath.

His hands rub along the sides of my arms. Thankfully, my long sleeves act as a barrier against his warm calloused fingers. "Just breathe, give yourself a minute". I take a few more breaths in and out, his energy calming me down the longer I stand with him.

After a minute, I finally feel like I'm able to function properly again and glance up at him. "All right, now you seem to have calmed down enough; tell me why you're so worried. We said we were going to tell them we were seeing each other, didn't we? Has that plan changed for you?"

"I… Well, I don't know, do you really think this is a good idea, lying to them? I'm not even sure what to say, I'm a shit liar Luca", I whine to him, praying he can fix this solution by himself.

I blow out another breath as his hands continue to rub soothing sweeps up and down my arms, "Look if you want to tell them, then that's fine. It's not fair of me to expect you to lie to them on top of everything else going on. Just make sure they don't say anything to anyone".

I really don't think that any of this will go down well but I nod to him anyway. He presses a light kiss to my head "You go deal with them, I'll be here if you need me when you get back".

.....

I make my way over to meet the girls at Bread & Coffee, the local café, my mind trying to figure out what the hell I'm going to say to them the entire drive over. They're already waiting when I enter, nestled together in a booth in the back as I sheepishly make my way over to them, they've both got a look that tells me I'm not in for an easy ride right now.

I've barely sat down before they start, "All right. Spill, what's going on?" Grace's tone isn't full of accusation like I thought it might be, she seems more curious than anything. I inhale a deep breath, looking around the café to make sure no one is close enough to hear us.

"Okay, so you know how his dad wants him to take over the company?" They nod in acknowledgement and I continue, "Well, he's basically told Luca, that unless he settles down and marries someone then he has to step back from the company, Luca then panicked and said we were engaged; something about me texting him and my name popped in his head", I roll my eyes at the memory of us in his living room.

"Anyway, after what he's done for me, helping to sort the bakery and putting me up, I can't see him have to go through that, and so I agreed I'd be his fake fiancé until his dad sees that he is capable of running the company, and when the time comes, we'll end our agreement".

Both girls stare back at me, mouths wide open as I finish telling them everything. Hallie is the first to speak, "Damm, I really didn't think his dad would do that, but I suppose we don't know what goes on behind closed doors". She arches a brow at me as she says it. I read between the lines, "I'm not sleeping with him Hallie, I'm just trying to help him out. His dad was trying to arrange his marriage to a friend's daughter, and anyway, he's helping me too".

I try to keep my tone calm, but anticipation jolts through me and part of me wants to just up and walk away already. I'm not sure I can face them trying to talk me out of it.

"What's in it for you then? I'm really not sure how I feel about this all of a sudden. Do you not think you need to be just a little more cautious with this?" Grace asks, and I glance over to her. She's always been worried about me like I'm a livewire, but I really don't think she needs to this time. "He's helping me by fixing the bakery after the flood. You both know how long I've wanted this, and I couldn't afford to do it by myself, the offer was too good to turn down. I get that it's not an ideal situation, but I want to help him too".

Grace nods thoughtfully, "I get that, I just have my reservations about the whole engagement thing, like I know you said it's not real but it's still a lot".

I wrap my hands around my coffee cup, forgetting that I still have the ring on, but Hallie has a completely different outlook to Grace. "Oh my gosh! Is that what he gave you?" Hallie grabs my hand, examining the ring as she moves my hand in every direction so she can get a good look at it. "Damm, I wish I moved in with him now, are you sure you two aren't engaged for real?"

Grace nudges Hallie for her outburst at the ring. I frown at her, pulling my hand back slightly, "Why would you think that?" She scoffs, "That ring must have been specifically designed to look like that. It's stunning, he's gone into so much thought for the sake of a fake engagement".

She voices what I had already thought myself about the ring, and I glance down at it, twisting it on my finger. "Yeah, it is pretty isn't it". Grace presses her hand to mine, and I glance up at her, a concerned expression marking her features, "We just want what's best for you. As long as he doesn't hurt you and you think you're doing the right thing, then go for it. But I'm not sure that this is the best way forward if you want to see how things go with him".

I know they have mixed views, and Grace seems more reserved about it than Hallie does, but I'm doing this for me, not them.

"So, you don't think I'm being stupid by doing this?" Hallie lets out a small chuckle "Hell yeah, this is possibly the most stupid thing you've ever done, but you need to live a little. What's the worst that could happen really?"

I fall for him, and he breaks my heart. I push those thoughts aside. I know he's got a past reputation, but all he's shown me so far is how far he's willing to go to prove his worth to his father and I just want things to go right for him too. I sit a little taller in my seat. "I know this could very well blow up in my face, but something in the way he told me niggled at me, and I feel bad for him, and it makes me want to help him, and if this is the way to do it then so be it".

"Well, that's all you can do then. Just don't let him take advantage of you in this situation yeah?" Hallie keeps her tone light, but I know she's worried about me. They both are. I nod to them, grabbing a menu as I do. "Shall we order some food anyway? I'm starving."

They share a look, one I'm not quite ready to delve into, so I ignore them, pushing Luca out of my mind for the rest of the day.

17

Luca

By the time I'd made my way out of my office on Sunday, I'd missed Rose coming home and sneaking into her room. We didn't get a chance to talk about what had happened that morning, between her panicking about the girls finding out we were 'engaged' and me having to work until the last minute to get a job completed, and if I didn't know any better, I'd say she was avoiding me.

I would have wondered if she'd been home at all the past three days too, but she's left me notes each morning by the coffee machine, telling me she won't be home for dinner.

By Wednesday morning, I'd grown tired of dancing around what we did on my kitchen counter, and now she was running away from me like she does each time we get close to each other. I took a peek at her schedule to see she's home mid-day. Most days, between the running around she's busied herself with, she has filled her time with orders for new customers. I told Cora I'd be working from home again, and after trying to hide her pout, she told me she would send everything I needed to my email.

I make my way into the house, announcing my entrance as I come into the living room to avoid being scolded for sneaking up on Rose again and stop short when I catch her bent over with a tiny pair of workout shorts on and a sports bra that barely seems to cover her. She's stretching out on a yoga mat in what looks like the downward dog position, and my dick twitches at the thought of just sliding right in behind her and keeping her on all fours.

Her head appears between her arms as she watches me from her upside-down position before coming to sit on the mat. "Hey, what are you doing home?" She says breathlessly, causing me to harden almost painfully in my pants, her voice takes me back to Sunday morning when I had her literally in the palm of my hands, and it takes all my focus not to rip those little shorts down her legs and fuck her right here.

I clear my throat, hoping that will clear my dirty thoughts, too, as I make my way over to where she is sitting and take a seat directly in front of her, getting a perfect view of her body as she moves into a new position. If she knows I'm watching her like the pervert I know I am, then she doesn't show it as she carries on her workout.

"What are your plans tonight?" She looks over to me, confused by my question, "Um, not much. It's Wednesday, so I was just planning on having tea and going to bed. What about you?"

I have to concentrate on her words so I don't get distracted anymore as she moves into a new position, bringing one leg in front of her and reaching to touch her toes, "It's Valentine's Day today, and since you have nothing else to do, I'm taking you out".

She laughs at me, shaking her head a little as she moves to sit cross-legged facing me, clicking her fingers as if she just remembered something. "Oh shoot, yeah, I forgot I have a date tonight". She smirks over at me, and I have to tamp down the jealousy over some date she's not even going on, and instead, home in on the fact she's clearly trying to wind me up.

I lean in closer to her, allowing my gaze to sweep over her as I play along with her game. "I thought we agreed that you were mine, *Red*". She rolls her eyes at me, "I never said who the date was with. It could be one of the girls, but you just assumed".

She raises a brow at me in defiance, her attitude coming to the surface. A small smile tips the corner of my lips upwards as I bring my hand up to run along her jaw. Her breath hitches at the motion, and I stop when I reach her chin allowing my thumb to run along the edge of her lips.

"These will look beautiful wrapped around my dick because I promise you, I will fuck the attitude right out of that pretty little mouth of yours. But right now, I want you to go get ready because I'm taking you out".

She blinks back at me before batting my hand away, "Luca, don't be so crass" I smirk down at her. She's still made no move to get up, and I'm impatient to take her out. I raise a brow at her, "Would you like me to do it now, or are you going to do as you're told for once and go get ready?"

She rolls her eyes at me again, biting her bottom lip as she does, and my dick swells more in my pants at the motion. She gets to her feet and turns to walk towards the door, but before she can make it far enough, I call out to her, "Wear the little black dress you have in your wardrobe". She peeks at me over her shoulder, a scowl on her face as usual, "How did you..." I smirk at her, and she shakes her head, "Never mind, perv".

.....

Rose spends the majority of the afternoon locked in her bedroom, and I'd think she was just using it as another tactic to avoid me, but when she steps into the living room just after six in the evening, I know she spent plenty of time preening and primping herself for this evening.

My mouth goes dry at the sight of her. Her auburn hair is in loose waves around her shoulders, a light makeup on her face, with a smoked eye and red lip that makes me hard just at the sight. I thought she would wear something different than what I'd asked of her when she ran off upstairs, but she surprised me by wearing the little black velvet dress with a bow on the back that comes to just above mid-thigh.

Her heels match in a velvet pump with a pointed toe, and I have to give her a twice over, because she looks fucking stunning. The only thing she's missing is some jewellery.

I stand, coming to meet her at the entrance to the door, pulling out a box and presenting it to her. She looks at it wide-eyed before bringing her hazel eyes back to meet mine. "Luca, I don't…" I ignore her as I open the box, revealing a necklace with a diamond edge and a Citrine pendant in the centre to match her ring, taking it out to place on her, "I knew this dress would go perfectly, that's why I asked you to wear it. Sorry for sneaking through your wardrobe but I wanted to make sure it was right. Turn around so I can put it on you". She stares back at me momentarily, before nodding and turning as I move her so she's facing the large mirror that's leaning against the wall.

She pulls her hair to one side, a few small curls escaping the hold she has on them as I place the necklace around her neck. I feel the goosebumps rise on the back of her neck as my fingers brush the delicate skin there. My fingers work to secure the clasp, and once it's fixed in place I let them drift over her shoulders, leaning down and placing a light kiss on the top of her bare arm.

When I look up, Rose is watching me, her lips are slightly parted as she takes shallow breaths, and my fingers trail down her arms as I bring my hands to rest on her waist. We look good together, I just hope she sees that too. I lean down to her ear and speak lowly when I say, "You look beautiful, Rose". Her breath hitches slightly at the use of her name, because she isn't used to me saying it. But I want her to know how serious I am when I say those words to her, because I mean them.

Her mouth tilts up slightly as her fingers absently come up to play with the necklace I've placed on her, "Thank you Luca, you don't look too bad yourself either". I didn't think it would be long before that sassy mouth came back as I smirk back at her, my fingers digging into the sides of her waist a little, "Thank you for this, you really didn't have to". She toys with the pendant, looking down at it. "Yes, I did. You don't understand how much all of this means to me, and I wanted to show my appreciation to you for it. For what you may have had to do or say to people, for the sake of this arrangement".

Hurt flickers in her eyes at my words, and I realise a little too late that what I just said sounded like I only want her for the lie we have created, as she quickly smooths her features and steps out of my hold. "Rose I…" She waves me off, "Shall we. We don't want to be late". Just like that, our little moment is gone, as she rushes out of the house and to my truck, I follow her feeling like a fucking idiot for what I just said.

She doesn't wait for me as she opens the car door, her heels not bothering her in the slightest as she hoists herself into the passenger seat. I make my way to the driver's side, turning to face her before I start the engine. "I don't think what I said in there came out right then, I didn't mean it…" She turns to look at me, a stern look on her face. "Luca, it's fine, I know what this is, and you just reminded me that this is purely an arrangement. Let's just forget about it and enjoy the rest of the evening". She turns to face out the window and dismisses me, and as much as I want to argue with her, I feel her pulling away from me the more I open my mouth, so instead, I let out a small sigh and turn back in my seat to drive us to the restaurant.

The drive to get there is quick but quiet, with the only sounds coming from the tunes on the radio and the low hum from the engine as it cruises down the quiet roads. I feel like I've fucked up with my comment earlier, and as we pull up and Rose jumps straight out of the truck, not even waiting for me.

I drop my keys with the valet and am thankful when I look up to see Rose waiting for me at the bottom of the steps. I give her a small smile, and she returns it before turning away from me to walk up the steps to the restaurant. I place my hand on her lower back as I guide her up the steps, wanting to be close in case she missteps in her heels. Of course, she doesn't because she's a pro in them and would probably stab me with one if I pissed her off enough.

I picked the nicest restaurant in town, somewhere we could dress up a little, rather than the smaller places where everything is more casual. It's nice and intimate, just what I want this evening for our non-date night. I take in the space around me as we're shown to our table, the place is packed out with couples celebrating their love for each other, and I'm reminded once more of the fuck up I made earlier when she takes her seat and instantly begins reading the menu without even looking up at me.

The waiter eventually comes over, and I order us a bottle of wine, Rose mumbles something to herself as they walk away, and I know she's still pissed at me. I pull on the top of her menu, dragging it down so I can get her attention, and she scowls back up at me. "What are you mumbling to yourself?"

She rolls her eyes at me, like I should know what she said, and lets out a sigh sitting back in her chair. "Nothing, I'm just in my head a bit tonight". I reach for her hand, taking it in my own as I try to figure out how to fix her mood. "Then tell me what's wrong, and I'll try to help. Is it what I said earlier because it didn't come out the way it was intended".

She nods to me, "Luca honestly, let's just not talk about it anymore, it's ruining the evening, and you've gone out of your way to make it nice so let's just enjoy it, yeah?" I go to carry on explaining myself, but the waiter comes back with our wine, cutting our conversation short.

Rose pulls the menu back up, attempting to get away from conversation too, and I let out an annoyed sigh, picking up my wine and taking a long drink. She's so fucking stubborn and won't listen to me, so I just let it go for now, deciding to just try and enjoy our meal.

We finally order food, and I'm about to update her on the bakery, when I feel a firm hand on my shoulder. I blink up at the owner of the hand, to see a slightly pissed-looking Jaxx standing above me,

Grace looking like she wants the ground to swallow her up beside him, and I realise that I haven't had a chance to speak to Jaxx or Tristan in person since the pictures came out of the pair of us.

I beam up at my friend, ignoring the looks he's giving me as I stand and embrace him in a hug. "What are you doing here, together?" Jaxx asks into my ear, low enough so the girls don't hear us. I pull back from him slightly, clearly he's not seen our little outing from the weekend. I look back to Rose briefly, and she gives me a small smile, not giving anything away either, so I turn back to Jaxx, "It's Valentine's Day, and I thought I'd treat Rose to a meal out for a change".

He looks pissed, but I push forward, trying not to egg him on anymore. "Why don't the two of you join us, we can make this a double date", I say as I look over to the girls, Grace smiles brightly nodding along with Rose, who looks like she could do with the break from just the two of us right now, and Jaxx reluctantly agrees.

The girls dive deep into conversation, and it seems that Grace already knows about Rose and me, so it's confusing me that Jaxx hasn't a clue. I turn to my friend, motioning to the girls, "Did Grace not tell you about Rose and me?"

He looks over to his girlfriend, who has a sheepish look on her face and shakes his head at me. "No, we haven't seen each other much the last couple of weeks. The station has been busy, and there's been a new guy starting at the ranch, so Grace has been there a lot. I guess it slipped her mind".

Grace overhears us and turns her attention to our conversation, "Actually, I only found out about the two of you on Sunday when Hallie called me up. She'd seen it online and called Rose who confirmed it when we met up". I nod to her, and my eyes flit to Rose as she avoids eye contact with me, and Jaxx takes the chance to find out everything he can.

"So how did this all start then?" He's not caught onto the fact this isn't even real, let alone the fact Rose is sporting a ring on her finger, so I fuck with him a little "It just kind of happened, I'm a one-woman man now, Jaxx, and I don't intend to change that anytime soon". He gives me a sceptical look, and Rose nudges me under the table. I glance in her direction shooting her a wink, so she knows I'll tell him eventually. Grace just rolls her eyes at me carrying on her conversation with Rose.

The conversation moves along, Grace tells us more about the new vet at the ranch, and I make a mental note to go and see Tristan. We order more drinks, enjoying the conversation as the evening flows. Rose becomes more animated the more she drinks, and I get carried away watching her talk about everything that she's been doing as she gives Grace a rundown of her life the past few weeks.

My eyes flit over to Jaxx as I notice he's watching me watch her, and I turn my gaze to him, raising my brow in question. He leans in, keeping his voice low so he can't be heard, "I know you're talking shit about being together, I just can't figure out why". I motion for him to join me outside, leaving the girls to their conversation as I follow my friend onto the patio out back.

He turns to face me once we reach the garden area, questions swirling in his eyes as he tries to figure me out. I let out a sigh as I walk over to the railing and lean on it, looking out onto the small lake that connects to the back patio of the restaurant "If I tell you what's going on Jaxx, I need you to keep it to yourself. No one can know I've told you anything, well apart from Grace and Tristan, but Rose already told her". I look over my shoulder to him and he gives me a blank stare but nods to me.

I already know this is a bad idea saying anything to him, but I do it anyway. "Rose and I, we aren't in a real relationship. My dad wants me to be settled down to take over the company and is trying to force me down the aisle with one of his friend's daughters, and I panicked and dragged Rose into this by saying we were engaged. He bought it, and she has agreed to go along with it, and she's getting something in return. And before you say how much of a stupid fucking idea this is, Jaxx, I already know, but I'm in too deep with this girl to even care. I want her to be mine, and I'll do whatever I can to hold on to that for as long as I can until I can convince her that she should be with me for real".

I blow out a breath as I finish my sentence, turning to my friend to gauge his reaction. He steps up next to me, keeping his breathing slow and measured like he always does, he's not a hot head like me or Tristan, the calm and collected one of the group. That's what makes him such a good sheriff. He puffs out one long breath that shows in the cold February evening as he places his hands on the railing next to mine.

"Jesus Luca, that's fucked up from your dad. I don't know what's got into him as he's gotten older, but I really hope it doesn't come down to that. I get it, Luca. I really do get how hard it is to be so infatuated with someone that you would do anything you could to have them be with you. But at the same time, I also see how you look at her, and I'm not sure that she is going to be one to return the love you seem to have for her".

I shake my head quickly as his words process, "I'm not saying I'm in love with her, but I can't get her out of my head, and she wouldn't have agreed to a date before any of this, so this is the best I can get from her for now. I want to show her that I'm not the asshole I used to be, and I think I can do it, but I need more time with her".

He hums in agreement next to me, and I turn to face him, "You know, I thought you would have lost your shit with me, after the way you were so protective over her the last time I mentioned her, telling me to stay away from her".

He smirks at me, "Oh, I still think this is a really fucking stupid idea, Luca. but I know you're smart and you will figure out what you need to do. At the end of the day, you're a grown man and I shouldn't have been as harsh on you as I was, and I'm sorry for that. I guess seeing you tonight and the way you look at her like you've got stars in your eyes helped me to see you're not just being a dick like you usually are". He nudges me a little with his shoulder, "C'mon let's go back inside, I have plans for my girl tonight that don't involve being sat at a table with you".

I bark out a laugh at Jaxx, following him back inside and slipping off to pay for the meal whilst he gets the girl's coats.

When I make it back to the table, Rose looks up at me, her pink cheeks light up her face as she beams at me. I've drunk too much to drive, so call us a cab as we make our way outside. She shivers from the cold, and I pull her into me to keep her warm, looking up to see Jaxx coming out behind us.

He smirks at me, and Grace is none the wiser as she says her goodbyes to Rose and me, but Jaxx leans in to hug Rose speaking to her just loud enough that I can hear him as he pulls her out of my arms, "You keep this one in line Rose, I know what a little trouble causer he is".

She lets out a breathy laugh at him, "Oh, don't you worry Jaxx, I've got plans for this one". I'm stunned into silence from the two of them as they laugh together, Rose plays her part beautifully, like we really are a couple, and if Jaxx and Grace didn't already know about us, I'd think we could have convinced them. "All right, that's enough you two.

Time for you to go home, Jaxx", I say, eyeing my friend as I pull Rose back from him.

He shoots me a wink as his car pulls up, and he opens the door for Grace and shouts over, "You two enjoy your night now", before climbing into the car and driving away. Rose peeks up at me through her thick lashes, a devious look in her eyes. Her tongue darts out as she leans up to me and murmurs into my ear "I definitely think we will".

18

Luca

I'm more drunk than I thought as we stumble back into the house after dinner. Rose clings onto me, trying to kick her shoes off as we make our way into the kitchen, I laugh at her as she tries to flick her foot, but her heels don't want to budge.

"Here, let me help" I pull her up and onto the countertop. She lets out a little squeal as I prop her on the side, bending a little to slide each shoe off her feet. Once free, she wiggles her toes at me, stretching them out after being trapped in the tight shoes all night. I grab one of her feet, taking a seat on the chair beside her and begin massaging the soles of them to relieve some of the pressure for her. She lets out a small moan as my fingers work to massage the tight balls of her small feet.

The noise she makes goes straight to my dick once again, as it does every time I hear something come out of her mouth, but I try to ignore it as I continue massaging her foot, bringing the other up to massage that once I'm done.

"Is there anything you aren't good at, Luca? Oh god that feels so good". I glance up at her and let out a small chuckle, shaking my head at her as I carry on. You'd think I was giving her an orgasm from the noises she was making. "I'm good at many things

Red, and some of those things, you'll just have to wait to find out". "Oh yeah, like what?" She's goading me for the answer we both know she wants.

I stop and glance back up at her. She's got a cheeky grin on her face, and I know she wants to cause some sort of trouble tonight, but because my alcohol-induced brain doesn't want to think straight, I go along with her, wanting to see what might happen too. I keep one hand holding her foot firmly in place and allow the other to slide carefully up the inside of her calve, stopping just below her knee. I lean into her, making sure to keep my eyes on hers the whole time.

"What I want to do to you would have you making your way to confession in the morning", my hand inches higher as I speak to her, giving her chance to back out. Our faces are so close, and the alcohol on our breath mixes in the air. "But if you're a good girl tonight, then I'll give you more of what you want".

She just nods, biting her lip as her eyes move down to where my hand is slowly disappearing under her skirt and my fingers brush against the lacy fabric that's barely covering her.

Her breathing becomes choppy as I tease her, my finger running along the side of her panties. I slide a finger just inside and feel the wetness that's already there and waiting for me.

She gasps at the contact as my fingers trace along her clit and I look back up to her, "Is this what you want?" She nods again, and I pull my hand away, watching as a scowl forms on her face. I let out a small laugh, "Patience Red, we have all night". She's not patient, and normally, neither am I, but right now, I want to savour every moment I have with her because I don't know if she will come to regret this in the morning, but I don't have it in me to stop right now to test that theory out.

I stand from my seat, pushing it out of the way as I move in between her legs. She's watching me, waiting for my next move and I slide her off the counter so she's standing before me, bending and pulling her up and over my shoulder in a fireman's lift.

She screeches from her position over my shoulder, and I slap her ass as it quickly turns into laughter when I march over to the stairs and up to my room. I make my way up the stairs quickly and place her down, turning her so she's facing the mirror in the corner of my room. It reminds me of earlier in the evening, except this time, I won't be putting my foot in my mouth.

I watch her reflection in the mirror, Rose watching the pair of us as I step in behind her, slowly unzipping the dress that has given me blue balls all night. Rose's eyes don't leave mine as I push it off her shoulders, letting it fall to the floor in a pool around her feet. She steps out of it, kicking it to the side and stands in her lacy black bra and panties, waiting for my next move. My fingers skim over her arms, coming up to the crook of her neck as I bring them around to trace over her collarbones.

Her skin breaks out in goosebumps from my touch, and I lean down inhaling her scent as I do. I kiss her cheek, making my way down to her jaw and down the column of her throat. Her head tilts to the side, allowing me more access, and her eyes close as I suck on the delicate skin there, "We don't have to do this if you don't want to. You can back out if you think this is too much" I murmur into her neck. I want this, want her to give in to me, but in the back of my mind I don't think I'll be able to let her go if she changes her mind after tonight.

She turns slowly so she's facing me and begins unbuttoning my shirt, "I don't want to think about anything other than this right now, Luca, can you do the same?" She peeks up at me through her lashes as she asks the question, a fire in her hazel eyes as they search mine. I let out a low groan, fuck I need her now.

I dip down, grabbing her by the legs and lifting her into my arms, my mouth finds hers and her arms come around my neck as we make our way to the bed. I place her down, undoing her bra and sliding it off her arms, my dick hardens at the sight of her perfect tits as I massage them in my hands. I push her back leaning over her to suck on her nipple as I take it in my mouth, swirling my tongue over the peak and enjoying the moans coming from her.

I sit back enough to watch as her chest rises and falls, and as her breathing becomes choppy my eyes make their way down to the last bit of fabric covering her. "These need to come off", I say as I stand, sliding her panties down her slender legs and tossing them across the room. She lies watching me as I make quick work of removing the rest of my clothes and I climb back onto the bed to settle between her legs.

Her arms come up as they wrap around my neck and she pulls me to her, and our lips meet in a hurried desperation that we haven't had before as I slide my hand between us, running my fingers up and down her slit as she writes beneath me, little moans leaving her mouth as my fingers play with her clit.

I dip a finger inside her, feeling her walls pulse around me, and let out a groan as my mouth crashes back down on hers and I push my finger in and out of her, adding a second to her tight entrance.

My lips move from hers as I pepper kisses down her jaw and neck and further down her body as I slowly make my way to her pussy. I peek back up to her and her eyes are closed, enjoying the moment she's getting lost in and take that moment to revel in the fact that I have her tonight, and she is mine. I don't know how long that will last until she tires of me, but for now, I'm going to enjoy every inch of her.

I press my lips along her pubic bone as I trail down until I hit what I've been waiting for. Her bare and ready for me, glistening with her juices. Sliding my tongue out I lick from one end of her opening to the other and hear Rose gasp. She moves as if to push me away, but my hands spread across her, gripping her sides as I glance back up to her. She looks at me as if she's about to protest but I pin her down by her thighs, keeping her spread open for me.

"If I hear anything come out of that pretty little mouth other than you moaning my name tonight, you are in for a world of trouble, Miss Adler. Do I make myself clear?". A pretty shade of pink covers her throat and cheeks as she nods to me in agreement, her lips tilting up slightly to one side as if she wants to protest just to see how far she can push me, and a satisfied smile takes over my face. "Good now lie back down so I can enjoy my dessert".

She giggles at me but lies back, allowing me to continue. I slide my arms around her and grab her ass as I pull her legs over my shoulders so I can really enjoy myself. I spread my tongue along her again, focusing on her clit as I circle the swollen little bundle of nerves there. As much as she seemed like she wasn't going to enjoy herself, her wriggling about beneath me tells me otherwise.

I bring a hand back around, keeping one leg over my shoulder as I slide my fingers back inside her, pumping them in and out as I continue to suck on her sensitive flesh, "Oh God, Luca, fuck I don't think I can take much more". Rose moans the words to me, like she doesn't really mean them, urging me to carry on as I bring her right to the edge, and I all but throw her over it as her legs begin to shake when she cries out, her orgasm taking over her whole body.

I slowly pull myself away, as she comes down from her high, quickly finding a condom in my side draw and sliding it on as I settle between her legs once more. She comes back around eventually, a lust-fuelled look on her face as I line myself up against her, leaning and pecking her on the lips. "Last chance to change your mind Red".

She blinks back up at me, momentarily confused by my statement, and I glance down to my dick pressing against her entrance. I sit back on my heels so I can get a good look at her, giving her time to back out as I run the head through her folds, coating it with her juices. I tease her clit as I do, pressing into it a little to give her some friction.

"Fuck me already Luca", she moans, and I look up to see her watching me play with her, her lip pulled between her teeth as the anticipation builds between us.

I push in little by little, letting out a low groan as I do, because *fuck me*, she's tight but takes me perfectly. I lean down, pushing into her a bit more, and she moans into my neck, giving me the go-ahead to push further in. I inch forward, pulling back a small amount each time I do, savouring every moment of our time together before she gets frustrated with me, locks her legs behind my ass and pulls me into her, letting out a sharp gasp as she does.

"Move Luca, now", she grits out as she grinds herself against me, and I pin her with my hips. "Stop moving, or I won't last much longer. You're so tight. Just give me a minute". She giggles, rolling her eyes dramatically at me, and I finally allow myself to begin moving in and out, building a rhythm but it doesn't last long as she begins moaning my name, making it hard to last much longer.

My movements become choppy as I come close to my climax, and push into her a few more times before I spill into the condom. I try not to collapse on her, but my arms give out as I pull out, rolling onto my side to catch my breath.

I press a quick kiss to Rose's lips before getting up and making my way to the bathroom to sort the condom, grabbing a fresh pair of boxers as I go and give myself a little pep talk whilst I'm in there because my dicks hard and ready to go again. But when I come out of my bathroom she's nowhere to be seen.

I'm pissed that she would just up and leave after that, like she can hide from me when we live in the same fucking house, and go on a hunt for her, stomping across the hall to her room.

She appears from the bathroom as I walk in, an oversized shirt barely covering her legs. She stops in her tracks, as if she can't figure out what I'm doing in her room and cocks her head at me in question. "What are you doing Luca?" She asks as I stalk towards her, "What do you mean what am I doing, what are you doing?"

Rose looks around for a moment, before looking to her bed, "Uh, going to bed, what do you think I'm doing?"

"Absolutely fucking not", I grit out bending down. I pick her up like I did before, and she yelps, "Put me down, Luca, what the fuck".

I march us back into my room, dumping her on the bed as I go. "You're sleeping in here. Don't think you can disappear off into your room after we just had sex, no chance". She glares at me for a moment from her position on the bed before realising what I'm talking about.

"Oh, I thought…" I cut her off. "Don't even finish that sentence, Red. Did you really think I'd just want to have sex with you and then ship you back off to your room? No, that is not happening".

Realisation crosses her face as it clicks that I want her with me all night. A small smile lifts on her lips as she sits back on the bed. "Alright I'm sorry, I didn't realise". I give her a firm nod as I come around to my side of the bed, climbing in and dragging her over to me. She lets out a small laugh, and I snuggle into her, wrapping my arms around her so she can't escape me for a second time tonight, "I didn't know this was part of the deal, Luca".

I ignore her comment, wanting her close to me for as long as possible before she inevitably changes her mind on us, "Shhh, go to sleep". She giggles a little more, before snuggling down into me, and I fall asleep wishing this was real life.

19

Luca

After what I thought was the best valentines I've had in a long time, one that wasn't taken up by women who only want one thing from me and actually getting to spend time with someone I enjoy being around, I feel deflated.

By the time the weekend has rolled back around I realise Rose has been different with me the past couple of days. She's been home more but has refused to stay in bed with me again since Wednesday, and now she's gone to stay with Hallie and Grace for a couple of days out of town.

And now since all I seem to want to do is be around her, I'm at a loss for what to do with myself. So, I called Tristan up to see if he had some time for me at the ranch and he was all too happy for me to go and see him for a couple of hours in exchange for coffee.

I pull up to the old blue and white painted farmhouse that Tristan has now moved into since his parents went travelling at the start of the year. The old place still looked like new since his dad kept on top of the maintenance, and the barn conversion they did last year is high spec. Grace moved into the new offices just before Christmas and I have yet to stop hearing Tristan moan about how his sister got the office with the better view.

I jump out of the truck and am instantly greeted by the golden retrievers his mom and dad left with him, Amber and Whiskey. They both come bounding up to me, yapping away, ready and waiting for the treats I bring them each time I come here, followed by Tristan who looks miserable as usual.

"Stop feeding them treats, they are going to get fat", he shouts over to me from the front porch, and I smirk back up at him "Don't worry about the dogs, worry about yourself. You look like you could do with getting in the gym with me a few days a week". He pats his belly, that's still rock hard from riding and training the horses all day, "Nothing wrong with me you fucker". His small smile betrays his usual grumpy look as he makes his way down the steps to greet me, embracing me in a firm hug and slap on the back.

"Come with me, I want to show you something" he motions to the back of the house, and I follow him around to the back porch where it overlooks the acres of land around him, and points to an area in the paddocks where there is an old house, "I want to do up the house over there for staff, we have that new vet that's in and around all the time and I'm hoping to extend the company, so having somewhere they can stay if we need them for a while will come in useful. Do you reckon you can put together some plans for me?"

I squint my eyes as my brain instantly gears up with ideas and nod to him, "Yeah, I'm sure we can work something out. It wouldn't take long to do up either. Is there a road that leads up to that house?" He points to the old dirt road that goes up the hill, "That one does". I give him a firm nod, already working out what I need to do, and we talk some more before heading inside for a drink.

Tristan pours us both a cup of coffee, before taking a seat in the kitchen area. "So, what's this new vet like then? How come you want him around more?" He shrugs his shoulder slightly, "He's new in town and wanted to get to know people better, so I said he could be a help around here when he doesn't need to be out on call as I think he's just doing it part-time at the minute. He's staying in the hotel down the road for now, but I'm not really sure why he's come here, other than he said he wanted to find someone. I didn't want to ask too many questions though, so I left him to it".

"Look at you making new friends" I tease, getting a blank stare in return. "I wouldn't go that far. Grace hired him. remember. He's all right, and he's technically staff. And anyway, talking of new friends, Grace told me about your little arrangement with Rose, thanks for leaving it to my sister to tell me". I grimace, knowing full well I should have told him myself.

"Ah yeah, I'm sorry about that, everything has just been up in the air with it, and I'm trying to find my feet with her. She blows hot and cold with me, but

I'm just trying to stay on her good side at the minute, and with me buying the bakery and getting it sorted after the flood, it's taking some time up. That and me trying to convince her she should be with me for real, but she's not quite caught up with me yet".

He glances up at me from his spot in the kitchen, his eyes narrowing in on me in accusation, "Wait hold up. You bought the bakery?" My head drops to my feet, shuffling them slightly on the spot "Uh, yeah, did I not tell you that? Her landlord couldn't do anything and is too ill, so I offered to take it off his hands".

I rush the words out, quickly wanting to move onto the next part of the conversation so he doesn't home in the fact I bought her premises. It doesn't deter him. "Does Rose know all of this? And have you actually told her how you feel too, or are you assuming she will just get the picture and fall madly in love with you?"

My brain scrambles to find a reasonable response as I stare back at him, but the words that come out are a far cry from that. "Um, well no, not in so many words, but I'm trying to just ease her in. you know, let my charm do the talking". He barks out a laugh at me, literally laughing at me as he shakes his head. "You're a fucking idiot, you know that don't you. Look, if you really want her then you've got to tell her how you feel. She's not a mind reader, and she's as stubborn as they come. You aren't going to woo her with your *charm"*.

"Thanks for the great advice" I grumble to him. Tristan doesn't seem to be fazed by my newfound relationship either way like he wasn't when Jaxx and his sister got together last year, either. "Well, if you think that will work, then go for it, bud. I'm happy for you, just don't screw it up because knowing Rose, if you piss her off, she will act like you don't exist". I don't doubt that she would do that very thing if I stepped a foot out of line when it comes to her, but the last thing I want is for anything to go wrong.

We carry on drinking coffee until the late hours of the evening when I would rather be switching my drink to whiskey, so I make my excuses and head out to grab some food before making my way home for the night, knowing I only have to be in there for one night by myself until Rose is back home. God, I feel pathetic that I need her home with me so badly.

I trudge through the front door, toeing my boots off and make my way to the kitchen to grab a drink. The house feels empty now I don't have her here, like she's just become a part of it, and I don't like that feeling one bit.

The lights are all off as I wander through the dark hallway, not paying attention to anything around me, but stop short when I hear movement coming from upstairs. I should be alone right now, and the last thing I need is to be dealing with some lowlife breaking into my house. I grab my gun from the cabinet as quietly as I can, making my way up the stairs. Whoever they are, they are in Rose's room and all I can think right now is thank God she isn't home.

I make my way quietly down the hall, attempting to avoid the small squeaks from the landing floor, and hoping to catch them off guard. The door is cracked slightly, and I quickly push it open as I point my gun at them, "Stop what you are doing right now. I've got a gun, and I will use it". A piercing scream leaves the intruder's mouth, followed by a thud as whoever it is just runs straight into the open bathroom door, knocking themselves over and letting out a groan.

Confused as to why the scream was quite clearly a female, I flick the light on, and all blood leaves my head as I stare down at a semi-conscious Rose. I toss the gun to the side and rush over to her, "Shit, Rose are you okay?"

She groans, her head rolling from side to side as she comes to, realising it's me beside her. "Owh, my head. Why would you point a gun at me". She touches the spot where she smacked her head off the door, hissing at the pain from the bump that's quickly forming on her head.

I help her up into a sitting position and run to grab a cold cloth from the bathroom. "Here", I say, pressing the compress to her head. She winces slightly at the pressure but takes over holding it as I check she hasn't hurt herself anywhere else. I sit back on my heels, staring at her in disbelief. "What are you doing home, you're supposed to be away until tomorrow. I thought someone was breaking in the house".

She chuckles a little at me, "God you're so dramatic. Hallie's dad had a fall, so she had to go to the hospital. The night out got cancelled, so Grace dropped me off about ten minutes ago. I was just coming out of the bathroom when you barged in".

I stare at her, trying to process her story because my mind just keeps pulling a blank when I'm around her. "Why are you walking around with the lights off? And why didn't you call to say you were coming home?"

She stares up at me, a confused look on her face, "I don't actually know, I just grabbed a water from the fridge and then came straight upstairs. I guess you weren't too far behind me. Sorry I didn't realise I needed to check in with you". The last part of her reply has more sarcasm and a little attitude, but I let it slide since she just smacked her head off the door.

"Well, next time, can you just let me know you're going to be home since I thought someone was breaking in". She rolls her eyes at me, removing the cloth from her head to reveal a little egg that's formed there and goes to stand up, wavering slightly as she does. "You might have a concussion. Just sit down a minute and don't make any fast movements". She nods as I help her to the bed, "You shouldn't stay alone tonight" I point to her head as I say it, attempting to make it clear why she needs to let me sleep in her bed with her. I can't seem to find any other way to be with her, so this will have to do.

She lets out a sigh shaking her head a little. "Yeah, I guess you're right. But I don't want to stay in your room, I like my own bed". I huff out a laugh, "Yeah I noticed since you won't stay with me". She glares at me, an annoyed look taking over her face, "Luca, I don't want to complicate things between us. We've already gone way further with things that I think we should have by sleeping together, and I don't know how long this arrangement is going to last, so I think it's best if we just stick to keeping things, you know".

She waves her arms around at me as she speaks like I should know where she's going with this, but I don't, because it's a load of bullshit she's giving me.

I wave my hands in the air, mimicking her actions, "No, I don't fucking know Red. I'd love for you to enlighten me though". She scowls at me, "Luca don't be a dick. You know full well this won't work if we keep sleeping together. I can't keep my feelings separate and I know I will be the one who ends up getting hurt. What we did the other night needs to not happen again".

My heart sinks at her words. She's so back and forth with me that I don't think she really knows what she wants, and as much as I know that I should give up trying to make her realise I'm not going to hurt her, I don't. Maybe I'm the one who will end up hurt in the end, but I'm a gluten for punishment. I don't press her, though. I need to figure out how to break down the walls she's so guarded by, and to do that, I should tread carefully, but before I get my words out, she speaks my thoughts to me.

"I know I've been so back and forth about this, but I just can't do it right now. It's too much". Making my way around to the other side of her bed, I pull back the covers and strip down to my boxers.

"All right, we'll talk about it more once you're not concussed. Get in bed and go to sleep". She watches me for a minute as her brows pull together and part of me thinks she'll kick me out of her room, "What? Do you want me to put some sweats on or something?" She doesn't respond but shakes her head and climbs into bed.

I pull her towards me to hold her, "Luca…" she starts, but I cut her off, not wanting any more rejection tonight. "Please, just let me have this tonight, you can go back to pretending you don't want me tomorrow". My voice has a hint of humour to it, betraying how I really feel, but she doesn't push me anymore and eventually falls asleep in my arms.

I watch her sleep until the early hours, her long lashes fluttering whilst she dreams. I wish I could get inside her head, to know what she's really thinking, but I know I can't, and I just hope that one day, she might just change her mind on us.

20

Rose

The house feels quieter than usual when I come downstairs on Sunday morning. The bed was cold and empty next to me when I woke up.

Luca must have gotten up and gone to the gym first thing, after leaving Tylenol and some water for my head that's still aching. But when I make it downstairs, he's nowhere to be seen as I come into the kitchen to make coffee. I can't help but feel guilty for pushing him away after sleeping with him, it niggles at me, and a small part of me craves him like I do sunlight, but my head is telling me to try and keep things less complicated. My body, not so much.

If he was hurt by my admission of wanting to keep things separate, he didn't show it, but who am I to know? My headache subsides a little as the tablets kick in, so I grab my coat and take my coffee to the back porch.

It's a little warmer than usual this morning so I can enjoy the sun rising over the lake. I never sat out at home because I was always either away or too busy with something else. But my not having to be at the bakery so early has given me a few mornings where I'm at a little bit of a loss for what to do.

I take a seat on one of the wooden garden chairs as the sun peeks up over the mountains in the distance, a pink glow covers the sky as it ascends, and the lake is still, apart from the odd droplet as a bird touches down over it.

It lifts my mood as I sip my coffee and allow myself to lounge back in the seat as my mind drifts back to Luca again. I don't know what to make of how unbothered he seemed that I didn't want to carry on the sexual side of our relationship, yet he carried on being just as attentive as he has been since I got here.

He held me all night last night. I woke once or twice, trying to roll over, but his grip tightened on me each time I did, and he twisted us into a more comfortable position, not breaking his hold on me once. I'd have been pissed that he was trapping me in his hold, but he lulled me back to sleep almost instantly each time.

The doorbell rings at the front of the house, pulling me from my thoughts and I get up to grab it, wondering who could be here so early on a Sunday as I pad through the house. I open the door and almost roll my eyes, thinking Luca has left his keys, but on a double take, I realise I'm not looking at him at all, but whoever is standing in front of me could easily be his twin.

The man in front of me, is a slightly broader version of Luca, with the same chocolate eyes and olive skin, but his hair is a little lighter with a slight wave to it. And he's got a slightly crooked nose, compared to Luca's straight one.

He stands around a similar height to Luca, and on a quick glance, he's dressed similarly in Jeans, boots, and a jumper with his coat over the top. If I didn't know better, I'd say this was his brother, but I know Luca is an only child.

"Um, can I help you?" His throat bobs as he looks back to me, then up to the house. "Oh, I was hoping to find Luca, is this his place?" I nod, folding my arms in front of me and leaning against the door frame. "It is. I'm um, his fiancé". I remember at the last minute we're supposed to be engaged, and I don't know who this guy is, so I don't want to slip up. His eyes widen slightly as he takes in the information, but he quickly smooths his features, nodding back to me, "Okay, do you know when he will be home?"

I don't know who this guy is, but he seems to be friendly enough, so I attempt to do a little digging of my own, "I'm not sure. He went out early this morning, do you want to tell me your name and I'll let him know you called".

He takes a slight step back, seemingly unsure of the situation. "I, um... He doesn't know who I am; we've never met. I'm just trying to piece together some information. I'll call back". I'm curious now but he turns to leave the house, and I panic, not wanting him to leave without me finding out something. "Can you at least tell me your name before you leave?" He looks back to me briefly, indecision in his features as his eyes bounce between me and then the house again. Eventually, he calls out "It's Ezra", before turning on his heel and making his way back to his car.

"Thanks!" I shout back to him, closing the door whilst my mind reels from what I just saw. Does Luca have a brother that I had no idea about? No, surely he would have told me. Maybe he's a cousin or something, a really friggin look-alike cousin. I call up Grace to see what she might know, but it rings out, and before trying anyone else I figure I should probably just wait until Luca is home to tell him.

I head upstairs, shooting off a text to my dad as I go to see if he wants to meet for lunch, he texts back within a couple of minutes, letting me know of a spot to meet him. I miss him so much and don't get to see him nearly as much as I want to, so I'm glad he was free.

I know I'm going to have to lie to him and tell him I'm engaged for real, and to be honest I'm surprised he hasn't seen the information already, but I shouldn't put it off any longer.

.....

I arrive a little later than I agreed, a given for me to never be on time anywhere. My dad is waiting patiently for me at a table for two, typing something out on his phone when I enter the small diner he picked out for us to eat at. It's a small hole in the wall we found years ago when we were taking a walk around the local town, and now we come here every so often for our catchups.

He beams up at me when he spots me, standing with his arms wide open for me, and I walk straight into his embrace, soaking him in. He's my favourite person, and I really wish I could spend more time with him, but he's married to the devil, aka my mother, so I avoid his house as much as I can.

"Missed you sweat pea". The term of endearment fills me with warmth as he presses a kiss to the top of my head, before releasing me and taking a seat. The waiter comes over to take our drinks order, and once he leaves, my dad gives me a pointed look, and I know he must have seen the news. I shrink back in my seat, waiting for him to berate me for not telling him, but instead, he just looks down at my hand where the ring is resting, "Have you got some news for me?"

I twist the ring on my finger, biting my lip as I figure out what to say to him. "It's all happened super-fast, I'm sorry I didn't tell you sooner. I'm still coming around to the idea myself". It's not a total lie, I'm still trying to wrap my head around this whole situation on a daily basis. Concern etches his features, and his eyes soften as he looks at me, "Tell me about him", he asks as he sits back in his seat, his fingers steepled on the table in front of him.

I inhale a deep breath before trying not to dive too deep into my new 'it's complicated' relationship status with Luca. "He's called Luca, and he's a friend of Grace's boyfriend, Jaxx. I've known him for a little while, and that's who I'm living with. We were spending some time together as he kept coming into the bakery, and then he offered me a place to stay after the flood at the shop and things just progressed quickly from there".

My dad nods, not saying a thing, and I suddenly feel the guilt rush through me at having to lie to him, but there's nothing I can do. "And why are you still feeling like you're getting used to it? Are you unsure it's the right thing to do?" I want to just blurt out that it's all fake, but I don't want my dad to catch onto anything, so I give him a small smile, hiding my inner turmoil. "No, it's not that at all, Luca's actually amazing. It's just all been a bit of a whirlwind, and I'm just trying to figure out what's going on with the bakery right now too, so there's just a lot going on at the minute".

His features remain the same the whole time I talk to him, and he gives nothing away, "Well I'm sure everything will work out like it's supposed to, and I'm happy for you so long as you're happy too. It sounds like you are settled down with a nice boy. I would like to meet him too since he never asked for your hand". There is a hint of humour in his voice, and I roll my eyes playfully at him.

We order food, and once we have it and I'm happily making my way through my burger, my dad clears his throat. I glance up at him, and he's got a serious expression on his face, causing me to place my burger down, wanting to give him all of my attention.

"I'm actually glad you asked to see me today because there's something I wanted to talk to you about". He pauses for a moment, and I'm suddenly not interested in my food. I sit a little straighter in my chair, wanting to make sure I'm properly listening to whatever he has to say. It must be serious if he's doing a face-to-face chat.

"I've decided to leave your mother. I haven't really had enough of a good reason before now, other than you two not getting along, but she's been having an affair with her personal trainer, so I think it's about time we call it a day on our marriage".

I blink back at him, lost for words. I can't actually believe this day is finally here. He sees the look on my face and confuses it for me being upset, "I'm sorry if that's not what you expected to hear, but I just can't do it any longer. I've tried to stay with her for as long as I can, even when it has pushed you away from me, but I can't do it anymore, and I feel like I'm really missing out on your life too, with you never coming around to visit". I finally get my bearings enough to force my body to move and reach over the table, grabbing hold of his hand and squeezing reassuringly.

"Dad, I've been waiting for you to tell me this was happening for so long. I'm glad you are leaving her. It means I get you back like before. We can have a proper relationship now without feeling like we have to sneak around". He seems to visibly relax at my statement, and I grin at him, glad that he's finally out of that miserable marriage. "So, are you keeping the house, or are you moving?"

He thinks for a minute, "You know, I've not decided. Your mother moved out a couple of weeks ago, so the house is mine to keep. She forgot that she signed a prenup when we got married, leaving everything to me if she ever was unfaithful or decided to leave since she refused to work and wanted to live off her inheritance, I looked after her just fine, but I drew the line at keeping her financially stable if we separated due to it being her doing. I think I'll sell the house, it's far too big for just me. I might even move a little closer to here, so I can be closer to you". I nod enthusiastically, I've always been a daddy's girl, and this is just making my day.

My mom always liked the bigger house, but it was never my dad's taste. He tried convincing her multiple times they should move somewhere smaller, but she dug her heels in, and now he's finally able to enjoy somewhere he wants to be.

"I feel like we should be celebrating right now". He grins at me, looking around the diner he chose. It's not really somewhere you can drink though. "How about we get one of those fancy milkshakes since we can't get alcohol here". A laugh spills out of me, I'm glad I get to see this side of him after so many years of him being down and not enjoying life.

He calls the waiter over, ordering the most ridiculous milkshakes and ice cream sundaes for dessert to go with it, and we catch up some more about how Grace is getting on since she worked for him for a short while. I convince him to have a look at some houses online and move around the table so we can both look at them on my phone to see what's around in the area near me.

The rest of the day goes by in a blur, and by the time I make it home it's late, Luca still isn't home, or he went back out, which one I'm not sure but I collapse onto my bed, exhaustion from a busy day pulling me quickly into a deep sleep.

21

Luca

"Okay, so I've moved your appointment this afternoon to next Thursday as Mr Johnson is out of town until then. He sends his apologies, but he's had a family emergency. And then I have a Miss Adler in at eleven to go over some designs for a bakery".

We've been sitting in my office for the past twenty minutes going over all the new projects that are coming in, and now Cora is taking me through today's schedule. She's wearing dark navy flared trousers and a cream frilled blouse, not something I'm used to seeing her in, but I'm happy that she's finally decided not to put herself through the pain of wearing obnoxiously tight dresses anymore.

She seems to have given up trying to flirt with me since the announcement of Rose and my engagement hit the papers, and I'm actually kind of relieved of the break it seems to have given me from women wanting to be taken out.

Cora blinks down at the tablet, pausing when she sees what we're working on. We normally take big projects, not something small like the bakery, so I can understand her confusion. Her eyes shift up to mine and then back down to the appointment she has booked in.

The corner of my lips twitch as I watch her try and figure it out, "It's my fiancé's bakery. I'm arranging for it to be renovated as it just had a flood, so she's coming in so we can put a plan together. I don't want to mess about with this. The work needs to be done efficiently and quickly as she's currently working out of the kitchen at home.

"She needs something bigger to work in, so if you can sort the logistics once she has decided what she wants, that would be great. And you can expect to see her in and around a little more whilst this is being done". Cora nods, making notes on her tablet whilst I sift through my emails. My dad has been out of town for the last week, so it's been me running things in his absence.

I'm happy that he's allowing me to take some more of the responsibility, I just wish it wasn't with the expectation of a marriage. Not that I mind having Rose pretend to be my fiancé. She's like a breath of fresh air compared to who he was trying to set me up with, and I'm glad she's finally coming into the office today so we can get her bakery refurb underway.

She's picked up quite a few clients already since opening, and I can tell trying to keep up with orders from the kitchen at home is driving her insane. It seems having her name in the papers has done good for her, the only downside is that she's taken over the kitchen at home. I don't mind one bit, coming home to the smell of freshly baked cupcakes, but she needs a bigger space to work out of.

Cora finishes up going through everything we need to and heads out of my office to get the rest of her work done for the day. Once I finish going through my emails, I sit back in my chair, feeling stiff from overdoing it at the gym the day before. I need to stretch my legs a little, so I make my way to the main kitchen to get myself a coffee. I'm rounding the corner to the kitchen when a burst of laughter catches my attention, mostly because I recognise the person that laugh belongs to instantly.

Spinning on my heel I spot Rose walking down the hall with my dad, chatting away whilst she carries a box in her hands. The weather has warmed up a little as we head into the back end of February, so she's ditched her winter coat for a leather jacket, a plain white T, jeans that hug her legs to perfection and some black leather biker boots. Her hair is pulled into a messy bun on top of her head as it bobs about when she talks animately to my dad. He must have come back early and decided not to tell me, not that he tells me much at all, but it would be nice to know when he is in the office.

I plaster a smile on my face as they come closer, and Rose is the first to spot me. She beams up at me, holding out the box in front of her, "I promised your dad I'd bake when I came to the office. Good job, he's back in today, or he would have missed out".

She winks up at my dad, and he lets out a small chuckle at her, I'm not sure when the last time was that I saw him this relaxed and carefree, but I'm not about to complain now.

I take the box from Rose, sliding my other arm around her and pressing a kiss to her lips. She responds to me instantly, leaning into the too-short kiss I give her, before pulling back, "Your dad was just helping me with my bag. You didn't tell me we were meant to be at a dinner next weekend".

My gaze shifts to my father, who didn't mention a thing to me about it either, luckily he notices my reaction and doesn't let me take the fall for not telling her. "It must have slipped my mind to mention it with me being away, but you're both free, aren't you?". Rose waits for me to answer, and I give him a firm nod, mostly because he seems smitten with Rose. A change I'm glad to see from the last time they met. "I'm just about to make a coffee, do you both want one?"

My dad's awfully cheery voice hits me first, "Yes, I'll take one, and I'll take one of those cakes to go with it too". He smiles down at Rose as he accepts, walking towards the kitchen with her as they begin another conversation, and I'm left standing in the hallway wondering how the hell I'm going to actually let her go once this is supposed to be over.

I shake my head, letting those thoughts go to the back of my mind for another day, as I make my way in behind them and make us all drinks. My back is turned to the pair as they chatter on more about my dad's trip away, and he asks her about how the bakery is coming along, "Oh, we're about to go over some plans for it. Would you like to join us?"

I squeeze my eyes shut, gripping the counter as I wait for my dad's response to Rose, "Oh, I wish I could, but I actually came in for a meeting that will be starting shortly, so I will have to catch up with you both some other time to see the plans".

I spin back around in time to see Rose taking my dad's rejection to stay in her stride as she beams back at him, "That's okay, I'm sure it's not something you normally work with". My dad actually looks like he cares about what she's doing, as his features soften towards her, "Please do keep me updated though, I'm looking forward to seeing my future daughter in laws business". Guilt creeps up me as I watch the exchange between the two of them, wondering how upset he really will be when this arrangement ends.

My dad stands, nodding to me as he takes his leave, grabbing a muffin from Rose as he does, and I slide my gaze back to hers. I don't know what to make of the expression on her face, she seems excited to be here, something I'm guessing has nothing to do with me or my dad. "Shall we go to my office? We can spread out whilst we go through the plans".

Her head bobs in agreement, and I carry our cups as we make our way down the corridor. Cora eyes her up and down, trying to be subtle and failing, but if Rose notices, she doesn't say a thing as we make our way into my office.

I set up next to the sofa so we can go through the plans in comfort, where they are already laid out for Rose to take a look at, and she does an excited little clap when she spots some of the designs. My heart melts a little more as I watch her get excited about fixing the place up. She's so fucking adorable when she's like this, and it makes me want to do everything I can for her, starting with this bakery.

She takes a seat on the sofa as I move around the small space to seat myself next to her, placing our coffee in front of us. She instantly grabs one of the sheets to start making her way through it, her eyes lighting up as she looks through each of the designs.

I enjoy seeing this side of her, being creative, and it gives me more inspiration for new projects that I want to work on and maybe bringing Rose on board as a side line if she enjoys it too. I point to the paper in her hands, "So this is what the new layout will look like, the open concept into the back would brighten up the place a little more, and we could even turn the apartment upstairs into another part of the bakery, for extra seating".

Waiting patiently, I sit watching her scan through the plans until she clicks on to the fact that she would have nowhere to live, and as she does, her brows scrunch together as she brings her face up to meet mine.

"I love the idea, but I don't know how long this will all take, and I also don't know if the landlord would be okay with that. Do you think we could speak to him before doing this? That and the fact I don't know how long Mine and Hallie's place would take to be finished, so for now, I wouldn't have anywhere to live".

My mind races as I bring myself around to the idea of having to tell her I bought the place, but right now, I can't do that, so instead, I tell her the white lie that slips from my lips, "I've already spoken to him, and he's agreed to a full renovation, don't worry about the cost of it, it's covered". She doesn't look convinced but nods anyway.

"And as far as living arrangements go, you have a place to live. You live with me". Rose's eyes roll so far back I'd wonder if she was having a seizure, but the little scoff that comes with it reminds me she's just testing my patience, and it takes all my restraint not to pull her over my lap and spank her ass until she can't sit down.

"Luca, we both know this isn't a permanent thing. I can't stay at yours forever, what if the house takes another year?" *Hopefully, by that point, you'll be madly in love with me and actually be my wife.* My brain screams at me to tell her what I so desperately want to, I want to shout those words so everyone can hear, but I know this is going to take every ounce of patience I have.

My hands work of their own accord as I reach out and take her hand in mine, "I don't care how long it takes. I want your bakery to be somewhere you can grow in, and if that means it takes another five years of you living with me, then so be it. I'd spend an eternity sharing my space with you if it meant I got to see how happy you are when you're looking at those plans".

A pink tint sweeps across her face as she takes in my words, giving me a glimpse of how much I have an effect on her. I brush a stray hair off her face, tucking it behind her ear and cupping her cheek in my hand as I bring my hand around, memorizing it like she might disappear. The delicate slope of her freckled-covered nose, the curve of her lips, the way her eyes soften when she looks at me. I want them to stare back at me like that for a lifetime.

"I want it to be perfect for you. The place was ruined like you saw yourself and there's no point in rushing it when I can make it your entire dream where you can stay for years to come". Her eyes flutter shut momentarily as she leans into my embrace.

"Okay".

The word comes out as barely a whisper, but I hear it well enough to break out into a grin. "That's my girl. Now, let's decide on some plans, shall we?" I bring my hand away, instantly missing the contact from her, but push forward with showing her more ideas. We order lunch into the office, working our way right through the afternoon, and by the time were finished, the rest of the office seems to be also.

Rose looks down at her watch, realising the time and glances up at me with a guilty expression, "I'm so sorry I didn't even realise the time. I've taken up your entire afternoon".

The corner of my lip tips up as I glance at all we have got through today. "Don't worry about it. I cleared my afternoon to do this with you. It needs to be right, but I think we've covered everything we need to. Why don't we head home, and I'll order something in for dinner, I don't want you cooking after we've been doing all this".

She easily agrees, and we head out for the evening. By the time we get back from the rush hour traffic, it's gone 7pm in the evening, too late for us to do anything other than veg out in front of the TV. I order dinner, and we settle in the living room for the rest of the night, making small talk as we watch the highlights from the ice hockey.

After finding out Rose enjoys the fighting more than watching the actual game, I put it on so she has some entertainment whilst I still get to keep up with the actual game. It's the team Hallie's brothers play for, so I feel like I'm supporting them too by watching.

Rose snuggles into me the more the night wears on. My fingers brush lazy circles up and down her arm whilst we watch the game. "Oh, I completely forgot to tell you the other day, a guy turned up at the house looking for you, has anyone got in contact with you since?"

I'm caught off guard by what she says and frown down at her. "What do you mean someone came looking for me? Did they leave a number or anything, or say what they wanted?" She shakes her head where it is resting against me, "He just said he was looking for some information, and his name was Ezra. He didn't give me a number or his surname though".

Ezra, I can't say I've ever heard that name before. My mind draws a blank each time I try to think of who it could be. "Did he say where he was staying or if he was going to call back?" She nods to me this time, half distracted by the fight that's broken out on the TV. "Yeah said he'd call back".

That's all she leaves me with as she begins to refocus on the game, I assume that's the end of the conversation, but she makes me jump by shouting out when she speaks again, spilling her words out in an excited rush as she remembers something else, "Oh, yeah actually, he also looked just like you. If I didn't already know you were an only child, I would have guessed he was your brother or something, weird, right?"

I feel like I remember Grace vaguely telling me the new vet looked like me too, and now I wonder if it's just a massive coincidence or if he's the same person. I pull my phone out, sending off a text to Jaxx.

Me: Hey, can you do me a favour and ask Grace what that new vet was called, please.

I only have to wait a few minutes before a message returns.

Jaxx: Um, yeah sure, I'll ask her now. Any particular reason? Did you buy a dog I don't know about or something?

Me: No. Grace said the new vet looks just like me, and now Rose has just mentioned that someone turned up at the house looking for me and that he looked like me also. I'm just wanting to see if he's the same person or if it's just a coincidence.

Half an hour passes, and I begin to think he's not going to bother responding to me, but eventually, I get a text.

Jaxx: Ezra James. Want me to see if Harris can run a background check for you?

Me: Yeah, actually, if you wouldn't mind. I don't want to speak to the guy until I find out what he might want.

Jaxx replies with a thumbs-up. His friend Harris is a detective and is the best at digging deep and finding out what I might need to know about this guy. My fingers grip my phone as I try to go back to watching the game, but my mind is stuck trying to figure out who the hell this guy could be and what he wants from me.

……

It takes Harris just under a week to find all the information I need about Ezra, and as Jaxx strolls into my office on Friday morning, shuts the door behind him and comes to take a seat across from me, a feeling settles in my gut, and I know this is going to be something I won't like.

Jaxx tosses the brown envelope over to me, a blank expression on his face. I steeple my fingers, and my foot taps rapidly against the wooden floors of my office as I become more nervous by the second. "Have you looked through them? You know, with him working with Grace and Tristan".

He shakes his head at me, "No, we did a basic background check when they first hired him, and that came up clean, I'm guessing this is something that is completely unrelated to that". I stare down at the manilla envelope that's atop my desk, trying to decide if this is something I really want to do when Jaxx pulls me from my thoughts, "If you want to be alone to read it, I can go".

I blink back up at him, he's already pressing his hands into the sides of the chair to stand, "No, don't go, I feel like I need the moral support for whatever is inside this".

I pause, my head going back and forth as to what the right thing to do really is. "Am I being paranoid for thinking it's more than it is?" He just shrugs at me, his expression remaining unreadable like it always is with him.

"I don't know, I think you should go with your gut if you think this could be something out of the ordinary. I mean, why would he randomly turn up on your doorstep and say he needs to talk to you if it wasn't something important?". I glance back down and decide I should just figure out what could be going on. There's, no point in me putting off the inevitable as I tear open the sealed edge and pull out the files Harris managed to pull for me.

I scan the pages, looking for something that could be out of the ordinary, but nothing jumps out at me, just simple things like where he grew up and what high school and college he attended. He got good grades and from the looks of it, has never been in trouble, so at least I know he's probably not after money.

It's not until I make it to a DNA document for paternity at the back of the files that my heart stops. There in black and white under father's name is my own father, Alistar Wilde.

All the blood drains from my face, and I instantly feel like I'm either going to pass out or throw up. My fingers scramble to find his birth certificate that's included in the files as I search for his date of birth. It's six years after mine, around a year after my mom found out she had cancer for the first time.

I swallow back the bile wanting to wretch from my throat, and glance up to Jaxx. He's watching me cautiously, trying to figure out what I've just seen. I can't speak, so I just hand him the piece of paper. His eyes scan it, quickly finding what he was meant to and widen almost comically. I'd laugh if I wasn't so shell-shocked right now.

"Surely this is just a sick joke. How can you have a brother, your mom and dad were together until she died when you were thirteen. This says he would only be six years younger than us".

My lids feel heavy as I blink slowly, unable to form a single word, whilst also trying to comprehend what I've just seen as my mind jumps back to me being five. I remember my mom being ill, I remember her crying a lot and being upset, and my dad was away a lot for work, although now I'm beginning to wonder if she knew about this all along and kicked him out. Or she could have just been upset because of the cancer.

Who am I to know though. I was never privy to any conversations that went on between the pair of them. They only argued a few times over the years, but now I think they just kept it from me.

My dad was 'working away' for a good six months at the start when my mom first got ill. I remember being so angry with him that he'd leave us for work, but Mom said he had to be away for us. I never understood it at the time, just that it needed to be done and to not be angry at him for missing my birthday or Christmas. He came back eventually, but the memories are hazy, they were such a long time ago I'm surprised I remember him leaving in the first place.

"I think he could actually be my brother. I remember my dad being away around the time I was five for a while but then he came back home. I don't know what might have gone on, but I need to find out. I'm going to have to find him and meet him".

I stand from my chair as I begin to pace the room and try to wrap my head around this whole situation. *I have a brother*. One who could very well hate me or want to get to know me, I don't know which one, but I'm dam well going to find out.

The tall glass windows that sit behind me, showing a view of the park and downtown Knoxville are covered in rain as it bounces off the window in the bleak February sky. I stare down to the street watching people running by, and knowing full well one of those people could be him. My brother. My own flesh and blood that I've gone years without knowing.

Anger floods through me at the thought of my father keeping this from me my entire life. Did he think I'd never find out, or that Ezra might not come looking for me eventually, or his own father for that matter? I spin and face Jaxx again, trying to form an idea in my head "Can you get hold of his phone number for me, from Grace or Tristan, I need to speak to him and get to the bottom of this, but I'm meant to be at my dad's tomorrow with Rose".

I run my fingers through my hair, tugging at the ends of it in frustration.

Fuck. What am I going to tell Rose? She'll have questions too, and whilst she's with me, fake or not, I want her to know everything. I just don't know how to tell her the guy who turned up at the house looking for me is, in fact, my brother, and she met the guy before me.

Jaxx leans forward in his seat, bringing his hands up to cover his mouth as his elbows rest on his knees. Frowning at me as he thinks, "I think you would be best avoiding him until you get your head straight, you don't want to do or say anything you might regret before you meet with Ezra, and the last thing you need is to be causing a scene when you're already trying to stay out of trouble with him".

I feel myself grinding my teeth from clenching my jaw so hard. I want to confront my dad, but I need to figure out what the hell to say to him. I can't do or say anything that could jeopardise my future. And this is the beginning of a long new road ahead for me.

22

Rose

The week after Luca and I spent that afternoon working on the bakery renovation, things felt different between us.

It seemed like our friendship had grown stronger in our complicated dynamic. The day after I saw him, his dad called and asked if I could start making pastries, muffins, and other treats for the office every Friday, and I began to think about branching out into deliveries for office meetings and other events, in addition to running the bakery.

I'm really glad that Luca insisted on creating more space for a bigger kitchen and work area instead of keeping the apartment upstairs as it was. Now, there will be more room to expand the business. It was incredible how I went from having the usual number of daily customers to now working at a higher rate and possibly needing to hire someone else once the shop reopens.

I won't lie and say I wasn't slightly disappointed when Luca told me there was more damage and we'd have to do a full refit, and I was also a little sceptical when he dropped into conversation that the landlord so easily agreed to the renovations, wondering if he had more to do with it than he is letting on.

Either way the shop has begun work this week, and it's nice to see it all coming to life from what we had down on the paper just a week ago. Things seem to be moving quickly when I pop in to check on things on Saturday and get a walk around from one of the guys on site.

They've ripped most things out, and it's back to bare brick downstairs. Apparently upstairs is too dangerous for me to go up into as they have ripped the flooring up, so I only spent a short time there before heading back home to Luca, who didn't seem so happy about having to go to his dads, informing me it's usually a dinner party. There will be more than a few people there instead of just us. But I'm more than happy to go along with it if his dad thinks I'm his fiancé, not just a woman taking up space in his son's house.

By the afternoon, Luca seems on edge about the whole situation, he's been pacing the floor for the last half an hour after a phone call he took in his office.

I watch him go back and forth from my spot on the sofa, my arms folded across my chest. He's not usually this worked up, but something tells me the phone call he took wasn't a good one. I huff out a breath, getting annoyed at his pacing, "Luca, will you just sit still for five minutes? I don't know what's got you like this, but will you take a breather?".

He stops on the spot, his chocolate eyes shooting to meet mine, a scowl on his usually calm face. Eventually he releases a long breath, placing his hands on his hips as his head drops to his chest. “I’m sorry, I just have a few things going on that I need to sort out, and it’s stressing me out a bit”. I nod to him, “Okay. Do you want to talk about it?”

He blinks up at me, his lips parting as if he’s about to tell me what’s going on, but just as quickly, he snaps his mouth back shut again, quickly shaking his head from side to side. “I need to figure everything out first before I say anything. I don’t want to have all my information wrong, and then it’s all been a big waste”.

He pauses momentarily, thinking over what he’s about to say, before shaking his head again as if he doesn’t want to come out with whatever he has going on in his brain. Watching him like this, having some problem with whatever is going on in his life, has me reaching out to motion for him to sit with me.

I wave him over and pat the seat next to me, and without any hesitation, he shuffles his way over to the sofa and plops down next to me.

I shift in my seat, allowing me to face him fully without craning my neck too much, and rest my hand on his leg. The action was meant to comfort him, but he stares down at the ring on my finger, bringing his hand up to cover mine and toy with it where it rests, reminding me that I should tread carefully and not get carried away.

I clear my throat, bringing his attention back up to me. Whatever is going on with him shows in the way he holds his body. His shoulders are slumped slightly, and that usually cheeky grin on his face is replaced with some emotion that I can't quite put my finger on.

He looks sad, but I know that's not all. Maybe anger too from the permanent frown on his face. I lean into him, causing my chest to brush against his arm, the feeling of friction against my nipple in my bra causes it to harden at the touch and sends a shot of heat to my core, a feeling I shouldn't be thinking about right now. I should be comforting him.

"I don't know what's going on, but let me be here for you as much as possible. If you want to sit and be miserable, we can do that. If you don't want to go to your dads tonight, then that's fine too". He shakes his head at me again, leaning into me too, "This is going to sound really pathetic right now, but can you just hug me? That's all I need".

His vulnerability hits me square in the chest. This is a side to him that I'm not sure I've ever seen before, nor do I think I might see again anytime soon. "It's not pathetic at all".

My arms open, letting him fall into me as we settle deeper into the couch. His arms come around my waist, squeezing me back like he really needs this right now, and the sigh that leaves him sounds like he's releasing every ounce of stress he's been carrying from whatever information he's having to hold onto.

I hold onto him for a while, not wanting to let him go too soon, and eventually, he pulls back just enough to look up at me. He looks like a lost child right now, and the emotion swirling in his eyes confirms that he's torn up by whatever is going on with him. "Thank you, I needed that".

We're so close as he shifts, adjusting himself, that my lips brush his cheek when he bumps into me, causing tingles and goosebumps to spread over my skin at the feel of him on me, and everything else seems so unimportant compared to this moment right now.

His eyes shift, becoming sharper and more intense as they lock onto mine. He adjusts himself again, aligning his gaze perfectly level with me, and my tongue darts out to wet my suddenly dry lips. His eyes follow the movement with unwavering focus. Every instinct tells me to get up, to create some distance between us, but the pull to stay close—to be here for him in any way he needs—overwhelms my better judgment.

His eyes flit up to mine for a moment, then back to my lips, not helping to break the intensity of his gaze as his eyes roam over my face. I want to say I'm a patient person, but right now, I don't care about anything else as I press my lips to his warm, soft ones.

The feeling of them reminds me how good it feels to be touched by this man, to have him pressed against my body. He deepens the kiss almost instantly, moving our bodies so he is lying on top of me on the couch, and I allow him to as I pull him onto me, wanting to have him as close as possible. His thighs push mine apart as he settles in between my legs.

One hand roams up my body whilst the other keeps him from falling on me as he moves his fingers around to my hair, tightening his grip on me as he pulls my head back, and tilting it up to allow him access to my neck. He peppers kisses down the side of my throat, and I feel my body reacting in the best possible way to him.

I know we shouldn't be doing this. I know it's a bad idea, yet I can't bring myself to stop wanting him. I keep telling myself all these things, that we're no good together, that he can do better than me, but it doesn't change the one constant. He's always there for me when I need him, and now I need to be here for him. He's been a perfect gentleman this last week, not coming too close to me or making his usual comments that remind me who he was before this, especially after I told him what we did shouldn't happen again.

It's made me miss him even more, even though he's been right next to me this whole time. Luca must notice I'm in my own head because he pulls back just a touch. His eyes roam over my face, searching as if trying to uncover something hidden beneath the surface.

They hold an intensity, a fire deep inside them that's drawing me in and leaving me unable to look away. "I can stop if you want me to", he murmurs the words like he doesn't mean them, but I don't want him to either, so I shake my head, "No, I want this. I just don't want you to think I'm only being like this because you're going through something. This won't change tomorrow".

His brow pulls together as he looks down at me, "Even if you changed your mind about this again, I wouldn't stop trying to convince you that this is right where I want to be. Today and every day. I'll fight to be in your life even if it's not always what you want because you make me feel like I want to be a better person for you and myself. I want you Rose, and I want you to see that too. Seeing my ring on your finger every day makes me want this to be real, to have you with me for real, to stay living here with me and fill this house with the happiness it deserves".

If my jaw could hit the floor from his words, it would hang so far down I'd have to scoop it up. I want to ask him '*Are you fucking with me right now*?' but the words can't seem to leave my mouth. The intensity and vulnerability of them leave me breathless.

His gaze locks onto mine, unwavering and filled with desperate hope. He wants me to agree to be with him, to share my life with him, and it's clear in every fibre of his being.

His eyes bounce between mine, seeing the indecision in them and releases a long breath, resting his forehead against mine. "I know you are the most indecisive person I think I've ever met, and I know I'm equally just as impatient, but we are good together. You're good for me, even if you don't always see it. You help me to be a better person every day". He pulls back, pausing momentarily, "Just don't think about anything right now. Think about this moment, us together, we can worry about everything else later".

My teeth skim over my bottom lip as I suck on it, using it to help ground me. I can't speak. He's flawed me with his words to the point where I can only convey how I feel to him by reaching forward and running my fingers through his dark hair.

I pause, holding my hand at the base of his head, and pull him closer to me until our lips are barely touching, "I'm scared Luca. I'm scared that you will change your mind and realise one day that I'm not who you want, and I'll be left to pick up the pieces, I don't know if I can do that".

His lip pulls slightly in the corner and forms into a ghost of a smile, "Let's just take this day by day then. No pressure to be anything other than the two of us enjoying each other's time together". I don't see how that's an unreasonable request, and right now, I'm getting sick of having to try and ignore the growing attraction I have to this beautiful man each day that I have to be near him.

I don't know how much longer I would have gone before I eventually made the decision to either act on it or leave to try and save my heart from the inevitable torture if I didn't act on my instincts. It would hurt when he gives up trying and finds someone else, but I would have to get over it.

Agreement or not, he wouldn't wait forever. I return his smile with one of my own, just a little bigger and brighter than his, and he reciprocates, widening his own smile to match mine. "That right there is the best thing I could see on you. That smile overrides everything else".

I tilt my head back, looking up at him through my lashes. His words sink into me, breaking down that wall I have spent my whole life building up. "Okay". I whisper, my voice barely audible as I lock my gaze with his.

He responds with a gentle kiss, one that feels more like a promise than a fleeting touch. His lips move softly against mine, exploring, savouring. The hand in my hair tightens, tilting my head to deepen the kiss as his other hand traces down my side, leaving a trail of heat in its wake.

Our connection feels electric, as if every touch, every kiss ignites a spark that courses through my veins. Luca's mouth leaves mine, trailing down my jaw to the sensitive spot just below my ear. My breath hitches, and I can feel the vibration of his low chuckle against my skin.

"I've wanted this for so long, wanted you to agree to try with me", he murmurs, his voice husky and filled with barely restrained desire as he continues working his way down my throat and across my collarbone and I become impatient, feeling myself getting more and more worked up the longer his hands are on me. I need to feel his skin against mine.

My hands find their way to his shirt, tugging and pulling at it to get it over his head. He breaks our contact just long enough to tug it over his head, tossing it on the floor beside us. My breath lodges in my throat, and I have to work to swallow as I watch his muscles ripple above me. My fingers reach out to touch his skin, my eyes following every move as he sucks in a breath the moment my cold fingers touch the olive skin of his body.

"I missed you".

The words leave my lips, and for a moment, I regret them coming out as I see the confusion on his face. He leans back into me, brushing his fingers across my cheek, caressing my skin.

"I've not gone anywhere, Red. I've been right here this whole time". I bite my lip and try to think how to rephrase what I've just said. He's not getting what I mean. I slowly release a shaky breath as I pull myself together. I can't think straight when I'm so close to him, like my brain decides it needs to switch off because he's here, and it somehow knows I'm safe.

"I mean, I missed you being like this with me. I missed your touch, the feel of you, the weight of you on me, keeping me grounded and making me forget everything else in the world".

Luca's eyes soften, and a tender smile curves his lips as he takes in my words. He leans down, pressing a gentle kiss to my forehead, his breath warm against my skin. "I've missed this too, more than you can imagine", he whispers, his voice filled with honesty. “Being close to you, feeling your touch, it's like a piece of me that was missing and couldn’t figure out how to get it back”.

He trails his fingers down my throat, sending shivers across my skin, and wraps them gently around the base of my throat, caressing the skin with his calloused thumb.

“I want to be here for you, to be the person you can rely on. I know things haven't always been easy between us, but I think we can make this work, if you’ll just let me in”. His words scare the crap out of me, but at the same time, I feel a warmth spreading through my chest, something I don’t think I’ve ever felt. “I want that too”, I choke on my words as they leave my mouth, trying to keep my emotions under control so I’m not a blubbering mess.

“I want to try, to see where this can take us”. Luca's smile widens, and he presses another kiss to my lips. “Then let's not waste any more time”, he murmurs against my lips. The urgency I feel crawl through me, to make this man mine overtakes as I pull him into me. He deepens the kiss, his body pressing against mine, and I can feel the weight of his promise in every touch, every caress.

In this moment, nothing else matters except the two of us as his hands roam further down my body, testing the limits of my patience the slower he moves. His lips move down my neck as he makes his way down my body at a torturous pace, tugging at my shirt as he groans into my neck, “This needs to come off, now”.

I giggle into him, wiggling my way out of my t-shirt as Luca pulls it over my head, discarding it with his own on the floor. He pauses, leaning back on his heels between my legs.

I'm thankful for his oversized couch right now because we don't have to move from our spot. He sits back again and watches me appreciatively, scanning his eyes down my body, over my breasts and stopping when he reaches the top of my leggings. I didn't wear a bra today, and right now, I'm glad I didn't, as his hands kneed the flesh of my breasts, forcing a moan to slip free from me at the feeling of his rough hands on me before sliding them down to skim the top of my leggings, toying with the fabric.

I wiggle a little, bringing his attention back to me, and he raises a brow at me, "I think these need to come off too". I nod to him, biting my lip. Slowly, my leggings are slid down, my underwear coming with them, and my legs are pulled up and to one side so he can slide the fabric down more easily.

His gaze is intense and wanting as his eyes roam over my body, a sexy grin taking over his face, revealing that dimple I have a small obsession with seeing. I raise a brow at him, "I don't think this is very fair, you get me naked, and yet you are still wearing clothes".

Luca glances down at himself before leaning over me as his arms rest on either side of my head. Leaning in close, his breath fans my cheek, bringing goosebumps up all over my skin, he murmurs, "And you are about to get at least one orgasm before we even make it off this couch. I'm only interested in what I can do to your body, not mine".

His head dips, pulling one nipple into his mouth as he sucks and nips at the sensitive bud. I arch on instinct into him, feeling his arm come around my back and pull me closer, pinning me to him like he thinks I might escape, but the only place I'm going to right now is heaven from this man's touch.

Luca nips and sucks on one before moving to the other, giving it the same attention, and my hands come up to his hair, running my fingers through it, tugging at the thick locks on his head when he bites down harder. I cry out at the pain that turns quickly to pleasure as he licks where he bit, soothing it again. His lips move back up to my neck as he presses them to my skin, letting out a strangled groan.

"You drive me crazy, Red. Every time we're together, I could lose myself in you. I can't think of anything else but how much I want you, need you". His voice is a deep rumble against my skin. The words send a rush of desire coursing through me, pulling me deeper into him.

His hand trails down to the overly sensitive part of me that's begging for him to touch, sliding his fingers up and down my slit before dipping a finger into me, his lips never leaving my neck as he continues to caress my skin, his beard scratching and most definitely leaving marks all along the delicate skin.

I moan into him, and my hands squeeze at the back of his neck, begging for more from him as his finger strokes my inner walls. He pulls it back, bringing it up to my clit that pulses with need and uses firm strokes to bring me closer to my climax. I feel myself getting closer and closer to the edge, knowing it won't take much more.

Luca sits back on his heels again, keeping his fingers firmly in place as he moves his body down the couch and onto his knees beside me. He moves with so little effort, sliding himself into a position he's comfortable with.

When he gets there, he stops, moving his hands off me just long enough to pull my legs up and over his shoulders, sliding me around on the couch as he does. He has full access to me now, having me propped up with my body fully in front of him, open and ready.

It feels right to be doing this with him, even though I swore to myself that I wouldn't do this again. I just can't help myself, and the pull I have towards him doesn't help one bit.

He licks his lips as his eyes zone in on my core, and he doesn't waste any time before diving in and pressing his tongue to me, licking up and down from my clit to just above my ass and back up. He adds a finger, pushing it in and out of me as he continues to lick and suck on the bundle of nerves, quickly bringing me up and over the edge as an orgasm soars through me. "Luca", I breathe, barely able to utter anything more than a whisper as another strangled moan leaves my body.

I can't focus on anything other than the feel of his hands on me as my orgasm subsides, and I'm left wanting, no *needing* more of him.

23

Rose

I'm breathless from the orgasm I've just been given. Luca has me over his shoulder, practically running up the stairs with me, and I can't help the burst of laughter that flies out of me as he rushes up the stairs.

I expect him to make a left into his room, but he surprises me by swinging the door open to my room instead, dumping me on the bed. I'm still very naked compared to him as he tries to climb over me. His knee just about digs into the mattress when I put a hand up to stop him, pointing down at the jeans he has on.

"Those need to be off before you come anywhere near this bed". He grins at me, popping the button on his jeans and slowly pulling the teeth of the zipper down. It's like my own personal strip show. All I need is the song Pony to be playing in the background, and I'll have my own magic Mike with his magical dick.

After a torturously long few moments, his jeans hit the floor, followed by his boxers. He kicks them to the side, giving me a show of his glorious naked form with his erection jutting out in front of him and standing proudly. "Is this better for you?" I nod to him as my teeth pull at my lips, the only thing I'm capable of right now.

His seductively smooth voice does all sorts of things to me as he rolls on the condom he must have pulled from his jeans before he prowls towards me, climbing back onto the bed.

He settles between my legs, positioning himself at my entrance and propping himself up on his palms so he can get a good look at me. I run my hand across the stubble of his jaw, enjoying the feel of it on my skin. "Fuck me, Luca". My voice is barely above a whisper, but he hears it just fine because his lips tip up into that sexy grin once again. "Yes, ma'am".

I don't get a chance to do anything else before the air leaves me as he pushes himself to the hilt, stopping once he's inside me to allow me to at least adjust to him.

"You good?" He levels his gaze with me as he asks the question, his eyes searching mine for any hint that I don't, in fact, want to go through with this, and I have to work to stop my eyes from rolling in the back of my head from the pressure of him. I need him to move, and quickly, so I rapidly bob my head and squeeze at his shoulders to give him the go-ahead.

He pulls out of me, almost to the tip, before pushing back inside me, filling me with himself as he begins to build a rhythm, pushing himself into me as far as he can go.

"Harder", I moan, wanting him to give me all he has, and he delivers, driving himself in and out of me at such a pace that I feel myself moving up the bed with each thrust.

Tightness pulls at my lower belly as I feel my orgasm building for a second time, but just as I'm about to come, he pulls out. Before I have time to protest, I feel myself being flipped like I'm a ragdoll and hauled up against his muscular body.

One hand trails down my body as he presses his fingers against my sensitive clit, teasing me, putting pressure on and then removing them. He slides back into me, keeping me against him as his other hand comes up to cup around my throat, gently gripping me to hold me in place.

"Tell me you're mine, Rose. Tell me you only want me". Part of me wants to tell him to fuck off, that no one owns me. But if he keeps touching me like this, then he can have me.

When I take too long to answer, his fingers pinch at my clit again, sending my body into overdrive. "Rose", he murmurs against my ear. I know I won't get what I want until he hears the words he's desperate for.

"Yes, Luca. I'm yours". The chuckle that leaves him vibrates against my ear as he applies more pressure, sending me so close to the edge that I grind against his hand, trying to get myself there quicker.

"Good girl".

I swear I must have a praise kink because those words send me straight over the edge as he presses my body down onto the mattress and pounds into me. My screams are muffled by the duvet as I cry out into it. Fingers grip my hips so tightly that they very well could be bruised, but I don't care.

He consumes me. My thoughts and my body need him like I need oxygen.

Luca's movements become choppy as he pushes into me a few more times before giving over to his own climax, and his body drops down onto me, keeping me secure. He pulls out after a minute but freezes before he gets too far.

I crane my neck and see the shocked reaction on his face. "What, what's wrong?" The guilty look he's got on him makes me worry, but then he motions down to himself and the condom that's now split. "I don't know how that happened. *Shit*".

I see him start to panic and pull myself up and into sitting as he strides into the bathroom. "Luca, calm down, it's okay". He shakes his head rapidly as he comes back out, washcloth in hand to clean me up. "No, it's not, Rose. This is not okay", he says more to himself than me, panic lacing his tone as his fingers grab at me to clean me up.

I raise a brow at him, trying to figure out if he's just scared of accidental pregnancy or if he's actually not been for a recent health check, batting his hand away to sort myself out. "I'm on contraception if that's what you're worried about, and here's the shocker. I haven't got pregnant yet", I deadpan to him.

He blinks back at me for a moment as he figures out what I'm telling him. "What if I've got super sperm, though, and you got pregnant anyway?".

He's joking, I hope, from the look on his face, that cheeky grin. I think he is. Rolling my eyes, I shuffle to the end of the bed and make my way into the bathroom.

"If you believe that, then I have no hope for you, Luca Wilde". I turn the shower on, wanting to freshen up before going to dinner, and I'm followed by Luca, who props himself against the bathroom door. "You never know. I know people who have been on contraception and got pregnant anyway. It doesn't always work".

I glance over my shoulder at him before stepping into the hot steam of the shower and pulling myself under the waterfall. "No shit, your big dick broke the condom, so it's a good job I'm on something anyway, isn't it". His grin breaks across his face, pleased with my assessment.

I close my eyes, enjoying the feel of the hot water gliding down my skin, and jump when I feel hands on me. They slide up my body and to my breasts, squeezing gently at the flesh. A moan slips free, and if it were up to me, we'd be going again, but it seems Luca is paranoid about not using extra protection. I turn to him and peek up at him through wet lashes, "Why are you so worried? Have you got a kid I don't know about?"

He chuckles at me, burying his head into my neck as his arms encircle me and squeezes my ass. "No, thank God. I don't think I would have been grown up enough to deal with having a child when I was younger, and I'd like to be with my children's mother when they do come along".

He pauses for a moment, the heavy fall of the shower filling the silence between us. "A few years ago, someone I was seeing casually said she wanted more than I was willing to give, and tried to trap me by saying she was pregnant with my child. Long story short, it turned out it wasn't mine, but it panicked me all the same. I've not gone without protection with anyone since".

The vulnerability shows in his voice as he pulls back and watches me, waiting for me to say something. I drag my hand over the stubble of his jaw, resting it against the gruffness of his cheek as my other hand weaves its way through his damp hair. I have to crane my neck to look up to him, as he's a foot taller than me, and when I do, I catch the intensity of his stare on me.

I reach up, pressing a gentle kiss to his lips, and he brings his forehead down to rest against mine as the kiss breaks. "I wouldn't do that to you, but I understand why you have reservations".

He hums in agreement, but I know not to push him any further on it. "But since we don't have any more condoms in here, I guess we'll have to improvise, won't we?" I say as I drop to my knees, watching as his eyes pop in shock.

A smirk tips at the corner of my lips, enjoying watching the excitement in his eyes, knowing what I'm about to do. My hand slides along the smooth skin of his erection, gripping at the base as I push him into my mouth. A deep moan leaves his mouth as his hand comes up to cup the back of my head, fisting my hair as he guides me in and out. I swirl my tongue around the tip, enjoying what I'm doing to him as a small amount of pre cum hits my tongue, the saltiness seeping into my tastebuds.

"Fuck, I'm not going to last long if you keep doing that", he grunts, barely able to get the words out. The words push me to move quicker, sucking and licking at his length until he can't hold himself anymore and releases himself down the back of my throat. I'm not normally one to enjoy this, but knowing it's Luca who is at my mercy makes me want to do this to him more often.

He pulls me to my feet, pressing a kiss to my lips. It's deep and wanting, and I feel like my knees could give way if he weren't holding me up. "I don't think I can ever let you go after that. You shouldn't have been so good". He smirks down at me, but part of me thinks he's not joking.

"Well, I'm glad it's something in my favour then, nice to know I have good skills". Luca buries his head in my neck, almost growling as he replies, "You won't be using those skills on anyone else, so better not be getting any ideas, Red". I giggle into him, enjoying the possessiveness he gives off. I like the idea of him wanting only me, even if it won't last forever.

We somehow finish showering, and Luca disappears into his room to get re-dressed. I'm putting the last of my makeup on when he returns, sitting on the edge of my bed. He looks like he has something on his mind again, and I want to find out what's going on just so I can help his mood, even if just a little bit.

Turning to him, mascara brush still in hand, I ask, "Are you sure you don't want to tell me what's going on with you? I might be able to help". I turn back to the mirror to finish applying my mascara, catching his reflection in the mirror. He blows out a long breath, pressing the heels of his palms into his eyes and resting his elbows on his knees.

"I do want to tell you, but I also don't want to have gotten information wrong". His response confuses me, "Is this something to do with one of our friends or me? Is this why you can't tell me?" My question has his head shooting up, eyes wide, like he can't believe I just asked that.

"No, absolutely not".

He rises to his feet, making his way into the bathroom and leaning against the door frame with his arm propped up against the other side. I keep quiet, not wanting to say anything that might dissuade him from telling me.

Luca watches me for a minute longer before continuing, "You know what, I may as tell you. Do you remember that guy that came to the house looking for me? You told me about it last week".

I nod to him, allowing him to keep going, "I had Jaxx's friend, Harris, do a background check on him to see why he may want to see me, and we found a document that alludes to the fact he might very well be my brother".

I drop the mascara wand into the sink, the plastic clanking and spluttering black paste along the porcelain as I stare back at his reflection, open-mouthed. I blink several times, trying to process the information he's given me.

The silence between us thickens as I struggle to find the right words. "Your brother?" I manage to stammer out, my voice barely above a whisper. Luca's eyes remain fixed on me, and I can see the tension in his shoulders, the way he grips the door frame as if it's the only thing keeping him grounded.

He nods slowly, his gaze searching mine in the mirror. "Yeah, it seems like it. I don't have all the details yet, but there's enough to suggest he could be. I need to speak to my dad to confirm it though". His voice is strained, a mix of confusion and disbelief.

"But what, how?" I can't find the words to form a full sentence. He looks amused by my shock, a small smile tugging at the corner of his lips, "You seem more shocked about the news than I was. But it looks like my dad had an affair when I was younger". He shrugs like it's no big deal, but I see the tension and hurt seeping through him.

"I mean, if he is your brother, it makes sense. You both look really alike. I know that doesn't help the situation, but I could see the resemblance". He shakes his head, grinning at me, "It doesn't answer any of my questions, but it does make sense what you just said. Grace said the same the other week. He's the new vet that's been working on their ranch, so she and Tristan already know him quite well".

I turn fully to him, propping my hip against the counter, "Do you want to meet him?" He nods, digging his hands into the pockets of his dark blue Levis. "Yeah, I think I do, I just haven't confronted my dad about it yet. I found out last week, and I'm still processing the information. I don't even know if he knows he has another son or not".

I shake my head, confused by this whole situation, but also a little hurt that he's kept this from me for so long. I brush that thought to the side, this isn't about me, it's about Luca and this shitty situation he's found himself in. "I don't even know what to suggest. Do you still want to go to your dad's today, or would you prefer to miss it?"

Luca's chocolate eyes meet mine, a small frown pulling at his brow. "I think I want to ask him tonight, get it over and done with. A part of me doesn't want to cause a scene if there are many people there, but I also don't think I can wait any longer to ask him".

I bob my head once in agreement. "I think you should talk to him as soon as possible. You've already waited a week". He sighs, running his hand through his hair as he pulls himself from the door frame and walks over to the window in my room.

"I'm just so fucking angry with him, why would he do this". Luca turns back to look at me, "If Ezra really is my brother, it means my dad slept with his mother when my own had just found out she had cancer. How could someone do that to their own wife?".

My heart breaks for Luca and all the things he must have gone through as a child, growing up and losing his mom at such a young age, and now knowing that his dad was playing away when his mom was so ill.

I force my feet to move, making my way over to where he is on the other side of the room and wrap my arms around him from behind. He sighs, twisting his body just enough to bring his arm around me and pulls me into his embrace. We stand there for a moment, holding each other. I don't know what else I can do or say to make the moment feel any better. All I know he has to confront his dad. I don't even know if I can bear to look at him and pretend to be nice to his face, knowing what I now do.

Luca presses a kiss to the top of my head. "Finish getting ready, we should get going soon. I want to try and catch him early in case he does have other people there." I nod, pulling away from his embrace and quickly throwing on some clothes.

When I meet him downstairs, he looks like a man torn between dread and determination. The tension in his posture speaks volumes, but I know this confrontation is something he needs to face. Taking a deep breath, I offer him a reassuring smile, hoping to lend him some strength as we head out to his truck.

The drive is silent and thick, with an unspoken tension in the air, knowing that the conversation ahead could change everything.

24

Luca

Nerves and dread fill me equally as I pull up to my father's house. I sit in the car, unmoving and staring ahead, willing myself to move and go in.

It's something that needs to be done, although I'm not sure what I should even say to him. '*Hey, Dad, I heard you had another kid you forgot to mention'*. I shake my head, trying and failing to keep it and my thoughts as clear as possible.

Rose sits patiently beside me, being my constant support and somehow not allowing me to fall in on myself like I want to. She barely said two words on the drive over, but I could feel the reassurance she was pushing through to me from the gentle grip she kept on my hand as we made the drive here.

I take a deep breath, finally unlocking the car door and stepping out, my movements slow and deliberate. Rose follows me, silently cheering me on with her gentle smile over at me. We walk up to the front door, the familiar creak of the porch steps echoing our footsteps.

My heart races as I hesitate for a moment before reaching out to ring the doorbell. The seconds stretch into what feels like an eternity until the door opens, revealing my dad with a welcoming smile.

"Luca, Rose, come in, come in", he says, stepping aside to let us enter. The warmth of the house contrasts sharply with the cold knot in my stomach as I glance around, noting the familiar decor and the faint scent of Dad's cologne mingling with the aroma of freshly brewed coffee and spot a few people milling around in the kitchen to the back of the house.

"Hey, Dad," I start, trying to keep my voice steady, "Can we talk for a minute? In private?" His brow furrows slightly, concern flickering in his eyes. "Of course, son. Let's go to the study. Rose, feel free to grab yourself a drink from the kitchen".

I spare a glance at her and nod once. She doesn't look like she wants to leave me alone but gives me a tight smile and my hand a reassuring squeeze before letting go, staying behind to give us the privacy we need before turning and making her way down the hall to the other guests he has here. He leads the way down the hallway, the sound of our footsteps muffled by the plush carpet.

Once inside the study, he closes the door and gestures for me to sit, but I gently shake my head at him, choosing to remain standing as I try to gather my thoughts. He watches me, a mix of curiosity and worry etched on his face as he rounds his desk and takes a seat. "What's on your mind, Luca?" he asks, confusion lacing his tone. I'm not used to seeing him so uneasy, and it gives me a small burst of satisfaction that, for once, it's not me doing something I shouldn't, giving me the momentum to carry on.

I take a deep breath, the words tumbling out before I can second-guess myself. “Did you know you have another son?”

My dad’s face pales, his eyes widening in shock. “What are you talking about?” My voice grows firmer, the weight of my emotions driving me forward. “It seems that you had an affair when Mom was sick. And now, I have a brother I never knew about. Is it true?” There is a heavy silence, the air thick with the gravity of the revelation. I watch as he sinks into the chair further, his head in his hands, as he tries to process the bombshell I've just dropped.

“How did you find out about him?” I blanch, almost stumbling as his words hit me.

“It’s true”.

My own flesh and blood have been trying to find me, and I’ve been none the wiser about the whole situation. I have to keep my anger in check, needing to hear his version of the story and hoping he’s just honest with me. “Last week, Rose told me about a man who came looking for me. I had a friend do a background check on him, as he’s working in town, and when he got information back to me, your name was on a DNA certificate in the paperwork”. I keep my voice level, not letting it waver as I keep my gaze locked on him.

My hands clench into fists at my side as I find the words I need. “Were you ever going to tell me about him, or were you planning on taking this to the grave with you?” He blinks up at me, his face returning to the dark olive it usually is.

"I… I don't even know where to begin". I inhale a deep breath as I clench my jaw, grinding my teeth to try and ease the tension, but it doesn't help. "The start would be good". He motions for me to sit again, but I shake my head, firmer this time, wanting to have the easiest exit possible when I need to leave.

He brings his hands down, clasping them in front of him, "When your mom got sick, I didn't handle it well. I began drinking and ended up staying out, either at bars or at the office, so late that she would be asleep by the time I got home. I knew I was going to lose her at some point, and I was selfish and only thought about myself in that situation".

He pauses briefly, his worried eyes flitting up to mine, and I nod for him to carry on. "One night, I was at work, and my assistant at the time was there, working late with me. One thing led to another, and a few weeks later, she found out she was pregnant".

He takes a breath, watching me and waiting for me to say anything. I nod again, not able to speak for fear of saying something I might regret, grinding my teeth so hard that my jaw begins to ache as his head dips before carrying on.

"She told me she was going to keep the baby, and I told your mother. She kicked me out of the house, and it stayed that way for a good six months until I finally convinced her to let me come home to look after her like I knew I should have done from the start". My mind races to keep up with what he's telling me, but he's not getting to the point any quicker. "What happened then?"

He clears his throat before continuing, "I sorted maintenance payments after having a paternity test done to confirm he was mine and told her I wanted to be a part of his life, but she didn't want to be known as the woman who had an affair with her boss. So, she upped and left a couple of weeks after he was born. I tried to fight it for a few years, but she kept moving, hiding from me. Eventually, your mom got worse, and she was my priority, so I had to forget about him. I guess now he wants to find out about his other family. You would have to speak to him. I haven't seen him since he was a baby".

I want to believe that he tried to do right by us and even my brother, but I can't help the hurt ripping me apart after what he did to my mom. "I'm not sure if I can forgive you for what you did to Mom. She might have, but I just don't have it in me to right now". He nods, a solemn expression on his face. "Your mother never forgave me for it; she just learned to live with it, and eventually, we adjusted. I don't expect you to forgive me either. I just hope that we can figure out a way past this".

The man in front of me isn't someone I recognise. My dad is someone who is fierce and also a little terrifying at times if you cross him. But this version of him is just a shell of that, one whom I can't decide if he deserves my pity for the son he never got a chance to meet or my anger for what he did to my mother.

I clear my throat, pulling his attention back to me. "I'm going to work from home for the next few weeks while figuring out how I want to proceed with this. I haven't met him yet and don't know what to say to him. I also don't know if I want to stay a part of your company anymore. If I can't be around you, then I need to figure out what I'm going to do".

My dad's eyes widen in surprise at my words, the last thing he expected of me would be for me to leave the company I've spent years working my way to the top of. But right now, I need to be as far away from him as possible. He nods to me, choosing not to say anything, and right now, I couldn't be more thankful for that as I turn to leave the room.

My hand reaches the doorknob just as he calls out, "I have always loved your mother, and that never changed, not once. Even now she's gone". I clench my jaw, leaning into the door as I try not to retaliate against him, but I can't help it. "You should have remembered that before you knocked your assistant up".

I don't say anything else as I swing open the office door, storming to the kitchen in search of Rose. I find her standing by the counter, a glass of wine in her hand as she talks to one of Dad's colleagues. She looks up and sees me, her eyes immediately filling with concern.

Excusing herself, she makes her way over, her hand gently touching my arm. "How did it go?" She asks softly, searching my face for answers. "Let's just get out of here", I reply, my voice strained. Without another word, she nods, setting her glass on the counter and taking my hand as we weave through the kitchen that's slowly filling with guests, the weight of the conversation with my dad pressing down on me with every step.

The crisp air hits me as we step into the evening, and I take a deep breath, trying to steady myself. "I need to figure out what to do next," I murmur, more to myself than to Rose. She squeezes my hand reassuringly, her presence a comfort, holding me together as my mind works out how to get past this. "We'll figure it out," she says, her voice filling me with hope that I can get through this if I have her.

I drive and drive, not having a destination in mind. I feel bad dragging her along with me tonight, she didn't need to be here for that. Reaching across the console, I grab her hand. "Do you want me to drop you home?" Her head flips in my direction, a scowl crossing her face as she glances back at me, "Why, where are you going?" I shrug, not having a clue myself, "I don't actually know. I just know I don't want to stay in the house right now".

Her features soften as she mulls over my answer for a moment, not allowing me to get a gauge on what she's thinking. "I'm pretty hungry if you want to grab something to eat. Or if you'd prefer to be alone, then just drop me home". I grin at her, thankful that she's choosing to be with me even though I'm no fun and really miserable right now.

"I know just the place". She nods, staying quiet as I make the drive a few miles out of town to a little diner I come to when I'm not feeling like being healthy.

Rose looks a little sceptical as we pull up to the run-down-looking building, jumping out of the truck and tucking her hands into the back pockets of her jeans. For someone who dresses so casually most of the time, she sure knows how to pull it off.

Her hair is pulled into a messy bun, and she's wearing a black camisole with an oversized green shirt and dark blue Levis that hug her ass to perfection. I told her not to bother dressing up to go to my dad's, knowing I wouldn't be able to stay any longer once I'd spoken to him.

I laugh at her expression as I round my truck to get to her, placing a hand on her back to guide her to the door. I lean in close as we reach the front door, murmuring into her ear, "Trust me, it's the best". She raises a brow back at me as I pull the door open, ushering her inside.

The place is dated, with worn-out paper on the walls and chairs and tables that have seen better days, but the food has always been good, so as long as that stays, I'd be happy to keep coming back. We find a booth in the back, and she pulls a menu out, trying to figure out what to eat when a waitress comes over.

"What will y'all be having this evening?" I spare a glance at Rose, who looks like she has no clue, "If you don't mind, can I order for you?" I ask her. She shrugs, nodding at me as I order two of the bacon cheeseburgers and a portion of fries for us to share, along with some drinks. The waitress writes down the order and returns to the kitchen.

My eyes move back to Rose, she's sitting back in the seat, arms folded over her with a smirk on her face. I clasp my hands in front of me, narrowing my eyes on her and leaning forward just enough to catch the smell of her scent.

"What are you looking at me like that for?" She attempts to hide her smile, but it creeps in, "Just wondering how you keep a figure like that when you eat this stuff". I grin back at her, "I don't come here too often, but when I do, I make sure to enjoy it thoroughly. We can work it off when we get back if you like?"

Her face turns a pretty shade of pink, and she bites her lip, not giving me the answer I need from her. "Is that a yes, Red? Are you gonna help me work up a sweat when we get home? Cuz you sure as shit aren't sleeping back in your room again".

She rolls her eyes dramatically at me, and my dick twitches, wanting to spank her for her attitude. I lower my voice, steadying it so she doesn't know just how worked up she gets me. "Roll your eyes like that again, and you won't be able to sit down for a week".

Her hazel eyes widen in front of me, the swirls of the golden flecks and the dilatating of her pupils giving away how much she wants me right now. She tugs her lip further between her teeth and I have to adjust myself in my seat, my pants becoming a little uncomfortable from how tight they're getting. My lips tip up in a small smile as I watch her squirm in her seat from across the booth, but I need to feed her before doing anything else.

The waitress comes back over with our drinks, and Rose takes a long sip of hers, before placing it back in front of her and playing with the glass between her hands, twisting it in her fingers.

"Have you thought about when you're going to speak to Ezra?" I blink back at her, my mind drawing a blank, and shrug my shoulder as I watch the crease deepen between her brows, concern etched in her features. "I don't know yet. I have his number, so I might see if I can get him to meet up tomorrow or something. But right now, that isn't really my biggest priority. I told my dad I don't know if I want to stay at the company anymore".

Roses' eyes flit up to mine as she nods in agreement. "I think you should give this situation the time it needs and don't make any rash decisions. Has this come out of the blue, wanting to not stay there anymore, or have you thought about leaving in the past?"

I know where she is coming from with this; she thinks that I'm just now deciding that I don't want to work for the company anymore, but I've been finding ways to make my own money for a while now, something even my dad doesn't know.

"I have thought about leaving in the past, but I don't know if I would want another architectural firm or whether I would start a full construction firm. We have the odd people who contract for us already, but I think I'd like to have a company where everything can be under one roof. My guys would do the job from start to finish. I've been setting myself up for a while, in case I ever decided I really didn't want to stay here at the firm. I love my dad in a weird way, but not how a son should love his parent.

He's always been there to protect me but never really looked after me, I had to work from the bottom to get where I am today, and ever since he said I have to marry to get where I want to be in the firm, to take over like I was supposed to, I have been thinking about pulling back".

The added bonus to this whole situation was that I finally got Rose, even if in the wrong capacity to begin with. But I'm determined to keep breaking down the walls she has built, guarding her.

Rose's eyes soften as I talk about my father, and I can see the empathy in her gaze. "It must have been hard, knowing that your dad had expectations for you that didn't align with what you wanted for yourself," she says gently. I nod, feeling a lump form in my throat.

"He always had this vision for me, one that required me to make sacrifices that I wasn't prepared to make. It wasn't just about the job or the company, it was about following a path that didn't feel like mine." I take a deep breath, the weight of my words hanging in the air. "And then, when he demanded that I marry to secure my position, it was like the final straw. It felt like he cared more about the company's legacy than my happiness".

Rose reaches across the table, her hand finding mine and giving it a reassuring squeeze. "I get it," she says. "You've been fighting for your place in the world, and it feels like he's been fighting against you rather than with you. But you've done an incredible job getting to where you are, and you don't need his validation to know your worth, and you shouldn't have to marry someone just because he decides that's how it should be".

Her words hit me, a tightening in my chest forming, and I don't know what to do about it. She could pull back from me at any point, but I tamp down the growing anxiety that she will realise I'm not enough for her either and leave. I squeeze her hand back, grateful for her understanding of the situation either way. "Thanks, Red. It means a lot to hear you say that. I wish he could see things the way I do."

She smiles softly at me, "Maybe he will, one day. But until then, you need to do what makes you happy. Build a life and a career you're proud of, and everything else will fall into place."

I nod, feeling more relaxed about the whole situation than I have since before I had the obligation of a married man to fill. "You're right. I need to move forward on my terms, not his." I look at Rose, my heart rate increasing as the words I want to tell her stick on my tongue, but I don't say them. "And having you by my side, whether you keep wearing my ring or not, I want to show you too that I can be a better person". She doesn't give anything away as she smiles back at me, the feeling sending warmth through me. She may not be giving me answers, but she's still here, and that's all I need right now.

25

Rose

I think I'm in a food coma from my burger as I sit back in my seat, tapping my over-full stomach. "Okay, you were right. That was really good, and now I think I might have an addiction to it. You need to bring me here at least once a month from now on".

Luca grins over to me, wiping his hands on his napkin. "I told you. Would I ever lie to you?" I don't even get a chance to respond before he points a finger at me, "The answer to that is no, by the way". I chuckle at the boyish behaviour that has come out, lifting his mood from the earlier conversation weighing heavy on him all day.

It seems like that weight has been lifted off his shoulders since he's told me that he hasn't always wanted to do this and just did it to please his dad, and I find it sad that he didn't pursue his dreams in favour of pleasing a parent. Something I'm now glad I never did and followed my own dreams.

"I'm really glad we came here tonight. I think we both needed this". He nods to me, picking at the last of the fries in front of him. "I'm glad too. I haven't told anyone else I'm thinking of setting something up on my own yet, even the guys don't know, and I tell them everything. I just need to figure out whether it's the right choice or not. It's been playing on my mind for the last few weeks, and I think this weekend has just made it clearer that I need to do what I want".

I hum in agreement, taking a sip from my drink before I delve deeper into this conversation. "You and I are a lot more alike than I first thought. I could say that worries me a little, but on the other hand I'm also kind of glad for it".

Luca leans forward in his seat, a curious look on his face, the remnants of his food now forgotten. "Oh yeah, how so?" I suck in a breath, not sure why I'm suddenly compelled to dive into my childhood trauma from my mother.

"Well, my mom always disapproved of my dream to become a baker. She had this idea of what I should be, and it definitely wasn't working in a bakery. She wanted me to follow a higher-end path, you know, something she could brag about to her friends".

Luca's eyes soften with understanding as he listens. "That must have been tough", he says quietly. "It was", I admit, my voice tinged with the remnants of old pain. "It felt like no matter what I did, it wasn't good enough for her, hell it still isn't good enough now. I remember sneaking out early in the mornings to work at the bakery down the road just so I could get some practice in. It was the only place I felt truly happy and free. But at home, there was always this tension, this constant feeling of not measuring up".

I pause, gathering my thoughts before continuing. "Her disapproval really affected me. It made me doubt myself, my choices, and my worth. I spent years trying to please her, trying to be what she wanted, but it just made me miserable. Eventually, I realised that I had to live for myself, not for her. I had to pursue my passion, even if it meant disappointing her. So, I went away to college and did my culinary degree to prove to myself more than anyone that I could do it".

Luca nods, his expression contemplative. "Did your dad never say anything to her about it? I know the two of you are close". I shrug, "He tried, but she was just set in her ways about everything. He actually told me the other week that he's finally leaving her after all these years. When he told me, I felt happier, for him and myself, that she won't be a permanent fixture in my life anymore".

I pause, suddenly feeling bad for talking crap about my mom when his isn't even here, "Do you think that makes me a bad person, for not wanting her in my life?"

A small smile tugs at his lips. "It sounds like you made the right choice. You shouldn't have to put up with a parent who treats you like that. My dad was no angel, but he did what he thought was right for me, knowing I didn't have my mom. And well, if just what I have tasted is anything to go off, then I think the world would be missing out on your talent. And brownies”.

A small smile tugs at my lips. “Thanks, Luca. It wasn't easy, but it was worth it. Despite her disapproval, following my dreams taught me a lot about resilience and self-worth. It made me stronger and more determined to succeed on my own terms. And now, whenever I create something new in the bakery, I feel this incredible sense of accomplishment and joy. That's something no one's opinion can take away from me”.

Luca reaches across the table, taking my hand in his. “I'm really proud of you, Rose. It takes a lot of courage to follow your dreams, especially when the people you care about the most don't support them.” A shiver runs down my spine. The sincerity in his voice and the joy I get from him saying my name every so often gives me a glimpse of how genuine he is.

I squeeze his hand, “And I hope you find that same courage to follow your own path, no matter what anyone else thinks. You deserve to be happy and fulfilled, just like everyone else”.

He smiles, a determined glint in his eye. “You're right. I think it's time I start making decisions for myself, too. But I think that’s enough deep talk for this evening. Let’s go home”. It’s three simple words, but it tugs at my heart all the same. I feel like I’m slipping down a dangerous path by falling for Luca, but my head and heart are in a standoff, neither wanting to listen to the other.

He stands and drops some bills on the table, taking my hand in his and pulling me out of the booth as he walks us towards the exit. I wrap my hand around his upper arm, leaning into him as we make the walk to his truck, opening the door for me and allowing me to climb in before he closes it again.

I'm on pins the entire drive home, hyper-aware of every little movement he makes. It's like my body now reacts every time he does or says something, lighting a fire inside me that I swear wasn't there before.

As we drive in comfortable silence, I can't help but replay the evening in my mind. The way he opened up to me about wanting to leave the company, I was sure he was only saying it now that all this had come out about his dad, but he stood firm in his resolve that it was in his mind before all this.

I feel like a weight has been lifted off me too, from telling him about my mother's own disapproval of me, thinking that us having this thing in common was a good thing, I'm not sure how any form of childhood trauma is a good thing to bond over, but the fact we are both coming out the other side of our parents less than ethical ways of trying to raise us, held my hopes up that things could work out for the better.

I know I still have my dad, and I do feel bad that he doesn't really have anyone to rely on, and him saying what he did about my own mother and how I pushed through her barriers, was a validation I hadn't realized I needed, a confirmation that my decision to pursue my own happiness wasn't selfish but necessary, and the way he related his own struggles with his father, made me feel less alone and more understood.

I glance at Luca, his profile illuminated by the soft glow of the dashboard lights. He looks lighter than he has in the past week. Waiting for the details on Ezra must have been tearing him apart inside and then having kept what he knew to himself until tonight, I'm surprised he is as calm as he is.

His eyes flit to the side, catching me examining him, and I'm suddenly embarrassed about being caught in the act. Instead of teasing me for gawping at him, he takes my hand in his, lifting it to his mouth and pressing a tender kiss to my knuckles. "Thank you for today. I'm glad you were here with me". I smile over to him, resting my head on the headrest as he keeps his eyes firmly back on the road, my hand still in his. I don't try to pull away, and I'm beginning to wonder what the point was in fighting this between us.

"I'll be here for you whenever you need me, Luca". His eyes move from the road, meeting mine briefly. He doesn't say anything else but squeezes my hand in acknowledgement.

We arrive home a short while later, and whilst my legs don't want to carry me into the house, I know I need a good night's sleep. I head straight to the stairs when we come in, closely followed by Luca, and as I approach my bedroom door, my fingers barely graze the handle when I'm swept off my feet, literally.

I squeal as Luca pulls me into his arms, walking us straight into his room and dumping me back on the bed. Deja vu hits me, bringing me back to the first night I slept in this room.

A satisfied grin is plastered across Luca's face as he looks appreciatively down at me. His hands slide across the cotton bedding as he bends his body, meeting my gaze head-on. Our noses brush as his velvet voice hits my right in the core, sending a flood of warmth there.

"Right where you belong. I'm moving all your things in here, you're not escaping me again." I giggle at him, raising my brow in defiance, but knowing full well I don't want to argue against him for once. "Is that right?" He nods slowly, brushing his lips against mine, "Yep. And you better believe I'm going to make sure it stays that way for as long as I can".

I don't know what to make of his admission, but I don't want to question it as I press my lips to his, drawing a moan from him. His body presses into mine as I wrap my arms around his neck, tugging him closer to me to deepen the kiss.

Our clothes disappear, item by item, until we are tangled deep in the covers, exploring each other's bodies, touching and feeling, getting to know each other's likes and what feels good. The caress of his calloused hands on my skin does something to me, drawing me to him with each sweep of my body, and I'm lost in the feel of him, vaguely hearing the tearing of foil before he fills me to the brim and sucks the air from my lungs.

I drown in him as he lazily pushes in and out of me, teetering on the edge each time. I'm not sure I've ever felt so connected to someone on another level than just fucking, because this isn't that.

This is something else entirely. I don't want to say making love, because I'm still not sure if I do love him or if it is, in fact, just the situation we find ourselves in. I push those thoughts to the side, bringing myself back to this incredible man who seems to want to do just about anything for me.

A moan tears from my throat as he plunges deeper inside of me, making me impossibly fuller from him. "I could stay inside you forever, the sweetness of heaven if I could call it a place". His words are quickly swallowed by the deep and sensual kiss he presses to my lips, pulling me closer and closer until we both fall together, our orgasms hitting at the same time.

I already feel my eyes closing as Luca takes care of the condom, sleep beckons, pulling me closer as he slips back into bed. Strong arms wrap around me, cradling and drawing me deeper into his soothing embrace. "Sleep now, my sweet Rose", Luca murmurs, pressing a gentle kiss to my forehead. He holds me tighter, and I drift into the peaceful depths of darkness.

26

Luca

My feet pound against the concrete as I push through a gruelling ten-mile run. Sweat drips down my face, neck and back, and my clothes cling to me from the amount I've worked out today.

None of it has helped the headache I have had since yesterday evening. I thought confronting my dad would help me figure things out, but instead, my head is mashed up even more. The only saving grace is Rose, who I left sound asleep in my bed this morning when I snuck out at the crack of dawn to clear my head.

She's honestly been a breath of fresh air for me and surprised me by telling me about how hard it's been for her with her mom. They clearly don't get along, and I'm unsure if I'd ever want to meet the woman. She sounds worse than my dad, and that's saying something. Rose told me her dad would be moving back to town soon after putting his house up for sale amid the divorce he's going through with her mom.

As I have yet to meet him, and he still thinks we are engaged for real, I need to put my best foot forward, knowing that if I leave my dad's company, Rose might very well think that I don't want her for good. I need to make that Fake engagement a real one, but I also don't want to scare her off either.

My inner turmoil slows as I approach my house, slowing to a jog as I round the corner on my street. The anticipation of waking Rose up for another round of glorious sex this morning gives me the last boost I need to shift my feet and get home quicker.

As I crack the door open, I hear her music coming from the kitchen, and know she's beaten me by getting up already. I stroll into the kitchen, attempting to catch my breath, but it's taken straight from me again when I catch sight of her in one of my T-shirts, her auburn hair piled on top of her head with curls hanging down around her face and neck.

She's mixing something in a bowl, singing away like she does every time she's in this kitchen. I prop myself against the wall, watching her for a moment before she realises I'm in the room, cocking her head to the side before beaming at me.

"Luca! Just in time, I'm making pancakes, come sit down, or do you want a shower first?" I round the counter to get to her, wrapping my arms around her middle and resting my chin on her shoulder as she continues stirring the mix. "I'll get a shower afterwards. How long have you been up?" She leans into my embrace whilst still managing to keep working as I press my lips to her cheek. "Mm, about an hour ago, did you have a good run?"

The simple conversation between us fills me with something I feel like I've been missing for a long time, something that seems so mundane as having a conversation like this on a Sunday morning makes me realise how much of my life I spent wasted on countless one-night stands, instead of just enjoying the simple things in life. Although, no one seems to have made me want to settle down before. Not Like Rose does. Call me soft, but I don't care. I'd take these mornings over nights out or drunken one-night stands, any day.

Rose wiggles her ass against me as she moves, leaning over the counter to grab something from the other side. I use the opportunity to slide my hand under her shirt, feeling the soft lace of her shorts, as I slide my hand around her front. She gasps as I press my fingers into her folds, pushing the fabric inside her and creating friction. "Luca", she breathes my name. It's barely above a whisper, but it urges me on more as I feel myself harden behind her.

I push the mixture aside, and if she finds it annoying that I've interrupted her cooking session, she doesn't say anything as I bring my other hand up, brushing it along her neck and turning her head towards me just enough that our lips almost touch and our breath mingles. "Lie down, Red", I rasp. Her lips open as if to protest, but I raise a brow at her, squeezing her delicate neck just enough that I feel the pulse in her throat.

"Lie down, so I can fuck you in our kitchen". Her throat bobs, but she nods as her lips tip up into a mischievous smile. Lowering herself onto the oak countertop, she comes up on the tips of her toes.

I push the fabric of my shirt up and over her head, twisting it when it reaches her arms and locking them in place. “Do you think you can do as you're told for once and keep your hands there, Red?” She pulls her lip between her teeth and nods to me. Her face rests on the cool counter, giving me a side view of her beautiful features.

I stand back and dig my fingers into the sides of the panties, pulling them down her legs and tapping her right leg and then her left to step out of them. I lean over her, brushing my hands up the side of her body and back down, watching the goosebumps that appear all over her creamy skin and squeezing when I reach her hips.

“Spread those pretty thighs for me, sweetheart”. Her breath hitches, but she does as I say without question, allowing me access to her. I drop to my knees, my height giving me the advantage of being head height to her perfect pussy when I’m in this position.

I spread her so that she’s open to me and suck on the sensitive bundles of nerves there, causing Rose to jolt and yelp in surprise, but as I keep sucking and licking the sensitive flesh, her cries turn into moans, urging me on further. I can’t get enough of this woman, and I’m not even mad about it. I pull an orgasm from her quickly, feeling her tense up under my hands and shudder as her release takes over.

A satisfied smile takes over my face as I lick my lips, standing behind her again and peppering kisses along her spine. She’s practically melted against the countertop as I make quick work of removing my own shorts, and without a thought, I ram myself into her.

She gasps at the sudden intrusion, and at the same time, a moan leaves my throat. *Fuck* she feels so good. I continue moving at a fast and hard pace, the sound of our flesh slamming together echoing through the kitchen as Rose moans and writhes under me. Whimpers and moaning from her give me the encouragement to continue as I bring us both to the edge. Spilling myself as I reach my climax.

It's only then I realise why she felt so good, why I didn't even think as I was inside of her and didn't want to pull out. *The condom.* I didn't even think about using one, and now I'm frozen in the spot. Too scared to move for fear of what might happen when I do.

The consequences of not being careful nearly cost me once, and I'm not sure if I'm ready to admit that I've done it again in the short space of a few days. "Fuck", I say again, but out loud as I pull out, my seed spilling out of her as I do. But *shit,* if it isn't a turn-on watching it as it slides back out of her.

The idiot in me wants to reach down and push it back inside to see if she did end up pregnant with my kid. Would that be such a bad thing? I shake my head. *No,* not right now. I have a million other things to worry about, and Rose getting pregnant should not be one of them.

Rose notices my reaction, pulling herself to stand, I'm so close to her that my semi-hard-on rubs against her ass as she does, and I let out a groan, pressing my head into her shoulder. We've only just gone, but I feel myself getting hard again as my dick rests between her legs. She makes me insatiable and apparently turns my brain off too, because this is not the first time I've fucked up when it comes to her.

My arms wrap around her middle, and she rests her hands on mine, where they are clasped in front of her. "What's wrong?" She asks, tipping her head back as she leans into me. "I forgot a condom".

The words feel bitter leaving my mouth. I shouldn't feel like I do when it comes to using them, but past experiences panic me every time. She shrugs, completely unaffected by my panic and twists herself around so she's resting her back against the counter. Her hands lock around my neck as she stares up at me. Those innocent hazel eyes would make me say yes to anything she asked of me.

She purses her lips as her eyes bounce between mine. "Luca, I'm clean. I assume you're clean, and I'd like to assume you held true to your promise and aren't currently sleeping with anyone else. I'm on top of my contraception, and I really think you need to stop panicking. We're both adults and if you're panicking that much, I'll go get plan B".

I blow out a sigh, resting my forehead against hers. "I'm sorry, I need to get a grip of myself. It's just…" "I know". She cuts me off, not needing me to explain myself again. "You don't need to worry. I'm not here to trap you with a kid, Luca. We both have things going on in our lives, and well, I don't really know what we are right now, whatever this thing is. It needs to be worked out before we ever even consider bringing a child into this very confusing situation".

She takes a breath before continuing. "Use the condoms or don't. I'm not going anywhere right now, and if you decide to change your mind and we stop this, just tell me. I'm trying to make your life easier, not more difficult, but we can do whatever you want".

I groan into her. God, why does she always have to talk so much sense? "I'm not letting you go, Rose. I don't think I can now that I've been inside you and felt how good you feel without a barrier between us. I don't even think I want to go back to using them. Just promise me, if you need to change anything or stop taking your contraception, you tell me first".

Fuck what am I even saying? I've never had to worry about this before, and here I am, double-guessing her before she's even said anything. "Honestly, Luca, you could fuck me however you like, so long as you keep doing it, I don't care what you use". I could fuck this woman into an oblivion and not use any protection if she kept talking to me the way she is.

I press my forehead to hers, pulling her tighter against me, "You think I want to use them anymore after I've felt what you feel like, fuck no. You just sent me to pussy heaven. I don't think I could go back to using them even if I wanted to".

She grips my chin, pulling my gaze to her, a small smirk touching her lips, and fuck if it doesn't turn me on, her taking a little control over me. "Do you trust me?" *Do I?* It's not even a question as I bob my head at her. "With my whole heart Red". She grins up at me, her hazel eyes shining with something I can't quite put my finger on, but I would do anything for her.

"Good, then you have nothing to worry about, fuck me however you like; just don't fuck me over, and we're good, okay?" She grins at me, tapping my cheek before pressing her supple lips to mine. I tighten my grip on her, pulling her closer to me and wanting to take her again. *Fuck*, I'm head over heels in love with her, and she's asking me shit like that. Does she really think I don't trust her actions? I guess my past behaviour doesn't bode well for me right now.

I push my shitty thoughts aside as I drag my hands down her body and haul her up into my arms. "The only thing I need to worry about is the stress that smart mouth causes me most days". She smirks at me as I carry her back to bed for a couple of hours, breakfast long forgotten.

.....

I stare down at the text message on my phone, clicking it open for what must be the tenth time in the last two minutes as I sit in Bread & Coffee, waiting to meet Ezra. I texted him this morning telling him I knew about the situation and asked to meet up, and he responded almost instantly, telling me he was free today.

I arrived early, wanting to get a good table with some privacy from prying ears from the local town gossip, and maybe I was too eager, but as I made a start on my second coffee, a man walks through the door, a similar height to mine, wearing a jumper, jeans and boots. And yep, the girls were right.

We oddly look similar. I can easily pick out his features, matching them to my own or my dad's. Our hair colour and skin tone are almost identical, but where my hair is straight, his has a slight wave to it and is a touch lighter.

He grins at me as he weaves through the tables, making his way over to the back of the crowded café and pulling his hand out to shake mine when he reaches me. "You must be Luca". I shake it, grinning back at him. I didn't expect him to be this friendly on our first meet, but I'll take it.

We take our seats, and I call over to one of the girls to make him a coffee. Before Rose opened her place, I was always here for my morning coffee, but luckily, it's not close enough to her bakery that it would cause a problem, and since her place is still under construction, here was the next best option for our meeting.

Now that we are up close, I scan his features. His chocolate eyes match mine, and our face shapes are almost identical. He has a strong jawline and sharp eyes. My dad clearly has strong genes because we are almost clones of him. One thing I'm wishing wasn't true right now after everything he's done.

I clear my throat, "So, Rose said you came to the house looking for me. You already know I now know we share a father. What else did you want to know?" He suddenly looks nervous, and I hope to God he hasn't searched for me to ask for money. The waitress comes over and places his coffee down before retreating back to the counter and he wraps his hands around the mug before blowing out a long breath.

"I don't even know where to start. My mom died a couple of years ago, and before she did, she told me about my dad and you. I couldn't face looking for you before then, but I found out she had a paternity test done when I was born, so it was easy to find who you were, and as time passed, I wanted to find out who the rest of my family were.

"She didn't tell me much other than she got pregnant with a married man and had to leave. She spared me the details but said he tried to see me when I was younger, and she felt bad for keeping me from him but didn't want to break up a family, and then he stopped trying. I guess I wanted to find out why that happened, and since you are my only sibling, it would have been nice to get to know you".

I relax as he tells me what he knows, his story matching up with my dad's. At least his mom didn't lie to him, but now I have to fill in the gaps for him. I sigh, sitting up a little straighter in my seat as I delve into it, "From what I've been told, my mom was ill when my… Um, our dad had an affair with your mom, and he tried to keep seeing you, but then my mom got worse, and he focused on her instead of trying to fight to see you".

I wince as I say the words. It's not nice having to repeat them to him, but I feel like he should know everything. Maybe he should hear it from my dad, but I still don't know if he cares enough to have a relationship with him now.

"I don't know much else, so I'm sorry I can't help more, my dad is still here in town. If you do decide you want to meet him, I can give you his number, and you can contact him. We, um, we aren't really speaking right now after I found out about you". Ezra nods, taking in my words as he stares down at his coffee.

"I guess that's to be expected. I just turned up on your doorstep, and I don't know what I thought would happen, but I'm glad that we are finally doing this. I'm actually staying locally at the minute, I've taken a job at a local ranch as their vet and was hoping if this went well, meeting you, that maybe I might stick around. I have no family now my mom has gone, so technically, you are the only relative I have, apart from an aunt in Montana, but I haven't seen her in years".

I frown, feeling awful that he has no one, and I still have my dad, even though I seriously dislike him right now. My grandparents passed away a couple of years ago, and my mom had no other family, so he's right, we only really have each other.

"Yeah, it's actually my friend's place you work at. Grace went on about how much we looked alike, but I didn't put two and two together until Rose said the same thing last week".

He raises his head, grinning at me, "Yeah, I guess we look a lot alike. If it's okay with you, I'd really like to be a part of your life in whichever capacity you'll allow, but I would like to get to know you better. And you're getting married, right?" I stifle the groan that tries to leave me, knowing I have to lie to him, and I've only just met him. "Uh, yeah. Not been engaged long, but she's a keeper". It's only a partial lie, because I'm keeping Rose, even if it means I need to tie her to me.

Ezra's eyes light up with genuine interest. "That's great to hear. Maybe I could meet her properly sometime. I mean, if you're comfortable with that". I nod, trying to push away the knot of anxiety forming in my stomach at someone coming into our little bubble.

"Yeah, that sounds like a good idea. I'm sure she'd love to meet you properly too". We both fall silent for a moment, sipping our coffees and lost in thought. The café buzzes around us, but it feels like we're in our own little world, navigating our way through this newfound connection.

"I have to admit", Ezra says, breaking the silence, "I was really nervous about meeting you. I didn't know what to expect, but this has been... better than I could have hoped". I smile, feeling a warmth spread through me and excitement at knowing I have a sibling. “Me too. It's strange, but in a good way. I'm glad we're doing this and that we have finally met. I just wish so many years hadn’t passed before we did”.

Ezra leans back in his chair, relaxing a little more. “So, tell me more about yourself. You’re an architect. I think I read that right when I looked you up?” I clear my throat, suddenly nervous again. “Yeah, I work for my, um, our dad’s company, but I’ve been thinking about setting up by myself recently”, I say, feeling a little self-conscious.

“I work mostly from home, but we have an office in downtown Knoxville, too. It's nothing too exciting”. I don’t know what he’s seen or heard of the business, but I try to downplay it as much as I can for reasons I’m not even sure of myself right now.

He gives me a quick nod, seemingly impressed, and I divert the question to him, not wanting to talk too much about my dad and the business. “And what about you? You mentioned you're a vet?”

“Yeah,” he nods. “It's something I've always wanted to do. I love working with animals, mostly horses, and the ranch job seemed like the perfect opportunity”. We continue chatting and sharing stories about our lives and our interests. The initial awkwardness fades away, replaced by some sort of friendship that’s already forming between the pair of us. Despite the circumstances that brought us together, hope floods me at the thought of someone who I might be able to one day lean on more than I do my friends.

As we finish our coffees, I glance at my watch and realize how much time has passed. “I should probably get going”, I say reluctantly. I didn’t expect us to get along so well on the first meeting, but he seems to be all right from the couple of hours I’ve spent with him, “But I hope we can do this again soon”. He agrees, a hopeful look in his eyes. “Definitely. I'd like that a lot”. We stand up, and I offer him a genuine smile. “Welcome to the family, Ezra”. “Thanks, Luca”, he replies, returning the smile. “I'll see you soon”.

We part ways, and as I walk out of the café, I can't help but feel a sense of hope. Maybe, just maybe, this unexpected turn of events will lead to something good.

27

Rose

I blow a piece of hair out of my face that keeps falling every time I dip my head in the downward dog position, as a golden retriever puppy licks at my ear.

I giggle from the tickle of it, as I try to move the pup out of the way. Grace and Hallie are on either side of me, moving with more poise than I seem to have today as we finish up the rooftop puppy yoga in town.

The sun has finally started to make an appearance as spring arrives. Shining brightly above us, and it keeps us warm despite not yet reaching scorching temperatures as twelve puppies run around causing havoc in the best possible way. Grace insisted on us coming here, since Jaxx has been trying to convince her that the pair of them should get a dog in the coming months.

The instructor wraps up the session, leaving the three of us sitting cross-legged on our mats as the pups climb over us, and Grace grabs hold of a girl, giving her snuggles and love. Everyone else clears up their things around us, cooing at the dogs as they approach everyone. I lean back on my hands, using them to prop me up as I soak in the rays from the morning sky whilst one of the pups rests itself in my lap. I'm not usually into this outdoors kind of thing, nor something that includes this many animals, but Grace convinced us it was a good idea.

She's in heaven, cuddling the pup, and I could see her getting one. "How much more convincing does Jaxx need to do before you buy one, then?" She side-eyes me, a small grin tugging at her lips, "I actually think I'm going to let him get one in a couple of weeks. He swore that he would be looking after it, and if I have to I told him I'm giving him to my brother". I chuckle at her, she's been insistent that she wasn't getting one, and now the cracks in her façade are starting to show.

We eventually pull ourselves from the dogs and make our way to the local brunch spot for some much-needed mimosas and food. The place is busy, but since Hallie knows the owner, we snag a table they have kept for us and make our way over to it.

Hallie beams at the waiter her from her spot at the table as we make our drinks order, her blonde ponytail swishing as she looks between the two of us as we make our choices, and I push the conversation along asking her about her older brother and his son, who she currently lives with as his nanny while she waits for the house to be done.

"How's that going, living with him?" I ask, wondering more when the house will be done. She sighs at me, "He gets on my nerves, but I love Oliver, and spending time with him makes it worth it. He's starting at a daycare in a month or so though, so I need to start looking for new jobs". I nod to her, wondering if she will stay over that side or back around near us. "On a better note, though, the house will be ready next week, so you can move back in". She grins at me, and I pale slightly, unsure what to say. "I um.. yeah".

Grace raises her brow at me, knowing full well what I'm thinking. She taps her finger on the edge of her chin whilst she pretends to think, "You know, Hallie, I don't think Rose is going to be moving back in with you just yet. Something tells me she's going to be staying there a little while longer".

I scowl at her, unable to hide my emotions on my face like some people can. "We still have to pretend to be engaged, so it would look really weird if I suddenly moved out when we're supposed to be in love". "Mm-hmm", she nods, looking completely unconvinced, "You keep telling yourself that".

It's been a week since Luca confronted his dad and met his brother, and right now, life is all up in the air. He still isn't sure what he wants to do about his job, although he's started working on different things to change to in case he changes his mind, and I'm still waiting for the bakery to be finished. We've danced around all the difficult conversations we need to have this past week, and now I have the decision to make as to whether I'm staying with Luca or returning home.

I bite my lip as I regard the pair of them. Hallie doesn't miss a trick though as she narrows her gaze on me, "You've slept with him, haven't you".

The accusation in her tone isn't a harsh one, more of an observation, because I can't seem to hide shit from either of them. I roll my eyes, feigning ignorance as I bury my head in my menu. Hallie makes me jump as she claps her hands, squeaking her excitement a little too loudly "Oh my friggin God! You have, haven't you. Was he good?" She wiggles her brows at me, and Gace bursts out laughing at her as she taps excitedly on my arms.

I roll my eyes, batting her away, she's so loud I'm surprised half of the cafe hasn't heard her. "Fucks sake Hallie, yes, all right". Her hands fold over her chest. "And now you're dicked down for life. I see it. You also haven't made any of your usual comments about him being an asshole recently".

I go to protest but stop myself because she's right. I haven't. I actually like him too much to do that. "We are obviously spending a lot of time together, and things just… happened". I don't want to delve into details with the pair of them, but Hallie doesn't miss a beat as she continues her line of questioning, "Are you in love with him?" I blink back at her. I'm not even sure of the answer myself. "I… I don't know, I don't think so, but I do like him more than I first thought, and he seems pretty adamant about spending time with me. He's home most of the time at the minute, and we have dinner together almost every night. We spend a lot of time together". I shrug as I finish, wanting them to lay off it, but they don't.

"I told you he liked you, and now you're living together, engaged and are clearly falling in love with him". Grace pipes up from beside Hallie. I over at her, giving her my best death stare. "We aren't even engaged for real". She waves me off, not caring about what I have to say, "Pfft, that's just an excuse you're using to run away from your feelings like you always do, might I add. You did it with the last three guys you were seeing, and now you're doing it with Luca, who is smitten with you. Before he even convinced you to *marry him*, he tried to get you on a date. This seals the deal for me".

Are they right? Do I want to be with him for real? He said he's not going anywhere, but I've heard that in the past, and they have bolted as soon as anything came near to serious. So sue me for wanting to keep my heart closed off for just a little while longer. "I don't know, I'm… I'm scared. What if he hurts me? He has such a reputation, and I only went along with this to help him out. I told myself I wouldn't go anywhere near him, and now half the time, I don't know what's real and what isn't".

Hallie grins at me, "It's all real. All. Of. It. You just have to open your heart to it and let him woo you". I shake my head at her, a ghost of a smile on my lips. "You want him to woo me? What is this, the 1950s?" She waves me off, "You know exactly what I mean. Just let him take care of you, and wine and dine you, and fuck you like you'll never see each other again".

She wiggles her brows again and I roll my eyes at her in return. Although she is right. Maybe I can lower my guard enough to let him in a bit and open myself up to potential trauma at the same time, but if I don't, I'll never know.

I hear someone clearing their throat from behind me and freeze. Turning my head a finding my mother of all people standing a little too close to our table. *Shit* did she hear our conversation.

I turn slowly, trying to school my features as I face the woman who has the uncanny ability to make my life more complicated than it already is. Her perfectly coiffed hair and designer sunglasses do nothing to soften the sharpness of her gaze as she examines me from head to toe.

"Rose, darling, it's been too long", she declares with an exaggerated air of affection that makes my stomach churn. I glance back at the girls briefly, Hallie and Grace exchange knowing looks, already bracing themselves for whatever drama is about to unfold. "Mother", I reply, trying to keep my voice steady, "I didn't expect to see you here".

"Well, you know how it is", she waves a manicured hand dismissively, "I was just grabbing some lunch with the ladies and spotted you, so I thought I'd come over and see how my favourite daughter is doing". I resist the urge to roll my eyes at her theatrics. "I'm your only daughter, mom. Anyway, what brings you to town?"

"Oh, just some errands and a spot of lunch", she says vaguely, her eyes narrowing slightly as she glances at Hallie and Grace. "And who are these lovely friends of yours?" I huff at her, "You know who they are, I literally grew up with them". She gives the girls a tight smile as I re-introduce them quickly, hoping to steer the conversation away from anything that might trigger one of her infamous tirades. But it's too late, she's already zeroing in on Hallie. "Ah, yes, Hallie, the nanny". she says, her tone filled with condescension. "How's the job search going, dear? I heard you left your father's place after the fire, terrible that, isn't it?".

To her credit, Hallie smiles sweetly and replies, "It's going well, thank you. And who knows, maybe I'll find something even better than before". My mother's smile is as thin as ice. "I'm sure you will". She turns her attention back to me, her expression softening just a fraction. "Rose, darling, I heard about your *engagement* too, from your father no less". Crap, yeah, she definitely heard us. She stares down at the ring that glistens on my finger, and I get my hackles up and ready to defend myself.

I try to keep my cool, though, as I shrug, "Yeah, we kept it quiet, I didn't need everyone knowing my business". She knows I mean her when I say it, but I smile as sweetly as possible. "I heard about your *little* bakery too. I suppose it's better than what you did before that".

Her words cut deeper than I want them to, the condescending tone spewing from her words, but she brushes over the engagement, and I relax a little, hoping she didn't actually care. She's always been like this, and I don't know why I thought she might ever change. "Yeah, it's great. It's having some work at the moment, but I'll have it back open in a couple of weeks", I don't want to talk to her about something of mine that I've done by myself, without her. She doesn't get to enjoy my pride with me, so I change the subject to her.

"Dad told me you two are getting a divorce". Her eyes widen in surprise for a moment, but she quickly recovers. "Oh, your father doesn't know what he's talking about. I'll be back home soon, it's just a small spat, is all". I barely contain the laugh that threatens to escape, coughing to cover it, "I don't think he thinks that, but honestly, I'm really glad you aren't together anymore. You two weren't great for each other for a long time, so this way you can both move on. Won't that be nice". My words drip with sarcasm, and she takes the hint that I don't want to talk anymore as her eyes narrow in on me, showing her true colours before she rights herself, "Right, well I better be going. I'll speak to you soon, Rose".

"You won't", I mutter more to myself than her, but she's too far away to hear me as she swiftly makes her exit out of the door and into the car waiting across the road. Probably her new man, but I could actually care less right now. I turn in my seat, and the girls give me a sympathetic smile, "Don't look at me like that. I'm fine".

I'm not. But I'm pretty good at holding myself together these days. Hallie smiles sweetly at me. "Sweetie, you don't have to hold it together. It's just us, we don't judge you". "Only on your taste in men", Grace butts in. I bark a laugh at her, her smile turning more serious, "But seriously, Rose. We love you, and she is poison. We've all known this for a long time now. We don't want you to feel like you can't be sad around us, hell we'll all cry together if you want".

I smile over at the pair of them. I love the hell out of these girls, they have always been there for me, no matter what. I sigh, leaning further into my seat.

"I know, I just hate her". I say, pointing my finger at the pair of them. "And that's saying a lot because I don't use that word lightly. I just wish she was a better parent, or person. But I guess you can't win with everything". I shrug grabbing the menu again as I try to avoid the topic, attempting to figure out what to eat.

"I guess not," Hallie says softly, reaching out to touch my hand. "But we're here for you, always". The waiter brings our drinks, and I give Hallie a grateful smile, the weight of my mother's presence slowly lifting. "Thanks, guys. Now, let's forget about her and enjoy our brunch, shall we?"

Grace grins, lifting her glass, "To friends who are family". We clink our glasses together, laughter bubbling up as we finally turn our attention to better subjects. I feel like I'm waiting for the other shoe to drop, things are just too good. But for now, the world feels right again because I have these two in my life.

28

Rose

The other shoe dropped.

I feel like I'm drowning in my own breath as I listen to a recording of me talking to the girls the other day, every single word that leaves my mouth clear as day, as I reiterate the fact Luca and my relationship isn't real.

It's attached to an email from my mother, outlining all of the points I made of us not being together, and a line underneath it.

Call this number. We need to talk.

My pulse races as I try to calm my nerves. But I silently make my way into my old bedroom and sneak into the bathroom there, closing the door and pressing call. I need to know what she wants so that I can put this behind me. The last thing I want is for this to blow up in our faces, and it's going to be all my fault by the looks of it. I don't even know how she got hold of this recording, I didn't think she was behind me for that long to hear all of this, but we were hidden in a booth, and she could have caught it all without being seen.

I hold my breath as I wait for her to pick up, and when she does, I want the ground to swallow me up from how sickly sweet she speaks down the phone.

"Rose, my darling. I see you got my email". I hear the snarky tone her voice holds and suck in all the air I can as I reply. "Let's cut to the chase, Mom. What do you want?"

She chuckles down the phone like this isn't some trap for me, but I need to go along with it until I can figure out what her agenda is. "Now, that's no way to speak to me, is it. You wouldn't want that recording to fall into the wrong hands, would you? Imagine what it would do to Luca's image if that happened".

My pulse quickens as she speaks, and I scramble to put my phone on record to catch the conversation, praying that it doesn't alert her to me doing it. "I don't know what you think sending that to anyone will do. It could be forged for all I know". She clicks her tongue down the phone at me, and the urge to reach through it and strangle her comes to the surface. I like to think I'm not an angry or violent person, but she brings it out in me.

"If you want to keep this out of the papers, then I suggest you get that lovely man of yours to pay up before it hits the press. Your father left me with nothing, and I need to start my life fresh, away from here. Get Luca to give you a million and have it sent to me, and I can make this all go away".

I pale at her words, but it's quickly replaced with anger as I bark out a laugh at her delusions. "You seriously think Luca won't question why I need a million dollars from him. Are you really that delusional? Dad left you for good reason, and I can really see why now". I spit the words out, the anger in my voice coming to the surface as I drag this phone call out to her. I need to tell Luca, and quickly, but I don't want to cause an argument over it. The last thing I need is him thinking that I'm using him for his money.

"Unless you want this reaching the papers, I suggest you do what I tell you". I roll my eyes at my phone that's now resting on loudspeaker on the vanity, "I'm not giving you any money, go and ask someone who cares".

Her façade slips when she realises she isn't getting what she thought she might from me. "Listen to me, you little bitch. Go to Luca and tell him you need the money, or I will release this to the papers and make your lives a living hell". I feel sick. I can't listen to her anymore. "Goodbye, Mother". I hang up and spin on my heel, throwing up in the toilet behind me. How the fuck am I going to keep this from getting out. I need to talk to my dad, and quickly. He will forgive me at least when I tell him the truth.

I feel like I'm sitting against the unit in the small bathroom for a while, but in reality, it must only be a few moments because before I know it, Luca bursts into the room, a panicked look on his face. His wild eyes find mine and he instantly crouches to my side.

"Rose, what the fuck is going on, I can hear you retching from downstairs. Are you sick?" I screw my eyes shut, shaking my head almost violently as I'm pulled into strong arms, "Shh, it's okay, what happened?" His thumb swipes across my cheek, wiping away tears that seem to have appeared out of nowhere. I bury my face into his neck, not sure if I should tell him what's going on or if I should just seek help from my dad.

"I… I don't think I can tell you".

He stares down at me, concern written all over his face, "Why can't you tell me? does it concern us?" I nod to him, and his grip tightens on me, "Tell me, Rose. I'm trying to keep my cool right now, but I need you to tell me what's going on so I can fix it".

"I made a mistake. I'm sorry. I'm so sorry Luca". I sputter the words into his chest, scared to see his reaction. I feel myself being pulled up as Luca carries me over to the bed, gently putting me down on it as he settles on the bed with me.

Strong hands grip my face as I'm pulled to look at him, staring this beautiful man in the eyes and knowing I've potentially fucked everything up for him kills me, but all he shows me is warmth as he searches my face for the answers I don't have.

"Tell me what you've done so we can fix it". I didn't expect him to be as calm as he is being with me right now, and part of me worries that he's just holding everything in until he has all the information he needs. But I pull my shit together enough to look up to him and see the concern brimming in his eyes.

Luca is closer to the bathroom, so I motion in the direction of where my phone is, "Can you grab my phone from the bathroom, and I can show you". He nods, getting to his feet and retrieving my phone. I fumble with it, trying to get to the recording and press play.

I watch as his face drops, me telling the girls we aren't really together, that we've slept together, everything. I want to crawl in on myself when he looks down at the phone, not making eye contact with me. I know I've fucked up, but I don't know what else to do at this point.

"Luca, say something".

He doesn't at first. Instead, he gets to his feet and begins pacing the room. "Who took this recording?" I bite my lip, panic clawing up me, but I know I can't lie to him. "I think it was my mom. I didn't know she was in the restaurant when I was talking to the girls, and she must have been hiding in a booth behind me, recording everything. She did speak to me, but it was after I'd said what I did. I'm so sorry. I didn't mean for this to happen".

I start to well up again and shut my eyes, wanting this just to go away. Feeling the bed dip a few moments later, I crack them open and see Luca perched on the edge of the bed. He looks pissed, but his voice doesn't match his body language. "What does she want?"

I pull myself together enough to tell him everything else as the words spill from my mouth, "She wants money. My dad told her she wasn't getting anything from him when he left her because she cheated on him, and now she's trying to use this to get money to start a new life". Luca's jaw pulses as his hands flex in and out of a fist. "And how much did she want?"

"Um, she said she wanted a million dollars, or she was going to release the recording to the tabloids and ruin your name".

"Fuck". He pulls at his hair, shaking his head as his elbows rest on his knees. I don't know what else to say to him, so I sit quietly, pulling my legs into myself as I sit up against the headboard of the bed.

"I'm sorry", I say again, not really sure it means anything at this point. I should have kept my mouth shut and not said anything to him. His head finally turns in my direction, frustration clear in his face and body language.

After what feels like forever, he releases a breath, shaking his head again. "I'm not mad at you Rose, I'm mad at your fucking mother, trying to use you to get money out of me". I sit up a little taller in bed, feeling hopeful that he won't tell me to leave his house and his life.

Before I can say another word, he's on his feet, pulling his phone out and making a call. "Hey, yeah. No, I need a meeting with you and the legal team ASAP and keep my dad out of it. I don't want him to know what's going on. We need to meet somewhere else". Luca talks to whoever is on the other end of the phone for a short while before hanging up and looking over to where I'm perched, waiting on pins to see what he has to say.

"I need to go to this meeting with my lawyers. Can you hang tight whilst I get this sorted?"

I nod quickly, "Do you not need me to come with you?"

"No. Send me the recording and anything else you have. I'll be back later". His tone is sharp and no-nonsense, and before I even get a chance to say anything else, he's striding out of the room.

I roll my body over, burying my head in the pillow and let out a muffled scream. Tears stream down my face as the enormity of what I've done hits, and I just hope that Luca forgives me for potentially fucking everything up.

29

Luca

This is a fucking shit show.

I've listened to the recording of Rose talking to Grace and Hallie on repeat for the last forty-five minutes on the drive over to my lawyer's office to figure out how the hell I'm going to avoid this mess.

My PR team has been called in, all being told not to breathe a word of what goes on to my father. I might be wanting to leave the company, but I don't need this to make things any worse than they already are. The team are working around me as I attempt to stay focused in the glass meeting room, but I feel like my head is spinning.

Why did she have to say that to the girls? Why couldn't she just keep it to herself? I'm trying not to be pissed with her, but she just didn't think, and now I'm trying to sort this mess out. On top of being blackmailed, her mom is attempting to say she's going to release this to the press. We need to get on top of it and sort this out before it goes anywhere.

I'm thankful that I've got such a hands-on team to deal with everything at such short notice, and they are the best of the best. I pay them well enough for them to be, and right now, I just need this all to go away.

My head of the press team, Sam is quick to find out who Rose's mom has spoken to and tries to talk them down from posting anything. The last thing I want is to pay her off, and then it gets leaked anyway. "I think we may be able to find a way around this all, but you might have to tidy up a couple of stories and attend a few events to get them to lay off your back. Can you do that?" I glare at him, "Of course I can fucking do that. Just fix this mess, please".

I grab my phone and call up Jaxx who thankfully answers quickly, "Hey Luca, you alright?"

"Uh, no, not exactly. Listen, I need you to get hold of Harris again for me and see if he can come down to my lawyer's office. Rose's mom has a recording of her saying we aren't together, and she's trying to ruin my reputation if I don't give her money".

He's quiet for a minute, and the apprehension builds the longer I wait for him to respond. After a few moments, he finally answers, "Okay, I've sent over a quick message to Harris, we'll be down in the next couple of hours. Can you manage until then?" I let out a breath I didn't know I was holding, "Yeah, thank you. See you soon".

.....

Two days and a tonne of negotiating later, my team, Jaxx and Harris, work their magic and hunt down Rose's mom, forcing her to hand over her phone and any other copies of the recordings to the police, and she's been arrested for blackmail and extortion.

I'm impressed that they managed to work so quickly, but I feel like I haven't slept a wink since then. I've been stressing over this not going public, but more than that, I've been worried about what impact this might have on Rose. Yeah, she fucked up big time, talking so openly about it, but how was she to know the implications of her having a simple conversation with the girls. I've not seen or spoken to her since I stormed out of the house, and I feel pretty shitty that I've just left her to deal with her own guilt by herself. But I needed to fix everything before I saw her again.

It's late when I drag myself through the front door, knowing Rose probably went to bed a couple of hours before I got in. My feet feel heavy as I trudge up the stairs, wanting to just climb into bed and hold her, but I stop short when I get to my room, and my bed is untouched like it was when I left the house on Sunday.

I pull back, hoping she hasn't left, but see her old bedroom door cracked open slightly. When I stick my head in, the curtains are wide open, allowing the night sky to shine through the windows, and Rose is lying on the bed, fully clothed like she fell asleep as soon as she sat on the bed.

Her body is curled up tightly, and the sight guts me. I should have been here for her, or at least had her stay with me, or even someone check on her. But instead, I've left her in the dark without answering any of her questions.

I can't be away from her another night, so I climb onto the bed behind her, grabbing a blanket from the cupboard to pull over the two of us and pull her close to me, thankful that I have her, but in the back of my head, I know we need to have a conversation about what she wants, and soon.

30

Luca

My head is buried in paperwork from the moment I wake up until I go to sleep. I've barely seen Rose for the past week either and I know she thinks I'm avoiding her, but the truth is, I'm trying to figure out a plan that includes her in it. I don't want her to think I'm pushing anything, but I also don't want her to worry that I'm not doing enough to keep her.

I briefly filled her in the morning after I got back home, but she and I both had a shit tonne of work to catch up on, so we never ended up having the conversations that we needed to.

I've been working with a couple of different people, building a company that I can set up as my own but also something that could give me the time I need to be with her. The last thing I want is to start a company and completely neglect what I have at home.

My phone buzzes on my desk, which I've been practically glued to in my home office for the past week. I swipe to answer, keeping my eyes on the work as I put Jaxx on speaker. "Hey man, what's up?"

He chuckles down the phone. "What's up is Rose told the girls you've barely seen daylight for a week, and you need to get out. Tristan is having a barbeque at the ranch this afternoon, and it's going to be a nice evening, so bring your ass and your lovely lady over to see us, we miss you". I snort a laugh down the phone, "You sound like a pouty child, and I'm busy. I'll have to take a rain check, but I'll make sure Rose comes".

"Absolutely fucking not. If you aren't at this house by 3pm today, I will come and drag you over here myself. Put the paperwork down and come enjoy yourself. You need to blow off some steam, it's not healthy for you to be holed up in that office all the time. I get shit's going on, but you need to have a work-life balance".

I scoff at him. "That's the whole point of what I'm doing, so when I have the new company, I can do just that".

"Well, one afternoon off isn't going to be detrimental to that. Get your ass over here, you have two hours". He hangs up the phone, not allowing me to make any more excuses. I sigh, glancing at the time on my phone. Jesus, It's after one already.

We managed to avoid our relationship hitting any sort of media attention, and Rose's mom was slapped with a hefty load of jail time after we found out she had been trying to get money out of more than one person, but it still doesn't stop me from checking every news article in the whole south, every time they post something new.

I stand from my desk, stretching my legs out as I look out onto the lake. My office sits next to the kitchen at the back of the house, allowing me easy access to coffee and this spectacular view. That is the whole reason I bought this place to begin with. Rose is out in the garden, sitting on one of the deck chairs with a juice and her book in hand. Reminding me exactly why I'm doing all of this.

She doesn't know it yet, but I'm setting all of this up for our future if she wants to have me in her life that long. We still need to talk about what we will do about the fake engagement, and to be honest, I don't want her to ever take that ring off. I want to add a second band to it within the year. But I know I need to actually have these discussions with her first, rather than planning our marriage and 2.5 kids out in my head. And after what she said to the girls, I don't know if she wants to stay in this or not.

I wander into the garden, grabbing a bottle of water from the fridge on my way and joining her. I lean down, pressing a kiss to her head before sitting in the chair beside her.

She glances up at me as I take my seat before closing her book and placing it on the table to her side. "Hey, I didn't think I'd see you until later". I smile, shaking my head. "Yeah, I wasn't planning on stopping working until later, but Jaxx just called and invited us to Tristans for a barbeque. You good with that?"

A small part of me wants her to say she isn't interested in going, just so I can get back to work. But the excitement in her eyes and brisk nod of her head at seeing her friends again pushes that thought straight to the back of my head. I miss seeing her face light up and the smallest of things, like it is right now, and I instantly feel guilty for even wanting to get back to work and avoiding her any more than I have for the past week.

It's not that I would ever say no to her either way. But this is just the confirmation I needed that I do need to listen to my friend and put work aside, even for just a few hours, to enjoy time with my woman and our friends.

My woman, Jesus, who the fuck have I turned into. Wanting to spend time with just one person and tell them all of my fears, secrets and goals in life. The woman before me pulls that man out of me, wanting to do just about anything I can to see that excitement every time she enters a room or has a simple conversation with someone.

The urge to touch her pushes me to tap my knee, wanting her to be as close to me as possible. "Come sit here with me for a moment". Rose rolls her eyes at my command, but the small tug of her lips tells me she would have done it anyway as she comes to sit in my lap. I wrap my arms around her tiny frame, soaking in her scent as she rests her head against my shoulder. I suck in a deep breath, feeling at peace with the moment of calm we're enjoying together.

She's been in my bed every night after me battling to convince her I sleep better when she's around, and although I feel close to her then, this is different. I feel more connected to her now than when

I hold her as we sleep. I don't know what she has done to me, but I'm a love-sick fool because I do love her. I just need to figure out when I should tell her about that and the business I am building, and right now, it seems about as good as any.

I tilt my head to look at her, her face serene and content as she gazes out at the lake. "Rose", I begin softly, "There's something I need to talk to you about". Her eyes flick up to meet mine, curiosity and a hint of concern etched on her features.

"What's wrong?" She asks, her voice gentle, worry lacing it, and I can tell she's thinking something has kicked off again.

I take a deep breath, feeling the weight of my words before I let them out. "Nothing's wrong. I've been doing a lot of work on new business and thinking lately, about us, about our future, and I want to make sure we are on the same page with things".

She smiles warmly, her fingers tracing idle patterns on my arm. "I'm really grateful that you want me to be a part of your plans, Luca. But I think we need to talk more about other things going on in our lives right now first, like the fact Hallie asked me about my plans to move back home".

My body goes stiff, and I feel the blood drain from my face at the mention of the house she shares with Hallie. Or the one she used to. I forgot that little bit of information was on the recording. I pushed it all out of my head as much as I could, not wanting to think of Rose in any situation where she might not want me.

Right now, she lives with me, and I don't want anything to change that. But I also don't want to push her into living with me permanently if she isn't ready for it, so I nod, attempting to keep my voice under control when I reply.

"Okay, and have you thought about what you want to do? Do you want to stay here with me, or would you prefer to return home?" The words feel wrong, leaving a sour taste in my mouth. Of course I don't want her to leave, but I need the choice to be hers.

She sits up and turns to face me, biting her lip, her eyes darting between mine. I can't figure out what's going through her head right now, "Well, um… I kind of need to stay here with you, at least for a little while longer, because of this little situation". She wiggles her ring at me, reminding me how we even got like this in the first place and all the shit that's gone along with it.

"Right". I nod firmly. She is only staying with me because she feels like she has to. She doesn't want to stay with me, and she's doing exactly what I told her to do, make the most of this arrangement, and until her shop and house are sorted, she's been stuck with me.

"Is this how you feel, Rose? Like you're just stuck here with me because you have no other choice?" I try to keep my voice steady, but I can feel the frustration bubbling up inside me. Rose's eyes widen, and she shakes her head vehemently. "No, Luca, that's not what I meant at all. I just... I have a lot of things to figure out right now, and it feels like everything is piling up on me, that and I still don't know where we stand after everything with my mom".

I run a hand through my hair, feeling the tension in the air. "And you think I don't feel the same way? I'm trying to build something for us here, Rose. All this shit has piled on top of me too, I want to make a life with you, not just be a temporary solution".

Her eyes soften, but there's still a hint of frustration in her voice. "I get your saying you're doing this for us, but you literally decided properly, like a couple of weeks ago, that you were leaving your dad's company. Do you not feel like this is all just a little quick? Especially with everything that's gone on. There's a lot to think about here, and sometimes it feels like you're not listening to me. Like you're so focused on the future that you're not seeing what's happening right now".

I take a deep breath, trying to calm myself. "I'm listening, Rose. But it feels like every time we talk about the future, you have one foot out the door. Like you're already planning your escape". She looks hurt, and her voice trembles slightly. "That's not fair, Luca. I did this whole thing to help you in the first place, and the plan was to keep your place at the company, and now you aren't even going to be staying there, so how am I supposed to know what the next steps are?"

I feel myself getting more and more frustrated the longer this conversation goes on, and I try and fail to hide my annoyance at the turn this conversation is taking. "I'm not asking you to have all the answers right now, Rose. I just want to know where you stand. This business is important to me, but so are you. I need to know if you're in this with me or if you're planning to leave as soon as you can."

She takes a deep breath, her eyes searching mine. "Luca, I'm not sure if I'm ready to make a decision like that right now". She pulls herself off me, walking back towards the house. My frustration boils over and turns into anger as she walks off mid-conversation. "Where the hell are you going?"

She stops at the door, turning to face me, her face flushed from the argument that just sprung out of nowhere, "To shower, we have a barbeque to go to". With that, she opens the door, walking through and slamming it behind her, causing the glass to wobble in the frame.

"For fucks sake", I mutter to myself, my head falling into my hands. How has my coming to talk to her about the business and us moving forward turned into a massive row? I stand and make my way down the small deck that leads out onto the lake, pressing my hands into my hips as I blow out a sharp breath.

We need to get on the same fucking page about all of this, and soon.

.....

The ride to Tristan's feels like it's drained all my energy. Rose didn't say a word to me as we made the twenty-minute journey to his house and didn't look in my direction once either. Her head stayed firmly glued to watching what was happening outside this car and ignoring the tension in the air from the argument earlier. I didn't want the others to know we were arguing, but Rose's dismissal of me every time I tried to say a single word to her made it difficult to keep our issues private.

I've barely got the car in park when she jumps out of it, hightailing it up the rest of the drive and around to the backyard where everyone is. I sit watching her figure retreat in the distance and feel like bashing my head against the steering wheel. "Fuck", I shout to no one, gripping my hands so tight against the wheel that I feel them begin to lose blood. Why can we not just fucking get along, I don't want to fight with her about something that hasn't even happened yet, and yet she's stubborn as always and won't just fucking talk to me.

I feel my temper getting to a point where I know I should just avoid the whole day and come back to get Rose later when she's calmed down enough to want to talk to me, but I know I can't do that.

I eventually calm myself down enough to get out of the car, and my feet crunch on the gravel as I make my way up the rest of the drive and around to the back of the house. Rose has already found the girls and the wine when I spot her. She avoids eye contact with me as she turns her head, blocking my view of her face as she engrosses herself in whatever the girls are discussing.

A hand lands on my shoulder, and I turn enough to see Tristan out of my peripheral as he hands me a beer. I take a long drink of it while he speaks, "What have you done to piss her off today?"

I frown at him, brushing his arm off my shoulder where he currently has it resting and manage to keep my voice neutral when I reply, "I haven't done anything. Why would you think that?" He scoffs at me, pointing to the wine in her hand, "She downed the first one, that's her second in the last ten minutes. She only does that when she's stressed or upset".

How the hell does he know that? As if reading my thoughts, Tristan moves so he's now facing me, blocking my view of Rose.

"I've known her almost twenty years. She's like another sister to me. Not that I need more than the two I have, but she's wormed her way into my life anyway. The same with Hallie. The three of them come as a package". He watches me momentarily, assessing me like I might crack, "So come on, what have you done?".

I roll my eyes at him and take another drink from the bottle, dragging it out before giving him an answer. I puff out a long breath before telling him what went down just a few short hours ago.

"I wanted to talk to her about the business and how I want her involved in it, making decisions with me because I want to be with her, and I want to clear the air after everything that went on last week. I want to fucking marry the girl, and all she had to say to me was that Hallie asked when she was returning to the house”.

I feel myself getting more annoyed the longer I let the conversation run over in my head, trying to pick out where it went wrong. “Have you actually asked her to move in with you permanently, or are you assuming that she wants to do whatever she wants?”

I shrug, knowing full well I’m too scared to hear her say she doesn’t want to stay with me again, especially after already hearing it last week. She swore it was just to get the girls off her back when I came back home, but after this, I’m not convinced.

“You need to talk to her, tell her how you feel, or you’ll lose her. She’s complicated at times, but she is a gem and one that is precious enough that if you lose her, you will never get over it”.

I mull over his words. “I know what I need to do, but with everything going on at the minute, I’m not sure if I can handle taking the rejection if she doesn’t want me”.

Tristan huffs a laugh at me and turns his body enough that he can see the girls. “Like I said, I’ve known her a long time, and if you think she doesn’t want you, then you may as well cut your losses now because you’re fucking stupid”.

I glare at Tristan, wanting to punch him for his comment, but my annoyance is disrupted by Jaxx as he makes his way away from the grill and over to us.

"Figured out what this idiot did to Rose yet?" He asks Tristan but watches me, a knowing smile on his face.

"Yeah, he's too chicken shit to tell her how he really feels because Hallie told her the house is almost ready and because of what she said on the recording last week". Jaxx blows out a low whistle, "I'm assuming you left your brain at your dad's office because it's not been working properly for the last few weeks since you left the place. Get your shit together and ask her to move in with you. Hell, tell the girl you love her because I bet you haven't done that yet either, have you?"

The silence on my part speaks volumes to the pair of them as they grin at each other, enjoying my misery. "I'll figure it out", I murmur to them, earning me another pat on the back from Tristan, "Atta boy. Now can we enjoy the evening without the pair of you killing each other before you have a chance to sort your shit out, or do I need to sit you both in a room until you kiss and make up?"

"I'll sort it". I grumble, done with this conversation. I leave the two of them and make my way across the yard to where the girls are in deep discussion about something, talking too quietly for me to listen in.

"Sorry ladies, I need to borrow Rose for a moment". She doesn't even flinch as she brings her glass to her lips, her eyes trained forward so she can avoid eye contact, "I don't need to talk to you. We'll talk later". *The fuck we will.* I try to contain my annoyance at her bratty attitude, but she really knows how to piss me off. “Red, get your ass up and in the house so I can talk to you for a minute, or I’ll carry you there myself”.

I should be surprised, but I’m not when she finally looks up at me, narrowing her eyes on me and utters the word, “No”. *Fuck it.* I tried to keep my cool whilst with friends, but apparently, Rose doesn’t like to play nice. I move towards her, plucking the glass from her hands and shoving it toward Grace.

She grips it before I drop it, and I grab Rose, hauling her up and over my shoulder. She yelps in surprise, “Luca, put me the fuck down, *now*. This is ridiculous”. I ignore her comment and slap her ass as I march inside, the others sniggering at my outburst, but I no longer give a shit what our friends think, as I dump her on the sofa in the living room and take a seat on the coffee table in front of her, pulling her legs towards me and trapping them between mine so that she can’t escape me. “We are going to talk now because I’m not spending the rest of the evening with you being a little brat and ignoring me”.

Rose folds her hands over her chest as it heaves with long breaths as she tries to calm herself down. I somehow manage to stay relatively calm on the outside, hiding the want to burst from annoyance at her. “There’s nothing to talk about Luca. I said I don’t know what I want to do, and you didn’t like it”.

My brows pull together as I look at her, “I never said I didn’t like it. I mean, I don’t, but that’s beside the point. I wanted you to decide what you wanted to do. But apparently, we aren’t on the same page right now when it comes to how we feel about each other and what we want our futures to look like. It's nice to know you can tell your friend things, but not me".

She glares at me, unmoving and not speaking. I know she knows I'm talking about what she said, but she still refuses to say a thing.

"All right then, I'll go first. I'm not mad at you for what your mom did. Yeah, you didn't think it through when you spoke openly to the girls in public, but it is what it is. I've not been mad at you through any of this, and I know you've been keeping out of my way, thinking that I'm pissed about the situation. It's shit, but we got a handle on it, and your mom is now out of the picture.

"And I want you to stay living with me. Forever. I want that ring to stay on your finger and you to be my wife, and I want you to stop acting like you're the only person this affects. Being a brat doesn't suit you, so will you fucking stop it and let me love you like I'm trying to do".

A small gasp leaves her lips as I utter the three simple words I should have said before we even began discussing our future. The words that I should have told her when her mom made the move to blackmail the pair of us, but I guess it's better late than never.

Wide hazel eyes stare back at me, the shock from my words hitting her. "You… You love me?"

I nod as I bring my hand up to cup her cheek, done with the animosity. "Yes, Red. I love you and want you to stop fighting me because I need you. I need you in my life, and I need you to get on the same page as me and love me back because it's fucking shit being here by myself".

She doesn't say it back, but instead lifts herself so we are eye level, her hazel eyes searching mine for any ounce of uncertainty she can find. But there is none, because I'm so far gone for this woman I couldn't be without her again. "Will you stay? Don't go back to Hallie's. I want you to live with me, and I'm sorry if I didn't make that clear before, but I don't want you to go anywhere".

"And what about this?" She wiggles her ring at me again, like she did before, but this time, I don't feel anger, just the knowledge that I will find a way to propose to her in a way that she deserves.

"Keep it on. We'll figure that out when the time comes, but right now, I want to stop fighting with you. Do you think we can put a pin in our discussions until tomorrow and enjoy the rest of the evening without bickering?"

Rose grins at me, nodding along as she leans in closer and presses her lips to mine. The kiss starts tenderly, her soft lips brushing against mine with a delicate hesitance, as if testing the waters of our hiatus on the argument we had. Warmth spreads through me as I deepen the kiss, wanting to have my hands all over her.

Her hands slide into my hair, pulling me closer, deepening the connection as if she's pouring all her unspoken words and emotions into this single moment. I didn't miss the fact that she didn't say she loves me back, but I can live with that. She's staying and that's all that matters.

My arms circle her waist, pulling her tightly against me. Every touch is electric, sending shivers down my spine and making my skin tingle with need. I push forward, pressing us both into the sofa and forgetting where we are as I settle between her legs. They wrap around me as a moan leaves her lips, urging me on.

Someone clearing their throat brings us back to the present, and I peek over at a very amused-looking Tristan leaning against the door frame of his living room. "Now that you love birds have settled your issues, would you kindly join the rest of us outside instead of fucking on my couch".

I grin at him, because I could do just that right now, but Rose pushes against me, tapping on my chest for me to move, and I reluctantly pull back, bringing her into sitting as I do. "Yeah, yeah. We'll be right there". He grins at me and spins on the spot as he makes his way back outside to join the others.

Rose giggles into me, and fuck if that laugh doesn't do something to me every time I hear it. "You heard him, no fucking on the couch". I raise a brow at her in challenge, "He didn't say we couldn't do it anywhere else… We have the wall, the coffee table, and even the rug". Her giggle turns into full-blown laughter, and before I know it, I'm laughing right along with her.

Eventually, we made our way outside to join the others. I had to give myself a minute to calm down, or everyone would have seen just how much making-up we had done.

I spot Ezra talking to Grace when we reappear, and he waves when he spots me. I didn't know how I'd feel about being with my brother among friends, but now he's here, even if it's just in passing, I kind of like it. He makes his way over to where I stand, "Hey, I was just sorting the horses for their vaccines. I didn't expect to see you here".

I nod over to Tristan, who's plating up the burgers on the grill, "We got invited for a barbeque. Why don't you stay and join us?" Ezra's eyes flit between mine and where Tristan stands over at the grill, a nervous expression on his face, "Oh… um, I wouldn't want to impose…" I cut him off before he can make any more excuses to leave, weirdly I want to spend more time with him.

"Nonsense. There's plenty to go around". I shout over to Tristan, "You don't mind if Ezra joins us, do you, Tris?" He nods and waves his cooking tongues at us in agreement, and I grin back at my brother, putting my arm around his shoulder as I turn us to move towards the rest of the group. "C'mon, I'll introduce you to Rose properly".

They get along like they have known each other for years. I'm thankful that he decided to stay because the evening turned out to be one of the best I've had in a while. As day turns to night, Tristan lights a fire and we settle around it, Grace curled up in Jaxx's lap and Rose in mine. Hallie is curled up with Amber on her lap whilst Whiskey paws at Tristan for attention as he sits deep in conversation with Ezra.

I nuzzle myself against Rose, and she shifts herself to a more comfortable position as I wrap my arms tighter around her. "I know we still have a lot to discuss, but I'm really happy you're staying with me". Rose smiles at me, and like every time she does, it takes my breath away. "Me too. We'll figure everything out, just don't stress about it, and enjoy the rest of the evening with me".

"Yes, Ma'am", I murmur, kissing her along her neck. She tries to hide her subtle moans, but one look from Tristan has me wanting to laugh. Instead, I stick my middle finger at him and enjoy reminding my girl how loved she is.

31

Rose

The sun peeks through the blinds, pulling me from my sleep. I crack an eye open, not wanting to fully wake myself up just yet if it's still early.

I reach behind me, searching for Luca in the sheets, but only find mildly warm cotton beneath my fingers. He must have got up early, but I'm in no mood to move myself this morning. After our argument last week and him probably trying to figure out why I'm such a bitch half the time, we enjoyed the rest of the evening with friends, and I really enjoyed getting to know his brother Ezra.

I snuggle down further into the covers, trying to grasp the last bit of sleep I can after one of the busiest weeks I've had yet, when the door cracks open, and Luca walks in, coffee and toast in hand. "Good morning, sleepy head. I brought you breakfast". I give him a sleepy smile as he places the food and drink on the side table before climbing on top of me, trapping me under the covers. "Luca, get on your own side". I laugh as he smothers me in kisses. "Eat up and get ready. I have a surprise for you", he says before jumping back off me.

I glance over at him as he makes his way into the bathroom, turning the shower on. He pulls his shorts down, grinning back at me as I watch him undress, "If you eat that, I'll wait for you, and you can shower with me". He points to the food, and I sit myself up, crunching through the toast. He laughs at my immediate enthusiasm, clearly amused by my sudden compliance.

"That's my girl", he says with a chuckle, his eyes twinkling with mischief. My heart flutters at his words, *my girl*. I never thought I'd see the day when I truly believed I could be *his girl*.

I make quick work of eating my breakfast and take a quick sip of coffee before joining him in the shower. It's a double unit in his bedroom, big enough for the pair of us to clean up without getting in each other's way, or even better, it's less cramped for our morning activities.

I'm pulled into strong arms, the feel of his hands sliding down my body makes my skin ripple with delight every time he touches me, and I'm yet to get used to the feeling.

I turn in his arms, pressing a needy kiss to his lips, and he responds instantly, picking me up and pushing me against the cool tile wall. My legs wrap around him on instinct, pulling him closer to me as he peppers kisses down my throat. A moan slips free from the contact, and he chuckles against my skin, his laugh vibrating against me and sending warmth straight to my core, I wiggle against him, needing him to give me more. "You're a needy girl this morning".

“I’m always needy for you, Luca. Now, can we do less talking, please?” He shakes his head at me but doesn’t say another word as he lines himself against me, pushing himself into me, inch by inch. The pressure sends tingles all over my body as he fills me, giving me what I need. “fuckkk”, he moans, as he buries himself inside me, my mouth forming into an ‘o’ as he pushes himself in and out of me.

The shower pours down us as we continue, a mixture of kisses and swallowed moans as we both come to our climax. If this is what makeup sex is always like then I’ll take it, and I get this for the rest of my life, then I am in no way going to complain about it.

.....

After attempting to dry off and being dragged back to bed for another round of glorious sex, I’m slightly sore and spent, but Luca insisted I needed to see the surprise he had for me. I quickly get dressed, and Luca guides me out to the car, a twinkle of excitement still visible in his eyes. “Where are we going?” I ask, but he just grins and shakes his head.

“It's a surprise, Rose”.

I settle into the passenger seat, curiosity bubbling within me. As we drive through the city, I watch the familiar streets pass by, trying to guess our destination. Luca's hand rests on my thigh, the feeling comforting and yet the anxiety that builds has me on pins for the whole drive. Eventually, we pull onto a familiar street, the blossom trees that line the sidewalk reminding me why I picked here in the first place as the bakery comes into view.

I jump up and down in my seat like a giddy child, and Luca grins over at me. “Is this really happening? Is it finally finished?” He nods, laughing at my reaction, “Yep, only took eight weeks and a tonne of mishaps along the way, but it’s all sorted”. He pulls the truck up outside the place, taking my hand in his, “You ready to see it?”

I nod enthusiastically, causing him to laugh more. We climb out, and I look around, trying to see if Mr Miller will be here to ensure everything is in order, “Who are you looking for?” Luca asks as he unlocks the front of the shop, the keys jingling in his hand cause excitement to ripple through me and I almost forget he just asked me a question. “Oh, um won’t the landlord be meeting us here? You know to make sure it’s all okay”. He looks sheepish, quickly pushing the door open and pushing me inside.

All thoughts leave my head as I see the inside of my bakery. All the plans I went through with Luca in the office are now brought to life. Wooden beams rest into the high arches of the building, exposed brick along the back wall with lit-up menus on them above a huge window that looks into the kitchen, and the side walls carry an earthy green tone with plants everywhere. A huge glass cabinet for cakes and pastries lines the back area of the shop, and a gorgeous coffee machine rests on the back unit.

Cosy booths have been fitted along the side walls, with plush chairs and oak tables lining the sides. A few smaller tables scatter through the main floor, allowing plenty of people to sit and eat.

I feel Luca's presence behind me as he rests a hand on my lower back, leaning in so close I can practically taste him. "The best bit is in the kitchen, go check it out". My smile gets impossibly wider as I rush into the kitchen. A huge industrial fridge sits along the back wall, with shelving on either side for utensils and three ovens on the other side, allowing me to cook so much more than before.

I turn to face Luca as he clasps his hands in front of him as he studies me, trying to figure out what I'm thinking. "Do you like it?".

"Fuck no!"

Luca's face drops as I take tentative steps towards him, keeping my expression neutral until I reach him. Wrapping my arms around him, a smile breaks free on my face as I beam up at him, "I fucking love it. This is more than I could have ever dreamed of for myself, it's so much better than I had before".

He visibly relaxes against me, wrapping his arms around my waist, a grin spreading across his face. "Little shit, I thought you hated it then". I press a kiss to his lips, a silent thank you for everything he has done to help me get this sorted. "I could never hate anything you've put work into Luca", I wave my hands around the space. "This place is amazing".

"I'm glad you like it so much, because you are the owner of the whole building now". I freeze, surely I didn't just hear him right. "What… what do you mean I'm the owner. How?" He shrugs like it's no big deal. "I may have convinced the owner to sell it to me, hence me being able to do so much work on it. But I've put it in your name, the place is yours, Red".

The sincerity in his voice has me crushing my lips against his. How could I ever thank this man for what he's done to help me, even after all he's been going through with his dad and my mom recently. I grip hold of him, pulling him impossibly closer to me as I deepen the kiss, pouring everything I have into it. I break away long enough to voice everything I need to, "Fuck Luca, it's perfect thank you. I love it. I love you".

He chuckles against my lips, the vibrations of his body against mine sending tingles through me, lighting my body on fire, like it does every time I'm in his proximity, I can't get enough of him, and I don't want that to ever change. "Jesus Red, if all it took was buying you your own bakery for you to love me I would have done it when I first met you".

I pull back from him, and my eyes search his deep chocolate ones, which melt with warmth the more he looks at me. "I didn't need you to do this for me to love you, Luca. I just needed you to be yourself and do everything you have done. You were so selfless with everything and always pulled through for me, even if I didn't think I needed it. And you still do that every single day. I've loved you longer than

I've thought to admit to myself, but you pushed through this bitchy façade and made me want to be loved by you".

I blink back tears that threaten to spill over. I never get this emotional, but Luca seems to bring out the softer side in me, the side I've always been missing.

"Sweetheart, even if you never loved me back, I'd love you until my last breath. You make me want to be a better man, and if I can give you everything you will ever need until the day I die, then you will never want for anything".

I lean my forehead against his, breathing in the moment and allowing the warmth of his embrace to envelop me. "You're incredible, Luca", I whisper, my voice thick with emotion. "I don't know how I'll ever repay you for this". The pad of his thumb brushes against my cheek, wiping away a tear that has escaped. "You don't owe me anything, Red. Just keep being you and let me love you".

I grin up to him as he holds me. "I've got one other surprise for you, it's upstairs. Wanna go see?" He grins down at me as he waits for my reply, and I nod enthusiastically. Luca leads me through a door I didn't see before, that's now attached to the upstairs from the shop and leads me up the stairs.

As I walk through the door that leads to the new upper section of the bakery, I shriek as our friends and my dad stand in front of us, screaming "surprise" as we enter.

Jaxx is the first to shout over the crowd, "Welcome to your new bakery Rose. We're only here so you feed us some of your treats". Grace elbows him for his comment, but he just keeps grinning at us.

Tears well in my eyes at my friends who have gathered to celebrate the new bakery with me, their faces beaming with pride and excitement. I can hardly believe my eyes as I take in the sight of colourful balloons, a beautifully decorated cake, and the warm, familiar faces of my loved ones.

My dad steps forward, his eyes glistening with unshed tears. "Rose, we're all so proud of you. This bakery is going to be the best thing this town has ever seen". I feel the tears finally spill over as I hug him tightly. "Thank you, Dad. Thank you, everyone for showing up for me".

Luca squeezes my shoulder, and I turn to him, my heart swelling with gratitude and love. "This is the best gift anyone could have ever given me. After all the hard work you did to get the place fixed up".

Luca smiles, his eyes twinkling with affection. "I'm glad you think so, but this was all your vision, I just gave a helping hand. Now let's celebrate".

As we all gather around the table filled with champagne and cake I feel a sense of contentment settle over me. Surrounded by friends and family, in my very own bakery, I know that this is just the beginning of a new and exciting chapter in my life.

32

Luca

"You decided to stop being a pussy yet and go talk to your dad?"

I glare at Tristan from across the island in his kitchen as he chews obnoxiously loud on an apple. He doesn't think half of the time before crap falls out of his mouth as he speaks. "No, I haven't", I say with a sigh as I lean back on the bar stool, gripping my coffee cup in front of me so hard I'm surprised it hasn't cracked. The longer the weeks stretch on without speaking to my dad, the harder I seem to find it to go and have a conversation with him.

A month has passed since I left his home office, and although Ezra says he's working on things with him, I can't bring myself to forgive him for everything. He's called and texted me a few times, asking to speak to me, but each time, I click off the message without responding or let the call roll to voicemail.

"You should really go clear the air at least, I get that he fucked up, but he's still your dad, and he wanted to do right by Ezra years ago, it just turned sour. I bet if Ezra had always been in your life, you wouldn't be hating on your dad so much". My brows pull together as I watch him across the space. Why does he think he knows me so well? He sees my reaction, pointing his apple-clad hand in my direction as he continues, "Think about it, if Ezra was brought into your life when you were a kid, and you were brought up together like your dad wanted, you wouldn't care how he got here, just that you had a brother who you want to be around".

Huh, maybe he does have a point. "It still doesn't excuse the fact that he hid it for so many years from me. He could have told me". I say, re-focusing on the anger I have towards him.

Tristan rolls his eyes at me. "Give the guy a break. Yeah, he did some shitty things, but if he genuinely never thought he'd hear from Ezra or his mom again, then why upset you by telling you about a brother you weren't allowed to see".

I push the cup away from me, bringing my hands up to my face and digging my palms into my eye sockets. It doesn't help one bit, but if I focus on the pain of shoving my hands in my eyes, the thought of having to deal with this seems a little less terrible. Every time I have thought about going to see him, I chicken out. I'm pulled from my dreary thoughts by Tristan giving me more unsolicited advice.

"You lied to him too. Maybe you're not quite as bad as hiding a child, but you lied about being engaged to Rose. He thinks you found the one you'll spend the rest of your life with, and you lied straight to his face".

My eyes take a minute to adjust. I have to blink a couple of times for the little white dots to disappear from my vision. "Technically, I didn't lie. I am going to spend the rest of my life with her. She just didn't know it at the time". Tristan barks out a laugh, shaking his head at me.

"Sometimes I wonder if I've stepped onto another universe when I get a glimpse into the inside of your head. Your fucking crazy for assuming she would even go along with everything in the first place". I grin back at him, sitting up a little straighter. "It worked, didn't it? I wanted her, and I got her. Alright maybe I didn't go the right way about it, and maybe I should have thought about it more at the time, but I love the bones of her. I would have worn her down eventually if she didn't agree to be my fiancé".

He raises a brow at me in question. I've never been like this with any woman before, so my obsession with Rose must still feel new to my friends. "I didn't think you had it this bad. I must say, I'm impressed you stuck it out this long with someone. I thought you would have got bored by now".

I scowl at him, wanting to be pissed at his comment, but equally, he is right. "I get you not understanding it, but when you find the one, you just know". He shrugs at me, finally finishing off his apple and throwing it in the trash before turning and pointing his finger at me again.

"Go and see him instead of moping around this place. I have work to do so you can see yourself out". With that, he spins on his heel and is out the back door and over to the waiting horses.

.....

The offices look different today, not where I thought I'd, be looking like an outsider, but I need to go and speak to him once and for all. The chat or rather telling off I had from Tristan put some things into perspective for me, and after a quick pep talk over the phone from Rose, I finally made it to the offices. Well, the café across the road, but it's close enough. I needed liquid courage for this, the hard liquor kind, but coffee will have to do.

I take a deep breath and step outside. The bitter smell of coffee mingling with the cool morning air clears my head in an unsettling way as I steel myself for what lies ahead. The tall glass building looms over me, its facade reflecting my anxious expression back at me. It's not just about Ezra or my father. It's about facing the past I've tried so hard to ignore.

The moment I step into the office building, the familiar hum of activity engulfs me as I stride over to the elevators, wanting to get this over and done with.

As the doors ping open and I step into the bright office space, I see him, just beyond the glass doors of his office, hunched over his desk, seemingly engrossed in his work.

As I approach, a wave of nausea hits me. My legs feel like lead, but I force myself to move forward. The receptionist does a double take, seemingly shocked to be seeing me for the first time in so long.

I give her a curt nod as I make my way down the hallway to his open door. Standing at the threshold of his office. I knock gently, and he looks up, surprise flickering in his eyes before he masks it with an unreadable expression. "Can I come in?" I ask, my voice strained and unsteady as the tension in the air rolls over me. He motions for me to sit. The silence between us is suffocating, a silent force pressing down on my chest. Finally, he breaks it.

"What brings you in today, Luca?" His voice is steady, but I can hear the underlying uncertainty at my presence. I take a deep breath, struggling to find the right words. "I've been doing a lot of thinking, about Ezra, about you, and about my place here in the company. I realized I've been holding on to a lot of anger and resentment and thought that maybe it's time to let some of it go". He leans back in his chair, studying me.

"Where do you want to start?"

"I'm going to start by saying, even though I don't now, nor do I ever think I can forgive you for the lies and deception surrounding my mother and now brother, but I can't hold a grudge forever. So, I'm willing to move forward. I know you and Ezra have been in contact, and as much as it pains me, I do miss you".

I see a glimmer of hope in his eyes, but I just as quickly squash it with my words. "I will be leaving the company, though. I have been working on various projects, and I think it is time for me to start anew independently without the constant pressure of striving to meet your expectations. I know it might not be what you want to hear, but I can't be in your shadow forever, and even if I took over this place, that's what will happen".

He nods thoughtfully, sitting back in his plush office chair as he regards me, "I think that's very brave of you Luca. I took a chance at starting this company against my own father's wishes. Did you know he wanted me to run the steel merchants that he owned? He didn't think there would be money in architecture, and I'm glad to say I proved him wrong. And now I want you to do the same with me.

"I want you to go out there and do everything you want because you are doing it for yourself and no one else. I'm incredibly proud of the man you have become Luca, and Rose brings out the best in you, I'm happy you found love in her too".

I swallow the lump in my throat, I want to tell him that my and Rose's relationship was fake. But it's not now, so what good would it do? I'm going to marry her either way, so him knowing that information wouldn't help our relationship mend.

I push past the burning in my chest and rise to my feet, sticking my hand out for my dad to take. "Thank you for the opportunity to build and grow under you, Sir". My dad grins at me, standing with me and gripping my hand to shake. "Good luck, son. I hope to see you and my daughter-in-law soon, get planning that wedding".

I grin at him as I leave his office and make a phone call.

.....

"Luca, what brings you to the office today. I hope you're not in any trouble". Rose's dad chuckles lightly from across his desk at me. I never got the chance to ask him for her hand properly the first time, so I want to clear the air and make sure I have his approval.

"I'm hoping not to need help with getting out of trouble anytime soon, sir". I grin at him as I run my palms up and down my thighs, attempting to calm my nerves, but it does nothing. "I actually wanted to come and speak to you, as I know I never did before Rose and I got engaged. I know it seemed as if we got engaged under the radar, but I wanted to confess something to you".

Her dad's eyes narrow in on me, and I feel like I shouldn't be telling him this now, but I'm not sure it would sit well with my conscience if I never told him the truth.

"Rose helped me out, and we weren't actually engaged in the first place. I was being pressured by my father into marrying someone to secure my place in the firm, and Rose agreed to be that person until the time came when my dad would take me seriously without marriage hanging over my head".

Her dad doesn't move, just nods once for me to carry on, I don't know if he's pissed right now, but his expression doesn't give anything away.

"That being said, I love your daughter and want to ask her to marry me, for real this time, and I wanted to get your approval before I did. I know I didn't go about it properly the first time, but I think I've always known I wanted to spend my life with her, it just took a bit of convincing for her to see that too".

I swallow, not knowing if I'm about to have my ass handed to me or not, as I stare back at the man that could tell me to fuck off and stay away from his daughter.

"Well. That's quite the story, Luca. I agree, it's not the right way you should have gone about any of this, making my daughter lie to me if not something I take easily".

Shit, he fucking hates my guts.

"That being said. I can see how happy you make her and how much of a difference you have made to her life by being in it. So, for keeping my baby smiling, I suppose all I need to say is, welcome to the family, son".

I grin at him, my heart going a mile a minute. I thought he would tell me to get out of his office, but this. This I can deal with. I stand to shake his hand, his grip is firm as he pulls me closer in warning, so we are eye to eye.

"But if you ever hurt her, I will find any way I can to bring you down. Do you understand?"

I nod to him, thankful I have his approval, even if it comes with a target on my back. “I won’t let Rose or you down, sir”.

Finally, he breaks out into a smile as he releases my hand, “Good, now get out of my office, and I’ll see you soon”.

I leave there feeling better than I have in a long time, knowing all I need to do now is find the perfect way to propose again.

33

Rose

Grace's new pup, Honey, sleeps in my lap peacefully as I sit on the outdoor sofa in her backyard. Her huge paws flop over the sides of my leg whilst she snores lightly.

Jaxx finally convinced Grace to get a dog, and they picked their new golden retriever up last week, and aside from her looking pretty sleep deprived, she's taken well to being a dog mom.

I grin at my friend as she comes out the back door with a wine in hand, "I might consider getting a dog too, I could do with getting out for some more exercise". She eyes me from where she has taken a seat on the other side of the sofa, her eyes flitting down to the sleepy pup and then back up to mine. "Just borrow mine for now. The sleepless nights aren't worth it". I snort a laugh at her, she loves her sleep so this must be killing her.

"How's the bakery going now anyway, did you find someone to replace Paisley?" I nod as I sip on my wine. Paisley started at her new job two weeks before the bakery re-opened. She told her new boss that she was pregnant before she started, expecting to lose her job since she would be going on maternity leave not long after starting, but he was surprisingly helpful and even suggested that she could bring the baby along with her to the grounds when it wasn't game days to help her out.

"Yeah, one of the neighbours a few doors down from the bakery saw the job sign and called in. She's the sweetest and said she just needed something to keep her busy since her husband died. I couldn't say no to her when I saw how she charmed half of the customers".

Grace grins at me, "I'm glad it all worked out for you. I still can't believe Luca bought you the shop though". I'm still in disbelief about that myself, but he finally started getting the plans together for his new construction firm and everything is coming together nicely. She reaches over, grabbing my hand, "I'm really happy for you, Rose, you deserve this".

"I know,". I've finally accepted that it's okay to lean on someone for help. My mother never wanted to, and my dad, as much as I love him, never could because of her. Grace scrunches her brow as she looks down at my hand.

"Have you and Luca decided to call off the engagement? That ring usually isn't off your finger". I glance down at my bare hand, biting my lip and dreading what I'm about to say, "I've not told Luca yet, but I think I've lost it. I swore I put it on the side while cleaning the other day, and I forgot to put it back on. When I went to find it, it was missing. I'm praying I can find it again before he catches on".

Grace shakes her head at me, a small smile playing on her lips. “You would lose your head if it wasn’t screwed on. Do you want me to come back and help you look for it?” I shake my head at her, letting out a sigh. “No, it’s okay, if I can’t find it by tomorrow I’ll have to tell him and hope he doesn’t want to murder me”.

As I say the words, my phone pings with a message, and when I check it, Luca’s name is on the screen, asking me to come home because he has something he needs to talk to me about, “His ears must be burning, he just texted me. I better get going, he said he needs to speak to me about something”.

Anxiety fills me. I really hope he hasn’t found out somehow that I’ve lost it already. I’ll just have to hide my hand until I can hunt it out. I say my goodbyes to Grace, heading back home as quickly as I can without causing an accident.

The sun is just setting as I pull up and look at the house. Pinks and reds swirl in the setting sky, calming me as I prepare to be berated for something I’m not sure of yet, but as I walk into the darkened house, I wonder if Luca meant to meet him somewhere because it doesn’t look like he’s home.

“Luca”, I call out as I slide my shoes off by the door. I hear shuffling in the front room and make my way in there, stopping short when I see the sight before me.

Candles fill the front room, and red roses are dotted about the place. I can’t take my eyes off it.

Because standing in the centre of the room in a suit and looking fucking edible, is Luca.

"What's going on?" I question. He still doesn't speak but holds a hand out to me, silently asking me to come to him.

I step forward, my heart pounding in my chest, and place my hand in his. He gently pulls me closer, his eyes never leaving mine, and I feel a warmth spread through me that has nothing to do with the candles.

"Rose", he begins, his voice deep and steady, "These past months with you have shown me what it means to truly love and be loved. I thought I knew what I wanted in life, but meeting you turned everything upside down in the best way possible". I can barely breathe as he continues, his words wrapping around my heart like a vice, tightening like my breath seems to be doing.

"Our engagement may have started as a charade, but somewhere along the way, it became real for me. You became real for me. You are my partner, my confidante, my love". He reaches into his pocket and pulls out a small velvet box, and my breath catches in my throat. He drops to one knee, opening the box to reveal my ring, the stone catching the flickering light of the candles.

"Rose, will you do me the incredible honour of becoming my wife? Will you marry me for real this time?"

Tears blur my vision as I look down at him, this man who has changed my life in ways I never imagined. "Yes", I whisper, my voice trembling with emotion. "Yes, Luca, I will marry you". He grins at me, bringing his dimple out as he slides the ring onto my finger, and as he stands, he sweeps me into his arms, capturing my lips in a kiss that sends shivers up my spine.

By the time I pull away from him, my brain has turned to mush. Who knew Luca could be such a romantic? "How… How did you get hold of my ring…" I glance up at him sheepishly, not sure I should be admitting this right now, "I thought I'd lost it".

He smirks at me, "I saw you take it off to clean the other day and swiped it so I could do this the right way". I smack his arm playfully, "Luca! I was worried I had lost this. I was so scared to tell you". He leans into me, his laugh vibrating through me, "I'm impressed you held it together this long, but from now on, that does not leave your finger". My smile widens as I grin back up at him, "I promise".

Luca presses a kiss to my lips, lingering for just a moment, "Good. Now get your ass upstairs so I can love you like I need to".

"Yes, sir".

I hightail it up the stairs, Luca hot on my heels and fall onto the bed, the laughter spilling from the pair of us from running around the house like a pair of kids. He rolls himself on top of me, a playful glint in his eyes. "I want to marry you as soon as I possibly can. I want you to be Mrs Wilde sooner rather than later. I don't want to waste another day without you being my wife". I smile up at him, my hand stroking along his jaw, "Becoming your wife tomorrow wouldn't be soon enough". His smouldering gaze has me wanting to marry him right now.

"Tomorrow it is then".

The end.

Want to see what Hallie is up to?

Want You, the next in the series, follows Hallie and her grumpy boss, West, as she takes a nannying job for him, which goes against her every instinct after she vows to avoid him at all costs.

Printed in Great Britain
by Amazon

60411186R10221